HAROLD

A boy looking for love

LORD RONALD VICTOR
ALAN STREETER

Harold as a boy

Harold reeled back against the wall with the force of the blow; he lay there his head ringing like a bell.

"The next time I tell you to do something, do it straight away" bellowed his father. His father was six feet tall and weighed about 18 stones and huge compared to a ten-year-old boy who was only 4 ft 10 in tall and weighed 8 stones. As usual he was drunk and in a vile temper, and when he was angry Harold was always the one to get the thick end of his anger.

"Now get yourself to your room. No supper for you tonight" he continued.

Harold slowly moved away from the wall almost on all fours, watching his father in case he attacked again. As he moved along the wall towards the door watching his father he fell to the ground as someone kicked his legs away. It was his elder sister, Mary, who took after her father in hatred of him. She was fifteen and her mother's favourite; she smirked as he lay there on the floor, then his mother grabbed hold of his hair and pulled him to his feet.

"Get up those stairs, your insolent boy! Or I'll give you a belting as well" she yelled.

Getting past the three of them Harold ran up the stairs to the safety of his room, he fell on his bed and buried his face in the scruffy blanket determined not to cry. But the tears came anyway; he tried to muffle them with the dirty blanket as he knew if they heard then he would get another beating. Gradually his sobs subsided, and he lay there in the semi-dark trying to get his feelings back under control. He was only ten and couldn't understand why all his family hated him so much. What had he done to them except being born? As for supper well, he was lucky to get anything anyway, more than not he went without for whatever reason they could think of.

Later that evening when he heard them go to bed, he cautiously opened the door and listened intently, trying to peer through the dark. Everything seemed to be quiet, so he crept along the landing keeping close to the wall, as he knew the floorboards did not creak if he kept to the wall. Slowly he descended the stairs, sliding along the grimy walls that had not seen any paint for years. Creeping into the kitchen he opened the larder door and went inside. Looking around he saw that there wasn't much to eat in there as usual; his parents spent all their money on drink and cigarettes. He managed to find some bread and a hunk of old cheese. There wasn't anything to drink so he got a tin cup and filled it up with water, and then he crept back upstairs to his lonely dark room.

"Come on your lazy sod, get out of bed. You must get to school" he was woken by his mother pulling him out of his dirty crumbled bed and dumping him on the floor. He leapt up and ran to the bathroom where he washed his face and hands with cold water and ran back to his room. He put on his crumpled shirt and trousers and socks and dirty shoes, it was a long time since he had any new clothes and his mother didn't wash his clothes very often. Coming downstairs he approached the table but before he got there his mother grabbed him and pushed him towards the door.

"No breakfast for insolent boys, get you off to school" she yelled. "What about Mary?" Harold said.

Softening his mother said, "The poor dear isn't well today so you can tell her teacher she won't be in" then angrily "Get on your way or you will be late",

Harold raced down the street then around the corner he slowed to a walk, why was it that Mary could stay at home when he had to go to school? Why was he punished for asking questions? He hadn't meant to be insolent he only asked if he could go to the park with his mates, and they had exploded. He never got to go anywhere, he was always hungry, his family didn't want him around, but he had nowhere to go so he had to put up with it.

Harold lived in Bristol on the river Avon and his family lived in a small terraced house not far from the docks where his father worked there as a day worker, which meant some days he didn't get any work. They were desperately underpaid anyway so losing even one day's pay was a burden, not being able to feed their families or pay the rent. The landlords had little sympathy and even missing one week they could find themselves evicted and, on the street, so it was a painful and desperate existence.

As he passed the bakers, he saw that there was a crowd in there so he joined them hoping that someone might take pity on him, but they all ignored him. Just by the door was the window display and there was a gap where he could just put his hand through, making sure everyone was busy he quickly put his hand through and grabbed a couple of bread rolls.

Then sidling out of the shop he ran down the street, pausing for breath he walked into the park and sitting on a bench greedily ate the two rolls. Later as he walked down the high street, he was able to steal an apple and a carrot, which he ate on the way to school. Reaching the school gates, he stopped, undecided whether he should go in.

"Look its horrible Harold!" somebody shouted.

Looking up Harold saw it was John Simpson one of his worst tormentors.

"Are you coming in to stink out the classroom today?" John shouted so that everyone could hear him.

Harold was used to this treatment and he rarely actually went into school so he said nothing, then he ran off to the canal, called the "new cut" that joined the river to the docks, and sat down under the bridge. He was lonely and unloved. he had no friends or anyone who he could go to for love, he didn't understand what love he was as had never had any. He vowed that one day when he grew up, he would find someone who loved him and who he could love, but for now he was just a little lost boy who had to make the best of it.

As he lay there all the hurts and beatings and hatred began to grow in his breast, he couldn't stop the emotions from rising and rising he tried to stop them, but they refused to stop. He was like a volcano and just like a volcano he exploded, all his hurts and lack of love exploded, and his thin wretched body began to sob.

The sobs grew stronger and stronger and as he lay on the grass his whole body convulsed as the tears flowed out of his eyes. All the torment of his 10 years became a storm of emotion that he was unable to stop, as if he wanted to anyway. He cried and cried until there was no moisture left in his body and then he collapsed into an exhausted sleep.

When he woke up, he felt new, refreshed although nothing had changed his emotions had been cleansed and now, he had new strength to face the world. The day was sunny and warm, so he got up and walked along the canal side towards the town Centre enjoying the pleasant weather and being alone. As he walked, he saw a bigger boy coming in his direction, looking around there was no way to avoid him so head down Harold ploughed on hoping to get by unscathed.

The boy went past him and then suddenly leaped on his back and pulled him to the ground. "Give me your money or I'll throttle you!" gasping for breath Harold said, "I don't have any money, let me go!" Wrestling on the ground Harold was at a disadvantage as the other boy was bigger than him so he kicked and punched as best he could by chance one of his wild kicks caught the other boy in the groin. Letting out a loud gasp he collapsed to the ground holding his injured part.

Finally, he gasped out "That wasn't fair kicking me in the balls", "Well you shouldn't have attacked me first" Having got his breath back but still sore the other boy replied "My name is John, what's yours?", "My name is Harold". "So why aren't you in school? Playing truant?". "I get bullied at school and my parents don't want me, so I decided to run away". "How old are you? You don't look very old" "I am ten going on eleven". "O.K. how about coming with me and seeing what we can get to eat, I'm starving" "So am I, I have only had a couple of bread rolls I snitched"

So, they started off together, Harold thought it was a great day, he had found a friend and now they were going to eat. They came into town and they saw a boy from the Grammar School coming their way, John looked at Harold and winked. Harold guessed what he was saying so as the boy passed, he grabbed him from behind and John grabbed hold of his tie and put his fist into his face. "Look grammar boy, hand over your money or you will get my fist in your face for sure". The boy terrified reached into his pocket and pulled out a shilling, "Great" said John and released his hold. The boy scampered off up the road as if the devil was chasing him.

Grinning at each other they walked off down the road and coming to a café they went in to see what they could get for the money they had stolen. "What's it to be?" said the man behind the counter. "Come on don't hang around I've customers to feed" he said as they stood looking at him. "How much is a breakfast?" John said at last. Looking at them quizzically the man said, "Full Breakfast is a shilling; do you want one?" "Yes, please" said Harold and nudged John to hand over the money, John did so reluctantly. "Go and find a table and Lucy will bring it over, Next!"

"Why did you do that? That's all our money gone". "You mean it's all that boys' money, anyway we can share the breakfast". They found an empty table and sat down, the place was very busy, and people were coming and going all the time. "Here you are boys, here's your food" a pleasant voice broke into their reverie. Looking up the boys saw a pretty girl who was about 15 holding a huge plate of food and a large mug of steaming tea. "O.K. who's having it?" she said in a smiling voice. "We want to share" Harold said in a timid voice. "Well I never who would have thought, right I'll go and get another plate".

She returned with not only another plate but another mug of steaming tea and a hunk of toast. "I thought you wouldn't want to share a mug, so I've brought another one". Smiling at their discomfort she said, "have a good meal" and glided away. Harold had never been treated so kindly and it brought tears to his eyes, but he quickly wiped them away, he didn't want John to think he was a cry baby.

Now looking at the plate of food they could see that they had two eggs, two rashers of bacon, 2 sausages, a pile of huge chips and a hunk of toasted bread. After they had stared at the food for what seemed ages, John began dividing the food onto the empty plate of Harold.

On the table was a large pot containing jam, so they piled that onto their toast and began to eat. Now Harold had never had much to eat and sitting before him was probably a couple of days' worth of his normal ration, so he was a bit overwhelmed. He began to eat. WOW! He had never had such good food, so slowly at first then faster he began to devour the food and wash it down with his mug of tea. Before he was halfway through his stomach began to tell him, it had enough. Looking at his half empty plate Harold couldn't decide what to do, at that moment Lucy came by and stopping at the table she said "me can't finish eh? That's O.K. I will bring you a bag to take the rest away".

She returned with a brown paper bag and gave it to Harold. "Sorry I can't give you a cup the boss would go mad". Harold was too stunned for words as he stared at her. She must be an angel he thought nobody else could do such kind things and the tears welled into his eyes again, this time he couldn't stop them. "There now, no need for tears" she said putting her arm around his thin shoulders and hugging him gently.

This was too much he burst into tears and sobbed "No-one has ever loved me before". Lucy knelt beside him and holding his hand gave him her handkerchief to dry his eyes. "There are some good people in this world you know". As his tears subsided she packed his left over's in the bag and helped him up, "now you go and enjoy your day and come back tomorrow, I'll see you then" All this time John had scoffed down his food and was ready to leave, she led Harold and John to the door where she gave them both a hug and sent them on their way.

Outside Harold said. "Well what shall we do now?" John said.

"Let's walk down to the Centre might find some odd jobs to do". They walked along in silence, Harold enjoying the feeling of having a full stomach, probably for the first time as far as he could remember and clutching his bag of leftovers as if someone was going to steal it from him, which someone usually did. Bristol at this time of the morning had started workday and the traffic was busy.

There were lots of people hurrying to their places of work not wanting to be late and incurring some punishment from the management. In the fifties although jobs were plentiful discipline at work was hard, many companies still thought they were in the thirties before the war and tried to keep their workers in the same state, but things were changing fast. As they came into Old Market, they saw that the produce market was closing, "We can probably get some work here" said John. They hurried across the street to where the market was set in the Centre of the very wide road. Approaching one of the men clearing away his debris John asked, "Any work for us today, Mister?"

He turned and looked quizzically at them "You should be in school, shouldn't you?" he asked. "Naw, we are 14 left school already" said John. "Well he looks a bit young" he said nodding at Harold. "I am nearly 14!" Harold said defensively. "O.K. you can give me a hand clearing all this stuff away" he said. John and Harold set to work moving all the old flower boxes to a big pile at the end of the market ready for the rubbish collectors to take away.

They put all the old flowers into a big bin that would be taken away to be dumped some- where. The work didn't take them long and when they had finished the man said "Well done, saved me a bit of time, here's some money" he gave them both six pence. "Mister" said John "could we come back tomorrow and help out?" "Well the market opens at 5 am so if you can get here before that I can probably use your help unloading the flowers". John looked at Harold and said "Sure, Sir. We will be here". "Right see you then" he said and marched off.

Harold looked at his sixpence; he had never had that much money before in fact he couldn't remember having ever had any money at all. Stuffing it securely into his pant pocket he joined John as they walked further into town. "That's great getting a regular job" he said. "Yah, so we can at least eat" said John. As they walked along the shops were now open and Harold gazed at all the wonderful things to be had if you had money, his sixpence was burning a hole in his pocket, but there was so much to buy he couldn't decide what to get.

John was more sensible and cautioned him about spending his money on silly things, "remember we have to eat" he said. So, Harold contented himself by just looking. The Centre of the town was still like a desert, during the war the Nazis had bombed Bristol and most of the Centre of town was razed: they clambered over some of the ruins to see if there was anything worth taking but the area had been picked clean already. As they walked around, they were able to do some odd jobs in various stores like sweeping the pavement, taking out the rubbish or loading a wagon. So, at the end of the day they had made three shillings and sixpence each, Harold was so pleased that he skipped along the pavement, he was so happy.

They bought a beef sandwich and a cup of tea for lunch and sat in the café for a while watching the people go by. Harold asked John "where are we going to sleep tonight?" "Well I usually find a corner and just sleep there, sometimes I find an old bit of cloth and cover me with that" he said. Harold thought that was alright for now but what about when it rained and snowed, but John didn't seem to think that far ahead.

That evening they were walking along and a lady from the Salvation Army stopped them. "Hello, Boys" she said, "are you on your way home?" "We ain't got no home" said John. "Well then let me get you a sandwich and a cup of tea, this way" she pointed the way and shooed them along like a mother hen and her chicks. Arriving at their cart they found about a dozen people there eating and drinking.

Once they had their food the lady said, "so where are you living?" Both didn't say anything for a moment, looking at each other. Then Harold said "we ain't got anywhere to stay". The lady didn't seem to be taken aback, she had heard this many time so she said, "We have a shelter in the next street; you can stay there for free. No soft bed but at least you will be dry and warm, and, in the morning, you can have a cup of tea and a piece of toast". "Thanks" said Harold.

The lady led them to the shelter and took them into a large hall with thin mattresses on the floor. "Here you are, you can stay until 7 am but then you have to leave". "we have to be at the market at 5 am so can someone wake us?' said John. "Of course, I will ask the warden to wake you up at 4.30" she then left them to get some sleep, which they did quickly as they had worked hard all day.

He had hardly seemed to have closed his eyes when he was woken by a loud voice in his ear "Time to get up!" He blearily opened his eyes and saw the warden looking at him, realizing where he was, he got out of bed and looked to see John awake as well. They went to the bathroom and splashed some cold water on their faces and then went back to the hall. The warden gave them a steaming mug of tea and a hunk of toast. They quickly gulped the tea down and set off to the market with their toast in their hands.

It was hard work in the market mainly carrying boxes and cartons from the delivery Lorries to the stall area, then when they had been purchased by the retailers to carry them to their vehicles. Once the day's work was done, they usually went to the local public house that could open early for the benefit of the workers in the market. Here they could get a breakfast of bacon, eggs, sausage, toast and beans with a large mug of Tea for only a shilling. Harold got to know most of the regulars and being a person who liked being with other people he got along with most of them.

One man called Charlie was always glad to see him and they chatted together about what was going on around them. As they finished work at 9 am they went to the pub and stayed there until about 11 am and then went out walking around the streets or down to the docks where they could usually pick up some casual work until 5 pm. Then they usually went to another pub, The Ship, down by the docks and spent the evening their drinking beer and having a laugh and joke with his friends, he had never been so happy. They both got on well with each other and enjoyed their work.

After breakfast they usually took a walk down to the Centre and sat in the gardens or by Queen Victoria s statue and looked out over the docks. At this time the docks were busy, but it was getting difficult for ships to get there because the river was silting up and had to be constantly dredged to enable the ships to get in and unload their cargoes. In the afternoon they usually tried to find somewhere to sleep, if the weather was good, they could sleep in the park but if it was raining then they tried to sleep in the bus station or a bus shelter.

The money they earned was enough for them to find a room to sleep in and most landlords didn't care who you were if you had the money to pay the rent. So, the problem of somewhere to sleep was solved and they were probably the happiest two boys in Bristol.

Sometimes Harold thought about his old life and wondered how they were doing but he felt nothing except anger and hate towards them because of the way they had treated him and made him so unhappy and wretched. The thought soon left him, and he carried on with his new life.

All in all, Harold loved his new life and his new friend, but it would not last, this is life.

CHAPTER 2

My Friend Jim

Harold and John spent all their time together and everything seemed to be great until one day John said to him,

"I am going away".

"Where to and why?"

"Well I want to see the world and I have saved up a fair sum to I am going to London first and then I will see. I might go to Italy; I have always thought that Italy would be a nice place to go to".

"I like it here; I don't want to go away".

"That's OK, you stay here, and I will come back some time and tell you all about my adventures".

True to his word John left the next day and Harold felt devastated. His first friend had left him, now he had nobody again what was he going to do?

But as we know life goes on and Harold spent most evenings in the pub, he didn't want to spend all his time in his small flat alone. He was able to sit in the pub with a pint of beer and watch and listen to all the noise around him. Sometimes others would talk to him and ask him to join them, he did willingly but because he had little social skills he didn't usually say very much. He had no knowledge of the topics they talked about, mostly foot- ball and as there were two teams in Bristol it was sometimes quite competitive. At this time Bristol City, who played at Ashton Gate were in the second division of the Football League whereas Bristol Rovers, who played at Eastville were in the third division. So, the talk was mostly about how they were doing in their respective divisions.

Harold s family had no thoughts of anything outside their own area, in fact they had never, as far as he remembered, ever spoken of anything outside themselves. Harold was therefore not aware of any achievements of the teams. He also did not know anything about the political situation as he had never taken any interest. And he had never been to church, so he did not know anything about the Christian religion or any other religion. Some people might say he was ignorant or uncaring, but this was not really the case it was just that he had never been in the company of people who knew or talked about these things.

By listening to what his companions were saying he began to pick up and began to educate himself as far as the people around him were educated, and most of them had little formal education, they had left school at 11 or 12 to get work because their families needed the income. They could barely read or write; they had learnt all that they needed to know to get by. When it came to fill in official documents, they needed help from the officials.

So, Harold passed his evenings quite pleasantly to him, he had no ambition to do anything else. He enjoyed his work at the market, had a good boss, enough money to do what he wanted and was even able to save some. When it came to save his money, he did not know about banks and even if he did, he probably wouldn't trust them. He didn't want to leave it in his flat, there were too many nosey people. So, he decided to hide it outside, he got hold of an old tin chest and put his money in it. Then during the evening, he walked around looking for a good place to hide it.

Bristol had suffered tremendous bombing during the war and there were acres of land with damaged or broken buildings. Near the pub there was such a site, Harold investigated careful that no one else could see him. Among the ruins he found a piece of concrete with a hole underneath. Examining it he thought it looked safe. So carefully pushing his box into the hole, he covered it with some larger stones and then examined his handiwork. It looked good; nobody would know there was his life savings there. So, each week after he was paid, he put some more money into the tin. He had no idea what he would use the money for but had nothing to spend it on so it was the only thing he could think of.

One evening he was approached by an old man who asked if he could sit with him as the pub was very crowded. Harold said yes and the old man sat down opposite him. "I've noticed you in here before and you don't appear to have any friends" the man said. Harold looked at him for a while and saw that he was old, and had a nice smiling face, the hair he had was greying and he was dressed like a labourer.

"That's true, I am not good at making friends. But I don't mind I am quite happy by myself". "Well, I don't have many friends either. I have been coming here for 15 years and I only know a few people well. My name is Jim what is yours?" "Harold". "and what do you do? I see you usually leave early do you have to get up early?". "Yes" Harold was puzzled how this man knew he had to get up early but continued "I work at the vegetable market, so I have to be at work by 4 am, I need some sleep. I find it difficult to sleep during the day". "I see. I used to be a labourer at the docks but now that they are closing down, I am probably going to lose my job and I am too old to really keep working".

"That's too bad". "But I was told at the unemployment office that I can apply for something called Old Age Pension. The labour government introduced this a few years ago for over 65 who couldn't work any-more. I filled in the forms, but I don't have a birth certificate and I am not sure when I was born. So, they said could I find someone who knew me when I was little to give some idea how old I am. I did find an uncle who could give me some idea so I hope that they will be able to give me some money.". "Well that's great. I hope you are successful".

The thought came into Harold s head that his money could be saved and used for when he retired. The thought of retirement never came into his head as he didn't know anybody who had retired, most people he knew worked until they died or lived on other people's charity. This Old Age Pension seemed a good thing so he hoped other old people could use it.

Harold and Jim had many pleasant evenings together, they both had a similar idea on things, and they became quite close. To Harold this was amazing he had never been close to anybody in his life enjoyed the experience.

Talking to Jim one evening Harold admitted he didn't know how to read or write so Jim said he would teach him. So, over their pints he learnt to write and to read, Harold was amazed how it opened up his life, now he could read the signs and know what they meant, before he just guessed from the store contents. He and Jim got along famously, and he began to think of him as his dad or even granddad because he never knew if he had one, and Jim was quite old, not sure how old.

They became great friends and some days they walked down to the river and sat and watched the boats coming and going. It was very peaceful, and they didn't need to say much the silence was companionable. Harold heard that Jim had been married but his wife had died some years before, they never had any children, so he had no family he was aware of. Harold felt that he had no family either as he had repudiated them as they treated him so badly and always felt he wasn't wanted. They started to go to a café to have a meal at lunch time and too Harold this was great, he and Jim really got on so well and he hoped that it would last forever. But nothing lasts forever as we all know it's just our hope to keep happy.

One day Jim took him to his flat in Bonnie Mansions. It didn't look much like a mansion just a 3-storey building that had seen better days. He had one room in what was probably a very nice Victorian building in its day but had not seen any good days for years, he saw a small poorly furnished room with one chair, a small grate and a bed. Jim gave him some books to read, Harold had never in his entire life had a book so treasured it. He read and re-read it many times, it was called The Adventures of Tom Sawyer. Harold could see that he was something like that boy and loved Jim for giving it to him.

Then one day Jim did not turn up for their lunch appointment, Harold waited a while then decided to go and see where he was, perhaps he was sick? Harold hurried along to the mansion and up the stairs to Jim's room, he then gave a loud knock. There was no answer, so he knocked even louder and thought he heard a sound, so he tried the door handle and it was not locked so he cautiously looked around the door.

On the bed lay Jim, Harold ran across the room and knelt beside the bed. 'Jim are you alright?", Jim barely moved and whispered in Harold's ear, "I think the Lord is calling me home", puzzled Harold at first didn't understand he had never had any religious education so didn't know about God. Then it occurred to him that was what Jim was saying. "Come on now, let me get a doctor and you will soon be right as rain", Jim waved a weak hand as if to say no, but Harold was determined to help.

He ran downstairs and asked a young lad if there was a doctor nearby and he said yes, so he gave him a sixpence and said if he brought a doctor to the third room on the first floor, he would give him another sixpence. The boy was delighted and dashed off on his errand. Harold ran back upstairs and sat with Jim, he managed to get him to have some water, there was no food in the place, so he didn't want to go and miss the doctor.

The doctor arrived with the boy looking a little puzzled; he had never been called to this place before because people didn't have any money. They didn't know that the National Health Service had started so it was free. Harold gave the boy his money and waited while the doctor examined Jim. Standing up he looked grim, "Sorry sir but your grandfather is dying, and I can't do anything for him, here is a prescription for some pain killers, give him one every 4 hours."

Harold ran down the stairs and went to the pharmacy to get the medicine, hastening back he ran into the room with the tablets and got a cup and filled it with water. Going over to the bed he lifted Jim up to give him some water and realized he was dead! Harold was so overcome that his friend had died that he collapsed on the bed and burst into tears. These were the first tears he had shed since that time on the canal when he first ran away. Now he had lost the only person who ever cared for him in his whole life, why was life so cruel to do this to him? Didn't he deserve more love?

Finally getting himself under control he had to get a funeral organized, he had no idea how to do it, so he went back to the pub and told them what had happened. There were some tears and many commiserations; he found that one of the regulars had recently buried his dad so knew something of what to do. He gave him the name and address of the undertaker and said his funeral would cost15 pounds.

Harold didn't worry he had a lot more than that hidden in his box at the bomb site. So, he went to the undertaker who was used to having paupers' funerals, so he knew what to do. Harold told him to take care as Jim was his only friend and he wanted him to have a decent burial, but he discovered that he needed a grave to bury Jim and of course he didn't have one. The undertaker told him to go to the cemetery near the hospital and get a plot which would cost him about 5 pounds.

Harold went to get his tin of money so he could pay the bills, he hadn't been there for a few weeks, so he was horrified to find that his stone was gone and the whole bomb site had been bulldozed flat. In desperation he began to dig with his hands where he thought his box should be. Ever more frantically he dug but he couldn't find it. Now he was desperate all his plans were gone, no money to pay for a funeral or buy a plot, so Jim would go to a common grave with only a pauper's funeral.

Slowly he made his way back to the pub and told them of his misfortune, some felt sorry others said it was his own fault he should have spent it. Anyway, he organized a whip round and came up with a sum of 10 pounds and 15 shillings and 3 pence. Harold couldn't decide whether to go and buy a plot or give the money to the under-taker, eventually he decided that Jim deserved a decent resting place, so he went to the cemetery. He managed to buy a plot near to the boundary for only 1 pound 10 shillings. So, went back to the under-taker and explained he had not been able to raise all the money but could he pay the rest at the end of the month, the undertaker took pity on him and send don't worry we will forget the money and give him a proper funeral.

Harold was overjoyed and felt like kissing the undertaker but thought better of it. The undertaker explained what was to happen now, the doctor had to give him a death certificate and it was to be registered at the office. Seeing Harold didn't really comprehend he said leave it to me and asked the name of the doctor. Harold remembered the name on the prescription so that was good. The funeral was set for the following Thursday, as Harold didn't know if Jim had a church it would be held in the funeral parlour and then the body would be taken to the cemetery.

On the day of the funeral Harold put on his best shirt and trousers gave his shoes a shine and went to the funeral parlour. He was a little surprised that only 5 people had turned up including the barman. The service was quickly over, and the body loaded on to the horse drawn hearse as nobody had any transport and it was a good half hour walk, only Harold followed the hearse.

Jim was laid to rest and Harold tried to say a prayer, of course he had never heard a prayer, so he just said goodbye in his own words. He then walked slowly back to the pub, he didn't stay long he was too upset and didn't want them to see so he walked down to the docks and sat on the wall looking at the water.

Later much later he realized it was dark and he felt hungry as he hadn't eaten all day, so he made his way back and went into a café and had meat pie and chips with tea. Now he wasn't sure what he wanted to do but eventually he went back to Jim's place and tidied it up a bit and exhausted fell asleep on the bed.

CHAPTER 3

Growing Up

He was woken by the manager demanding what he was doing there, Harold said he had just fallen asleep, and could he take over the room, the manager became much more pleased after all he needed the rent. It was 3 shillings a week, pay 2 weeks in advance, no women were allowed in and no fighting. Harold gave him the money; it was about all he had. So now he had a room to stay and felt much better. He felt more secure and a little bit happier despite his loss.

Nothing much changed over the next several years, he had a job he liked he had money and he was healthy, but he didn't make any friends. Now and then he would go back to the café and see Lucy and thank her for her help that first morning, she just blushed and said think nothing of it, didn't cost me a penny. Harold liked Lucy and she sat next to him as he ate his meal, smiled into his face and touched his hand.

"Got a girlfriend yet?"

"No, and I am not looking",

"But you need a friend who you can talk to and who will listen to your troubles. I know I do".

"I am all right by myself, I don't need anyone" said Harold but inside him he knew he did, just didn't want to admit it. Lucy was a nice girl but a bit older than Harold, she had a nice figure, he thought and a pretty face, but he had no intentions towards her other than being a friend, although she may have had other ideas.

He also took more care of his money after losing it all on the bomb site, but now he had a room to hide it in, he found a loose floorboard and put his tin in it and then put it back, there was an old carpet which he placed over the site. He was sure that no one was going to find it, he couldn't bear to lose all his money again. Sometimes he wondered what he was going to do in the future, did he want to always work in the market? Did he want to get married at some time? Have children? Well he liked his job in the market and the hours, so he had plenty of time for other things, he wasn't sure about getting married. His only experience was his parents who seemed to be always fighting usually over money. Children? Well his only experience was his and he vowed that if he had children, they would not be beaten like he was. So, for the time being he was quite content to carry on living as he was, it wasn't half bad, he thought.

Now Harold knew nothing about women and sex but had picked up some ideas from the talk of the other men and as he was now seventeen and he had feelings that he didn't quite understand but every time he saw these women, he felt a strange urge down below his belly. One night one of the women came to the table where he was sitting with two of his mates, she sat on the edge near him and said "Well my fine fellow you look as if you could give a lady a good time". He blushed and looked down into his pint glass; she put her hand under his chin and lifted his face up to look at her. He tried not to notice that her dress was very low, and he could see her breasts hanging there. Never having touched women's breasts before or been so close he went even redder in the face. "Come on my lad why not give a lady some pleasure, I am very reasonable". He looked at her and frowned thinking what does she mean by being reasonable? Jim whispered in his ear, "She will do a trick for two bob". Even more confused now Harold looked at Jim and whispered, "What sort of trick?" Jim laughed at loud; "I think you have a virgin here, treat him gently" he looked at the women as he said it. 'Go on, lad, she will show you what a trick is".

The women took hold of his hand and lifted him up "That's right I can teach you everything you want to know and more, if you want" Harold wasn't sure what was going on and didn't much like the laughter going on, at his expense he thought. So reluctantly he allowed himself to be pulled through the throng and up the stairs. At the top of the stairs was a corridor with doors on each side, on the floor was a strip of threadbare carpet that might have had some colour once but was now just a grey ribbon. The women gently pulled him along and then opened a door on the right, pulled him in and shut it behind them, locking it with a key.

"Right then first of all what shall I call you?" "Well my name is Harold"

"So that is what I shall call you, you can call me Mary"

Sitting on the side of the bed she patted a space beside her and beckoned him to come and sit there, Harold slowly moved across and sat a foot away from her. "Now Harold, is that right you have never slept with a woman before?" "No, I have never slept with any one before; they don't allow that at the Sally Army". She laughed, he quite liked her laugh it was merry and cheerful and filled him with happiness. "Well what I am going to do is to teach you something about men and women. First of all, I suppose you noticed that men and women are built differently, is that right?" "Yes" "Do you know how babies are made?" "No!" said Harold moving away "I don't want no baby!" "Well that's fine then, because only women can have babies" she laughed again. "Right so let's get down to business. I normally charge two bob for a trick but for you, as it's your first time I am going to only charge you a shilling, that OK?" Harold wasn't sure if it was or not but dipped into his pocket and pulled out two sixpences and put them in her hand. "Great, now we can start as you have paid your dues, I must pay mine!"

Reaching over she began to unbutton his shirt, "Oy!" he said pulling away. "What are you doing?" "Well we can't do a trick with our clothes on so you had better take them off" she smiled as she said this and Harold smiled back but wasn't sure why doing a trick you had to take your clothes off. So, he turned away from her and took his shirt off "you have to take all your clothes off, silly" she said.

Harold slowly took his clothes off and stood their naked not sure what to do next. "Right get into bed now" he half turned and saw that she was already in bed, lifting the sheet he slid under the covers not facing her. She put her arm around him and pulled him towards her, he realized she had no clothes on and was slow to come around. She pulled him to her and kissed him on the lips.

Harold had never been kissed by anybody especially on the lips and was surprised but it felt good. She pulled him down to the pillow and pulled his hand towards her breast, hesitatingly he followed her, and he was surprised how soft her breast was. "Just follow me and you will soon get the hang of it" she said. She said this is my nipple and it excites most women, some more than others. Just gently take the nipple between your thumb and finger and squeeze it and then pull it up. Do it gently and a woman will love it. Always be gently when you are making love to a woman and she will do whatever you want. So, for the next while she showed him a women's body, from head to toe. Telling him what was good to do and what was not good to do.

He began to get that burning feeling again and felt his penis expanding; pulling back he stared as it had never done that before. She took it in her hand and gently massaged it, the burning got stronger and his penis got harder, then she pulled him on top of her and pushed his penis inside her. What glories! What sensation! He soon got the hang of what to do and started going in and out fast, faster and faster than he felt as if he was going to explode, and then he did. He felt as if he was melting into her and then it was over. He lay on top of her exhausted but exhilarated. She smiled up at him and caressed his cheek. "Well that was your first trick. How did you like it?" "It was great" Harold looked at her and thought he had found someone who he could love and might love him as nobody ever had before. "Right" she said "times up let's get dressed" Harold looked at her, now so business-like and rolled onto the bed. As he dressed, he wondered what had happened.

"I love you" he said. "No, you don't you only think so because this is your first time, once you have done it a few times you won't think anything of it" she said. Puzzled Harold couldn't understand how her attitude had changed. "But you were so loving in bed, what now?" "Look she said I do this for a living, just like you work at the market, we all have to live". He stared at her, for a living he thought, he felt ashamed and angry. This woman had led him on thinking she cared for him, but she didn't she was doing a job!

He raced out of the room downstairs and out of the pub, ignoring the laughter from the people inside. He felt angry, betrayed. Everybody was the same, all they wanted was money, nobody did anything for love or friendship. Of course, he thought, I should have realised that because nobody has ever cared about me before so why should they now. He went back to join the queue at the Sally Army and got himself a bed. But he couldn't sleep even though he knew he had to get up in a few hours. The whole scenario played out in his mind and he relived the emotions he had felt, but at the end the emotion he had when he had come inside her was the one, he remembered most fondly and he determined he would do it again, and soon.

He was busy with work for the next few days and didn't get back to the pub until Friday evening. As he walked in it was full as usual with lots of noise from the people talking the thick fog of cigarette smoke covered them all. He walked to the bar looking for Mary, but he couldn't see her at first. He ordered a pint and looked around for somewhere to sit; eventually he found a space by the back wall. Sitting down he had a draw on his pint, felt good as he hadn't had a drink in two days. Satisfied he lay back in his chair surveying the crowd, he saw some people he recognized but they were busy talking to each other, in a way he was glad because he didn't want them to remind him of his last visit and the humiliation he felt then.

He had a second and a third pint and was now feeling quite mellow when he saw her! She was at a side table with a big man and they were laughing and touching each other, she motioned with her head and he nodded. They got up and started to make their way to the stairs through the crowded tables. He jumped up without realising so and began to move towards the stairs intending to cut them off. He felt angry and not sure what he was doing but he wanted to confront her and make her sorry for what she had done. He got to the stairs just as they did and grabbed her wrist and attempted to pull her towards him, but the man smacked his arm and made him let go. Harold cried out in pain and attempted to hit the man, but he was much too big and strong for him. "What do you think you are doing?" he demanded. "None of your business" said Harold, turning to Mary he said "I want to talk to you: "Not now sweetie I am busy as you can see" she replied with a slight smile on her face. "Well I want to talk to you now!" Harold shouted attempting to pull her back again. "Not now, little boy. I have a man to deal with: she replied with heavy sarcasm and pulled her arm away again and started up the stairs. "You can't treat me like this!" Harold shouted, "I love you and you can't have another man". She turned and looked into his face "You are only a boy, go away and come back when you are a real man and then I might see you' she said with anger in her voice. "No, you won't" he shouted and once more tried to grab her.

By now the man was fed up and he turned on Harold and said, "look sonny, the lady doesn't want anything to do with you so do as she says and go away". Harold turned to the man and tried to hit him with a swinging right but long before it would have reached him, he was lying on the floor semi-conscious from a blow from the man. As he lay there, he could hear the people laughing at him.

Groggily he got to his feet, face red with embarrassment and pushed his way through the crowd angry at his further humiliation at her hands. Outside the pub he leaned against the wall trying to clear his head of the alcohol and the punch he had suffered. He bitterly thought of what he would do to Mary to get back at her, but now all he could do was stumble away back home.

Out into the night Harold half ran half stumbled, not thinking or caring where he went, he was so devastated. It was dark and there were not many people around, so he did not meet anyone as he wandered around the city. His mind was in a turmoil trying to sort out his emotions following his humiliation at the pub. How could she be so callous, I thought she loved me, he thought. With his lack of experience of life outside of his work he was totally confused.

It started to rain but he didn't notice blindly he walked down one street then another not knowing or caring where he was going.

He found a late-night café that was still open and sat down, morosely looking in front of him but seeing nothing. "Can I help you, sir?" a pleasant voice woke him from his reverie, and he saw that a young waitress was smiling at him. "I would like a cup of tea", "OK, won't be long, anything to eat?". Remembering he had eaten since lunch time he said, "could I have a ham and cheese sandwich with some plain crisps?" "Certainly, won't be a mo'". Of she went and Harold began to calm down from his anger but was still fuming quietly.

"She was only a prostitute so I should have known better than to give her any love, people like her don't want love they just want the money as fast as they can. Next time I won't fall for their lies and then I won't get hurt".

The tea and sandwich arrived, and Harold actually was able to smile at her "Ta!" he started on his sandwich and found he was really hungry, and he soon finished off. Drinking his tea, he waved at the waitress, she came over and he noticed that she was about his age and quite pretty and had a lovely smile. "What is your name?". "Emily" "that's a nice name, I would like something else to eat I forgot I haven't eaten all day" "Would you like some fish and chips?" "Yes, that would be great and another cup of tea". "No, Prob".

While he waited for his food Harold looked around, there were no other customers and Emily was busy talking to someone in the kitchen. When she came over with his plate of fish and a huge pile of chips he said, "Thanks, would you like to sit and talk to me?" glancing around Emily said "Yes". She sat down opposite him and watched as he tackled his meal, "Emily, do you have a boy-friend?" she looked at him a while then said "No, not now. Working here I don't have much time to go out". "Don't you get any time off?" "Yes, I work until 1 am then go home to bed. I start work again at 5 o'clock. So, I am sleeping while the world is awake and I can't go out in the evening because I am working, but I do have Monday off".

"Well we do have similar lives, I work in the vegetable market and start at 4 in the morning, finishing about 10. So, I sleep most of the evening because I have to be up early" Harold was now feeling much better and enjoying his meal and his talk with Emily. Finishing his meal, he leaned back and smiled at her. "we don't know each other very well yet but I would like to get to know you better. Would you?" "No, thank you. We have only just met, and I don't know you at all".

His temper began rise again, he looked at her then abruptly got up, laid some money on the table and almost ran out of the door. Once more a woman had rejected him for no reason that he could see, fuming at his treatment by women he walked quickly down the road.

Looking at the clock on the wall he saw it was already ten and he needed to be at work at four so he began to hurry home, the rain had stopped now and the streets smelled clean and fresh and he felt that the world was a pretty good place after all.

He found himself near the docks in the city Centre and then he saw this girl walking alone towards Queen Square. For no particular reason he followed her and she realized this and began to walk faster, Harold pretended to go around the square the other way but halfway he ran across through the bushes and grabbed her as she passed, she screamed but he put his hand over her mouth and dragged her into the bushes.

Throwing her roughly to the ground he lay on her and ripped open her blouse, roughly fondling her large breasts he reached down, and she began to fight him. He slapped her on the face, and she stopped and then he reached down and lifted her skirt, pulled down her knickers and raped her. He felt good it was a long time since Mary and he had not had another woman, so the physical relief was wonderful. Rolling of her he did up his pants and noticed she hadn't moved, reaching over her lifted her head and realized she was dead!!

Harold was desperate, he hadn't meant to hurt her, and he was hurting himself and just wanted some love. Dropping her head, he looked around, they were well hidden in the bushes, so he carefully crawled out checking to make sure no-one was around then crossing the road he ran all the way back to his room.

Gasping for breath he tried to decide what to do. As far as he knew nobody had seen him so perhaps, he might get away with it, but somebody at the pub would tell the police of his fight and they would come looking for him. After some time, he decided his best option was to leave Bristol. Getting his money and few belongings he put them in a sack and made his way to the Railway Station at Temple Meads. Having no idea where he was going, he asked the ticket seller where the next train was going, last train tonight is going to London he said so Harold bought a ticket and made his way to the platform.

Looking around nervously he saw there were only 5 other people on the platform. He took a seat as far away from them as he could and had 45 minutes to worry about what was going to happen. Suddenly he saw a policeman enter the platform, he shrank back against the wall and prayed that the policeman wasn't looking for him, no, he just looked around spoke to the ticket collector and left. Relieved Harold impatiently waited for the train, at last it arrived in a cloud of steam and smoke, luckily it was one of those no corridor trains so he found an empty carriage and got in, pulled down the blinds and hoped no-one else would come in. the train was only stopping in Bath so once they left Harold felt relieved and managed to drop off to sleep.

CHAPTER 4

Penny and her school days

My name is Penny and I had grown up in the urban town of Ipswich; my parents both worked for the local council. Mum, Margaret, in the housing department and Dad, Albert, in planning. They had always worked there from leaving school, they would be considered boring, but they considered themselves to be contented. They had never wanted anything else, not wild parties; holidays charging down a wild waterway on a rubber raft, no hang-gliding. The most exciting thing they had ever done was probably buying their house from the council. They considered this a great risk, and for the generation born during the Second World War they were no exception to all their generation.

I was born 5th March 1945 in Ipswich Nursing Home right at the end of the war, so I had grown up in the days of rationing, never having known going shopping without coupons. Being born towards the end of the war was a terribly depressing and lonely time for most of my generation, having parents who did not understand that after the war everything was different, but they desperately tried to keep hold of their old values. By the time I was old enough to go to senior school I had begun to see what was happening around me and was struggling with trying to keep my parent's values in a rapidly changing world.

When I passed my eleven plus, I was looking forward to meeting new people and having a good time. I joined up with a couple of other girls in my class, Ruth and Ann. We liked each other and went around with each other that week as we discovered the school. Ruth was into music and was learning to play the piano and viola her father was a director of an engineering company and her mother stayed at home, Ann's parents were both civil servants working in the department of employment. We all enjoyed the same things and used to go the pictures on Friday evening and to the local dance hall on a Saturday where we met the local young people. Mostly we just drank soft drinks and made sure that we got home by 10 o'clock as our parents insisted. I did reasonably well at school, I was not the most brilliant scholar in the class, but I worked hard and didn't cause any trouble.

One topic we discussed of course was boyfriends and they eagerly discussed all the potential boyfriends and selected their favourite. Eventually a couple of boys from the second year began paying us more attention and they debated amongst ourselves which boy was interested in who. Eventually it was clear that Richard was interested in me and his friend Harry was after Ann, this made Ruth feel a bit out of it. I was excited and apprehensive, as she hadn't had a boyfriend before.

I noticed that quite a few boys seemed to be interested in me but never got any further than saying hello, which worried me a bit. After all I thought I was quite presentable, perhaps tending to be overweight, plump was the polite expression. I had developed large breasts like my mother early. When I was only ten, I had been a bit embarrassed about them and tried to hide them.

Eventually Richard had asked her if I would like to go to the pictures, shyly at first, I refused. This seemed to make him keener, I didn't realize that by refusing it seemed to him that I was playing hard to get, such a thought was furthest from my mind. He persisted and eventually I said o.k. but I had to ask my mother first. My parents said that they needed to meet him first, after all I had never had a boyfriend before. Richard agreed and said he would call around about 6 to pick me up.

I excitedly went through all my clothes looking for some- thing special, wailing to her mother that she had nothing to wear the cry of all women for 6 to 60 through the ages. Eventually with my mother's help I decided to wear my short sleeve white blouse with the ruffles around the neck. And my blue skirt that was dangerously short, so my dad said, as it came to just below my knees. Mother overruled him, so he demurred. I was ready by 5:30 and anxiously waited in my bedroom for Richard to knock. By 5:45 I thought he wasn't coming, by 6:00 I knew he wasn't. And thought what a laughingstock I would be at school on Monday when the heard of me being stood up.

Weighed down with misery I lay on my bed trying not to cry and cursing all boys for being so cruel. Suddenly the doorbell rang, I leapt up in a panic looked in the mirror to see if my first attempt, well her mother's mostly, had been ruined. Her mother called up that Richard was here, I panicked again did I look o.k., what would he think?

Then plucking up courage I opened the door and walked down the stairs. Trying to be erect and disdainful like a princess, but thinking I just looked a fool. Richard was standing in the hallway with her mother on one side and her father looking glumly on the other. Richard smiled and I coyly smiled back. My father said that they were to come straight back after the show. I was mortified. Dad was treating me like a baby, and I was all of 11!

Richard squirmed awkwardly as my parents instructed them again on what was expected. Finally, they got out of the house; Richard led the way and opened the gate for me. I could hear her mother saying what a gentleman he was and blushed in shame again. He didn't seem to notice and walked awkwardly beside me; a bit closer than you normally would but not close enough to actually touch me.

They talked in fits and starts, we both seemed unsure of what to do or say. We got on the bus and when we arrived at the cinema there was a queue. I wasn't sure whether to be proud or not because we were in public together. Then two of his mates came along, they winked at him and hoped he would have a good time but didn't speak to me it was as if I was not there. I wasn't sure whether to be upset about their attitude, but I decided to ignore them. He bought me some Black Magic chocolates and then we went in.

He immediately took me to the back row despite my quiet protestations, telling him that I preferred to be in the middle. He was silent as they waited for the film to start, through the adverts, trailers, coming soon etc. I wondered when the film would start, eventually it did.

It was a film and I had been looking forward to seeing it with her parents, but it was better with a boyfriend. First of all there was the B Feature and they sat through the first 20 minutes side by side and they could have been strangers, then he slid his arm round the back of my seat and it lay just barely touching my shoulders.

I sucked in my breath waiting for my first cuddle from any man other than my father. I watched the film but didn't see or hear anything as I waited for his next move, and waited, and waited. I thought he must have nodded off, the he brought his hand over my shoulder and gripped it hard. It hurt a bit but I didn't say anything, then I began to relax and moved closer to his seat beginning to enjoy the sensation when the film ended and he abruptly withdrew his arm looking around as if embarrassed to be seen.

They spoke a few words in the interval, he bought me an ice cream tub, and it seemed to be more to stop me talking than anything else. Then the main feature started. I waited for him to put his arm back, but he seemed reluctantly too so I moved across my seat and gently lay on his arm. He took the hint and put his arm around my shoulder again. I relaxed and was enjoying the film when I felt him turn towards me and bring his other arm across my lap; I tensed again not sure what to do or what he was doing.

His hand lay in my lap just below my waist and I began to accept it being there when he moved it up and grabbed my blouse and my breast. I pulled away turning to look at him, surprise anger registered on my face. Then I told him that he wasn't to do that.

He seemed to accept that and pulled me back towards him and gave me a cuddle. I was wary but thought that perhaps it was an accident. He seemed to be holding me a bit tightly and then he tried to kiss me. Well I had never been kissed by any boy before and didn't know what to do.

I just sat there as he brushed my lips. Well that wasn't too bad I thought and let him do it again, and he did but harder this time, which I didn't find so pleasing. Then as he kissed me again, he groped my breast again this time much harder. Alarmed I pulled away, tears welling into my eyes, what was he doing? I wasn't that sort of girl.

Nice girls didn't do that her mother had told me only two days ago. He turned away and for the rest of the film treated me as if I wasn't there. After the film he put me on the bus and said he had to get home. Miserably I sat on the bus wondering what had gone wrong. My first date and I had spoiled it. When I got home, I pretended that Richard had stayed on the bus and everything was fine. But I quickly went to my room and cried, why I wasn't sure.

On the Monday I was a bit apprehensive and as I walked to school I kept looking for Richard but was relieved not to see him. But on entering the school yard one of the first people I saw was Richard, he was with a group of boys and one of them nudged him and pointed.

He looked in my direction and then said something with a smile to his friends and they all laughed, then he turned away and ignored me. Mortified I carried on towards the entrance trying not to cry or let them see my distress. Of course, Ruth and Ann wanted to know everything that had happened and at first, I tried to pass it off but by lunchtime I had to tell them what had really happened. Ruth told her that I did the right thing and shouldn't have anything to do with Richard again, but Ann wasn't so sure. She thought that by doing what I had done I would be seen as being a bit of a prig. After all Richard had only done what she expected any boy to try, and she told them that Harry had also done the same to her and she enjoyed it. It was thrilling to have someone touch your body like that, but of course she only allowed Harry because she loved him.

I was aghast that Ann could do such things, how could she be so loose, and we had our very first argument, all over a boy.

That day I noticed that a lot of the older boys seemed to be laughing at me, but I dismissed it as my imagination especially when

Ronald from the third form asked me to the pictures on Saturday. I said O.K. as long as my parents agreed. My parents wanted to know what had happened to Richard and I said he was only a passing fancy, so they agreed. Ronald did not come to my house but arranged to meet me at the cinema at 5 o'clock so I spent the afternoon in town with the girls and we all walked to the cinema together.

Ann's boyfriend turned up at five to five and Ruth decided to go home so left me there by myself. By quarter past I was beginning to get a bit upset, standing there by myself I felt isolated and thought everyone was saying "she's been dumped". Then just as I was about to go home, he rushed around the corner, saying he was so sorry, but he had to help his dad in the garden and couldn't get away. Because the film started in five minutes we went straight in and he bought me a bar of fruit and nut chocolate and because we were late, we had to sit near the front. In a way I was dreading that something would go wrong again so when he held my hand in my lap, I smiled at him and squeezed his hand back. He didn't try to do anything else and I felt quite relaxed as we left the cinema and he suggested a cup of coffee before I caught my bus home. We had a cup of coffee in the new coffee bar and talked about the film and school, then he walked me to the bus stop, and I caught the bus home. On the bus I felt elated, at last I had found a boy who treated you with respect and didn't expect you to do things that other girls might do who were not as good as you.

On Monday I got to school as fast as I could looking for Ronald but when I found him, he was with his mates and as soon as he saw me coming, he disappeared. Puzzled I went into class. During the week I kept trying to see him, but he was always disappearing and then on Thursday I ran into him coming out of the library. He denied that he was avoiding me just hadn't been in the same place as me. Anyway, he said how about coming to a dance on Saturday at the town hall, I immediately forgave him and said yes. Happy again I skipped through the rest of the week looking forward to Saturday.

On Saturday I took ages to choose what to wear, Ruth and Ann came to help but I think made it ten times worse. Eventually I decided on a blue dress with a sailor neck and a dark blue belt. It came down to my knees and we agreed to take it up a bit, but as soon as dad saw it, he ordered me to take it down again saying he didn't want a tart for a daughter. Angry but obedient I did as he said but as soon as I was out, I went into the nearest ladies and hastily stitched it up again.

At the dance there were hundreds of people I had never been in such a crowd, but Ronald turned up on time and we went in and got ourselves some orange squash and lemonade. Ronald and I were not good dancers, so we basically walked around to the slow music but when the rock and roll started, we joined in with the others just copying what they did.

I was having a great time enjoying the music and Ronald's company so when he said let's go outside for some fresh air, I didn't expect anything. We went outside and as I leaned against the wall, he went to kiss me, but I had not expected it so drew away, he demanded to know what was wrong and I said nothing really. Then he said hadn't I been kissed before and I said not really, so he was much gentler and kissed me gently on the lips and I loved it. We then started kissing more urgently and my mind was in a turmoil I didn't understand what was going on in my mind. These feelings were new and unexpected but exciting as well then, he pressed his right hand on my breast, and it hurt. I pulled away and he looked strangely at me, he said it was typical of your sort of girl lead a boy on and then stopped. He stormed away and after a while I went back into the dance hall to find him, but I couldn't find him anywhere so eventually I went home.

On the Monday as I walked into school, I heard the boys muttering to each other, the words "slag" and "cock tickler" were said as they glanced over their shoulders at me. Even some of the girls in my year ignored me and I wondered what had happened. Then I met Ann and asked her what was going on. "Don't you know? What did you do to Ronald on Saturday?". "I didn't do anything" I replied defensively, I didn't want to tell about my humiliation at the dance. "Well he is putting it around that you led him on and then refused him. Did you do that?" "No, I didn't," I almost cried in horror, why was he saying such things, I hadn't done anything it was him. "Well you have been branded a slag because he says you lead boys on and then stop them". Tears were welling up into my eyes but then the bell went, and we had to go into assembly.

I found out that week that everyone believed I was the sort of girl to lead boys on to believe I was easy, and then at the critical moment stopped them. Someone drew a stick figure on the board and labelled it slag, when the teacher asked what was going on nobody said anything. She said that it was not nice to call someone a slag and she hoped that no one in her class said such things, there was a bit of a giggle and that was that.

Now I found that no one wanted to talk to me, even Ruth and Ann weren't as friendly as before. That night I went home and ran up to my room where I cried my eyes out, but only softly because I didn't want mum to hear me and make me even more ashamed. Somehow, I got through the week and the next, slowly things got back to normal but none of the boys asked me out again.

This situation carried on through the next two years, some boys did ask me out but none of them attempted anything sexual, I even got to a point of nearly asking them to do something. But in a way this was good because I had more time to study and to keep my mind of boyfriends. I was excluded from many social occasions because I was a single and nearly all my classmates were in some sort of relation-ship, a couple of times mum asked why I didn't go out on a weekend and I made some excuse about studying for a good result. Eventually I obtained eight GCE Ordinary Level Passes, which should have meant me going into the sixth form, but I couldn't bear the situation anymore, so I went to the local college and did my A Levels there. I passed Levels in English Language, History and Geography. This was enough for me to go to teacher training college in Manchester, and I hoped for a new and more exciting life.

That summer we went to Great Yarmouth for a week's holiday in a caravan. This was a typical holiday for many working-class people. At least it was a change of scenery and new things to see and do. Great Yarmouth is a very popular resort and all along the seafront are attractions like slot machines, rides, candy floss stall, souvenir shops and cafés, some called themselves restaurants, but this was just to appear better and could charge more. The beach is very long and lots of people would go down there and hire a deckchair and sit on the sand all day, bringing their own food and drink.

I laughed to see some people struggling to set up their deckchairs, it can be tricky if you don't know how to do it, she had seen some comedian making it funny and some of these people were the same.

This being only 1963 the attitude of most adults was still the same as before the war. For example, some men turned up in a suit and sweltered in the sun, the thought of taking anything off was not considered nice. To relieve the heat some of them knotted a handkerchief and put it on their head, there were some adventurous ones who did take of their jacket. The women were the same they wouldn't consider baring any part of their body, anyone who exposed their arms were considered adventurous, and showing any leg above the knee was being a "slut".

If they had children, they would take them down to the sea for a paddle so the men, if they could be persuaded to go, took of their socks and shoes and rolled up their trousers a few inches.

The children spent the day building sandcastles, playing football, or just running around, they were dressed as much like their parents so didn't get fresh air on their bodies. One of the highlights was when the man came with ice cream, all the parents were begged to buy them and being on holiday they usually did.

After a day on the beach all the family trooped of to a café for a meal, usually fish and chips. The national dish of England. There were other items on the menu like roast beef and Yorkshire puddings but not many people had them. For pudding the usual choice was ice cream. After dinner they walked around the amusements and the children played the penny games, when they won, they jumped for joy, but of course they lost more than they won. Then it was back to where they were staying. Many people stayed in boarding houses or B&B, others like my family stayed at a caravan park.

Caravan parks were cheaper but of course you had to do all your own catering whereas in the B&B breakfast was provided, but you had to be out by 9 am and not allowed back until 5 pm. This was OK if the weather was fine but if it was raining, it does a lot in England, then what were they to do all day? A nightmare for parents. If you had a caravan at least you could stay, there for as long as you wanted which was much more convenient.

Now being eighteen I did not want to sit on the beach all day I wanted to do and see things, my parents couldn't understand why, after all being on holiday was relaxing doing nothing. On the second day I managed to persuade them to let me go to look around the front, but they told me to be back by 12 for lunch. Happily, I ran off the beach and across the road to the attractions.

I had managed to save five shillings so had some money to spend. I walked around looking at the games, penny waterfall, ball drop, grab and go, and the first video games. I had a few goes but didn't win anything so went out. Walking along I came upon a group of people a bit older than me she stood outside the group, then one of the boys came over to me and asked my name. Smiling I told him, I was glad someone had noticed me.

I found out his name was Stephen and they were all from Norwich where they all belonged to the same youth club. They were about 20 years old so a bit older than me. I walked around with them for a while and they said they were going to have a party on the beach tonight, they said why not come along? I demurred I was sure my parents wouldn't let me out at night. Then I saw a clock on the wall 12.15! my goodness I had better get back to my parents. By time I got back it was 12.30 and a volley of anger met me. I didn't try to defend herself and just waited for them to finish. All afternoon I lay on the beach waiting for the time to go home. After their fish and chips, they silently went back to the caravan and waited to go to bed. Not a word was said just a sullen and angry silence.

The rest of the week was the same, such a fuss over being late but that was my parents. I was glad when we went home.

CHAPTER 5

Harold's Adventures in London

Harry woke up with a start as he felt the train come to a noisy halt with brakes grinding and steam whistling out of the carriages, then with a final heavy jolt it stopped. Carefully Harold looked out of the window, seeing only a few fellow passengers hurrying away he stepped out of the carriage and walked purposely down the platform to the ticket collector. At this time of the morning he was not very alert and took Harold's ticket without looking at it.

Harold moved away as quickly as he could without attracting any attention, he looked around and decided that he would spend some of his precious savings on a breakfast as he hadn't eaten since lunch time yesterday.

Entering the restaurant there were only about 6 patrons so he went to the counter and ordered a bacon sandwich and a cup of tea, he was shocked at the price not realizing that prices in London were a lot higher than in Bristol. Impatiently he waited for his order and then quickly went to a table near the back wall with a view of the door. He was still afraid that the police would walk in and arrest him, but he finished his sandwich and then watching carefully he walked out of the station.

To his mind there were police everywhere, but this was London and there were a lot more police to be seen than in Bristol, but he was not aware of that.

Now the next thing was to find a job, it was still only 4 am so he wondered if there were any markets around as that was where he had been working all his life. He asked a passer-by "Is there a market near here?" he said, "Of course Convent Garden". Harold had never heard of it "So how do I get there?"." Take the number 9 bus to Leicester Square and it's just around the corner". "Thanks" said Harold. Looking around all the buses he eventually found a number 9.

He jumped on the bus "How do I get to convent garden?" "That will be 3 pence" the conductor said. So, another bit of his savings had gone, but never mind he was sure he could get work there. The conductor called out "Leicester Square!" when he got off, he looked for a direction post but couldn't see any. So, he asked another man "Which is the way to the garden?" and he said, "Why it's just down there and around the corner", "Thanks" said Harold. He set off and within 5 minutes found the place.

It was much bigger than the one in Bristol.

He looked around at the stalls and found one that had flowers, he knew about them so approached the owner and asked, "Do you have any work today?" The man said, "Do you know anything about flowers?" And Harold said, "I worked at another market doing the flowers, so I do". The man, whose name was Sid, said "OK, I will give you a trial for a couple of days. start by clearing all those boxes away".

Harold was glad to have got a job so easily and set to work with energy, before Sid knew he was back. "Finished already?" "Yes, it was easy". Sid looked and saw everything was cleaned up. Impressed he asked, "What is your name?" for a moment Harold paused then looking across the road he saw a sign Be a Kings Man, so he said "King, John King". "O.K. John let's get to work".

Harold worked hard and when the market was closing Sid said "Well you certainly work hard. Would you like a permanent job?" Well Harold was over the moon and said "Yes please" without asking how much his pay was. Sid said, "well you seemed to know your job so I will start you on 2 pounds a day, is that O.K.?" Harold had never been paid so much so he said, "Thanks very much".

He did not know that London was much more expensive than Bristol. Sid asked, "Do you have anywhere to stay?" Harold said "No, I have only just arrived in town. Sid said "Go down that road over there and you will see a tall red brick building, it's about half a mile away. And tell them that Sid sent you and they will give you a room".

Harold said "Thanks" and then rather embarrassed asked Sid "Could you let me have my days' pay as I am a bit short". Sid looked at him for a moment and then said "Look you are a hard worker and I think I can trust you so I going to give you three days' pay in advance and will deduct it from next week's wages, OK?" "Thanks" said Harold and gratefully took the 6 pounds.

At that moment it seemed like a for- tune, he was soon to find out it wasn't. He found the building and saw it was a Victorian building that had been converted into small rooms, he saw there was a man at the desk so he walked up and said "I am looking for a room". The clerk looked at him and then said, "We're full".

Puzzled Harold said, "Well Sid, my employer said you had some rooms", immediately the man's demeanour changed. "Oh! You work for Sid Owens down at the market; well I always keep a room available for his friends so that's OK. Normally the rent is 4 pound a week but for Sid its three pounds 15 shillings that OK?" "Fine" said Harold appalled at the cost compared to his room in Bristol." I need a week in advance but as it's already Monday then 3 pounds will be fine, rent is due every Friday O.K.?"

Harold handed over 3 pounds, now he only had 3 pounds to live on till pay day then of course he had to pay back six pounds of his twelve pounds. Nevertheless, he had a room and a job so he would make it with what was left of his savings of ten pounds.

The room was on the second floor overlooking the street, quite a nice room as that sort of room was. It obviously had not seen any paint in years, there were some scraps of wallpaper with flowers hanging down, and on the floor was a small carpet in front of a small grate that probably wouldn't give much heat in the winter. There were no curtains on the window, Harold wasn't bothered as he was on the second floor, there was also armchair that might have survived since the First World War, but he sat in it and it was quite comfortable.

So, sitting there he looked around and was quite happy with the situation in general, he seemed to have fallen on his feet as the saying goes. He opened his parcel put his clothes in a small chest of drawers by the window then decided he needed to have a look around and get some lunch. Outside the street was busy now it was 8 am all the office and shop workers were rushing to their jobs, being late was a serious offence. Despite this being the 1960's many employers still lived in the 1930's and didn't understand that life was changing fast and would get faster. So those who didn't change with it would get left behind.

Harold saw that there were only a few shops here and, on the corner, a large one that seemed to sell everything under the sun. He wandered along looking for somewhere to eat and came into a square like area; it was called the Seven Dials. Where there were lots of shops and cafés. He stopped by one and asked for his usual full breakfast as he was starving having only had that bacon sandwich when he arrived.

He didn't like the price but felt he could afford it now and was well satisfied when his plate arrived piled high with 3 rashers of bacon, 2 eggs, a pile of chips, 2 pieces of toast with butter and marmalade, and a large mug of tea.

Having eaten that lot he lay back in his chair and felt very comfortable, he had almost forgotten the events of the previous day it seemed so long ago, suddenly the memory came back and he looked around to see if any police were heading his way. He couldn't see any, so relaxed a bit before deciding to have a walk around the area and see what London was like.

Compared to Bristol it was very busy with people everywhere and seemingly not taking notice of anyone else, just pushing them out of the way in their hurry to get wherever they were going. Harold didn't understand the rush; surely it wasn't that important to get somewhere?

There were many more shops here and an amazing variety of goods were for sale, but Harold still wasn't used to the prices.

Everything seemed so expensive and his wages seemed to get smaller as he saw how much he had to pay. There were also lots of people from other countries and he was surprised when he saw his first black man. He couldn't help staring and luckily the man just carried on.

He wasn't the last black person he saw because the government had persuaded many Jamaicans to come over and work in London because they didn't have enough workers. The country was still suffering from the effects of the war and all the men that had been lost. Jobs were available for everyone and most were reasonably paid, some hours were long, but people seemed quite content to do them. One of the biggest problems was housing. So many houses had been bombed flat by the Germans that there was a severe shortage. It took time for the council to clear the sites and start building. One solution had to build "new towns" these were about 30 miles outside London and people were encouraged to go and live there in new houses with new jobs. Many Londoners didn't want to go but some had no choice and found life was much better there than in their old neighbourhoods.

Harold eventually found himself in Leicester Square. This was very popular place for people to meet, day or night. There were cinemas, night clubs, café, restaurants shops; almost everything was available day or night including of course the prostitutes in Soho. He was approached several times and wondered why they were working at this time of the morning and there seemed to be a lot of them.

Harold was amazed and excited at this new place and was looking forward to living here and enjoying London. Eventually he felt tired as he hadn't had much sleep but then he couldn't remember where he was staying, for a moment he panicked but then he looked for the market. Eventually he found the market and was able to retrace his steps back to his flat. Collapsing on to the bed he fell asleep in no time, his first day in London had been revealing and exciting and he knew he would enjoy living here.

He woke early the next day and made his way to the market, outside was a cart selling bacon sandwiches and tea, so Harold bought some for breakfast and made his way to the stall. Sid was already there "Hello John, glad to see you made it I wasn't sure if you would wake up in time", "No problem I had an early night, so it was fine". "Right, let's get to work.

The van should get here in about 5 minutes and we need to get the best flowers before the others so be quick and grab what I tell you". Harold nodded in agreement and they made their way to the unloading area. The large lorry drew up and was surrounded by half a dozen other sellers, Harold being big was able to elbow his way to the front followed by Sid. As the boxes came off Sid looked and nodded to Harold which ones to pick. Harold picked them up and placed them on his cart. When it was full, he stacked them all around until Sid had enough stock, then he pushed the heavy cart back to their stall, returning for the rest whilst Sid paid the lorry man.

Having got their stock then they needed to display it to the best advantage so that the retailers would buy theirs not somebody else's. Having done this many times before Harold was quick and only had to make few adjustments as Sid preferred his stock arranged a little differently. In no time everything was ready, and Sid said, "Well done, you have definitely done this before and saved me half an hour". Then the retailers began to arrive, and Harold gently moved into their path, so they passed close to Sid's goods. By this tactic they sold their stock in record time.

Sid was really appreciative. "Come on let's clear up and I will treat you to breakfast". They cleared their pitch and made ready for tomorrow and then went to the Lord Nelson Pub. The Lord Nelson was unique in London being allowed to open from 6 am to 9 am for the benefit of the workers in the garden.

Sid and Harold enjoyed a great breakfast and a couple of pints of beer as they chatted together. Harold was very careful not to give any clues as to where he came from but when he pressed said Nottingham. He had no idea why as he had never been there but must have seen the name somewhere. At the end of breakfast Sid gave Harold two pounds, puzzled Harold said, "It isn't pay day is it?" "No" said Sid "You did such a good job today I was able to make more money so that is your share".

Happily, Harold took the money and said, "It has been my pleasure and I hope we will be working together for a while". "Sure thing, I think we will. Well cheers I will see you tomorrow morning". With a wave he stood up and walked out of the pub a very happy man, leaving behind another very happy man with unexpected money in his pocket.

Harold began exploring London; he walked down to the river Thames and towards Big Ben. He admired all the traffic, cars, red buses, Lorries, motor bikes and bicycles. He was amazed at all the traffic and wondered how so many vehicles got crammed onto the road. He stopped and leant against the wall watching the river traffic going up and down. Mostly they were small craft, tugs and lighters.

He entered Parliament Square and looked into Downing Street and then walked up Whitehall to Trafalgar square. The place was swarming with pigeons and they were a nuisance to people swooping down to pick up crumbs scattered by some people.

He then walked down Charing Cross road past the railway station and turned back into the garden. Now it was busy with people going to work or shopping, so he carried on back to his flat, there he lay down for a few hours' sleep.

When he woke up, he was hungry so set out to find somewhere to eat, from his previous walks he knew where some cafés were so went in that direction. Looking in the windows he saw that it was early yet for dinner so there were plenty of choices. He picked one that looked not too pricey and entered.

Inside there were about fifteen tables with nice blue and white tablecloths, metal cutlery and a small vase of flowers on each table. It looked a bit too expensive for him but now he was here he might as well try it, as he looked around he heard a cheerful voice "Good evening sir, how may I help you?" looking around he saw a pretty woman of about 20, 5ft 4 in tall and a curvy body smiling at him from the doorway.

"Let me find you the best table" she said and led him to a table near the back wall, just what Harold would have chosen himself. Her smiling caused Harold to smile back and felt quite at home already. "Here is the menu, tonight's soup is mushroom, I will be back in a little while so see what you might fancy" with another engaging smile she left.

For some time, Harold just sat and gazed at where she had gone then started to look at the menu. He was surprised to see that the prices were pretty good so looked more closely at the food. Now he had never eaten in a proper restaurant before so didn't recognize some of the dishes. But he saw Fish and Chips; well he knew what that was so decided on that. The waitress came back and said, "My name is Diane, what is yours" for a moment Harold forgot who he was then stammered "John" "Well John what would you like?" "I was thinking of having the Fish and Chips I haven't had any recently". "That's a good choice; would you like some bread and butter?"" Yes please" at this moment Harold would have said yes to anything she said.

He was bemused by her looks and manner. "Well the dinner will be about 20 minutes as I have to cook it, meanwhile would you like some tea?" "Yes, please" "OK I will be back soon" she then disappeared into her doorway. She soon came back with his tea and giving another of her smiles disappeared again.

Harold sat there with his tea thinking about this great woman, now of course Harold's track record with women was not very good so he was very hesitant at making any moves. She brought his plate, large piece of cod, pile of chips, a slice of lemon and two pieces of bread and butter. By now there were other customers, so she was busy most of the time, it seemed she ran the place by herself. Then about seven another girl came and put on her waitress costume.

Harold had been watching Diane and felt even more attracted to her. His thoughts were interrupted by "Can I get you anything else, sir?" it was the other waitress. Harold thought for a moment and she said, "We have some apple pie, would you like a slice with custard?" wishing to prolong his visit Harold nodded his head and she went off.

The pie was delicious, and Harold had not had such a good meal in his life. When the bill came, he really didn't care how much is was but was pleasantly surprised how little it was. No wonder the place was so busy. Reluctantly he paid his bill and wanted to speak to Diane before he left but she was not in sight, obviously in the kitchen cooking.

So slowly as he could he made his way to the door and went out. Just nearby was a pub so he went in there to have a few pints before bed. All the time he was thinking of Diane but eventually he left and went home as he had to be up at 3 am.

The following day Harold had his head full of Diane, but it did not interfere with his work and they had another successful day. At the end of the day the market manager came along and said, "Sid some of the other traders are complaining that you are preventing customers coming to their stalls". "How is that then?" "They say that your man here is blocking people's path to their stalls, so they are not getting the business and you are stealing it". "Well I have to stand somewhere" said Harold, "But not in the passageway so people cannot get past" said the manager. "Alright" said Sid "I will get him to stand somewhere else, I don't want any trouble here". "That's fine" said the manager "I don't want any trouble either, good day".

Sid said, "Tomorrow stand at the back of the stall near the gangway that, should be O.K.". Harold felt that coming to London had been a good thing, he tried not to think about why he had come that was too painful. Every evening he went to Diane's restaurant and had his dinner.

Harold couldn't wait to go to see Diane and he impatiently waited until 5 pm when she opened. He was there 15 minutes before and waited another 5 minutes as he didn't want to appear too eager, even though he was. He went in and was pleased to see that Diane was happy to see him. "Welcome John, I hoped you might come back" she said with that wonderful smile he already loved so much.

As per usual Harold was short on words so just said "I loved your food, so I came back". He tried to speak to Diane as often as he could and as the days passed, they became friends, and this made Harold very happy. He was still hesitant about making any romantic moves he was still hurting from his experience with Mary.

The work at the market was going well and Sid was very pleased with him, they began to strike up a friendship and they usually had a meal after work. Sid was married with three children so he tried to get home before they left for school, then he could sleep all day and be awake for them coming home. He obviously adored them all and he had a loving wife who kept the house and looked after him and the children. Harold was very envious as he had never had anyone who cared about him and his parents wished he had never been born.

One morning Sid said "Harold, it's my youngest fifth birthday so we are having a party on Saturday, would you like to come and meet the family?" Harold stopped for a moment; he had never been to a birthday party so was excited. "Yes, please I would love to meet your family". "Great. Don't worry about bringing her a present she will have lots more".

Harold nodded; he hadn't even thought about a present. He had never had any presents; nobody had celebrated his birthday and Christmas was the same as every other day. His sister got presents but he never did. That day he scoured the shops looking for something five-year-old would like. Eventually he came to a small toyshop and decided he needed some advice. "What would you suggest for a five-year-old girl?' "Well, all girls love dollies, here are some choose anyone you like". Harold looked at them all and finally decided on one with long blonde hair and eyes that opened and shut, he thought it was beautiful and not too pricey. He asked the shopkeeper to wrap it for him.

Then clutching his precious present, he hurried home.

Saturday came and he followed Sid's instructions to get to his house. He lived near Clapham Common, so he took the underground there and then asked for directions to Sid's house. He found it was only around the corner near the catholic church. There was no front garden the house was right on the pavement; he knew it was the right house by the noise of children coming from it.

Knocking loudly the door was opened by a middle-aged lady of about five feet five and quite tubby, she had a big smile and said, "Come in you must be Harold, Sid has told me so much about you". Walking in most of the children were in the back yard playing and someone was playing a violin. Sid came out and shook his hand, "Glad you could come, Rosie is looking forward to seeing you, you needn't have bought a present but thank you anyway".

"Rosie, you have a new visitor".

A small girl appeared a copy of her mother, she ran in and then coyly hid behind her father. "This is Harold, the best flower man in London" Sid said.

"Happy Birthday Rosie, I hope you like my present".

She rapidly tore of the paper and shouted with joy and happiness, "Look Daddy just what I wanted a Sleeping Beauty doll. How did you know?"

"Well I just asked the shop keeper"

She danced around with her doll and then ran off to show her friends.

"That was really great of you" said Sid.

"Well as I said I just asked the shop keeper".

Harold enjoyed the party, the fun and laughter, the food (and there were lots of it) and the sheer joy of being part of the celebration. Later he said his farewells and caught the train back to Leicester Square, he went home and fell asleep, this had been the happiest day of his life.

CHAPTER 6

Diane

He looked forward to his daily dinner at Diane's restaurant and usually turned up just after she opened so he might have a chance to talk to her before it got busy. Usually she showed him to the same table and she gave him a menu, "The soup today is tomato, if you would like some" he smiled as he had no words he could bring to mind, she smiled and moved away. He decided that today he would have beef pie with potatoes and cabbage so when she came back, he ordered that.

She brought his meal and didn't seem in a hurry to leave and sat down at the table. "Tell me, something about yourself as I can hear from your accent you are not a Londoner". Harold thought for a moment and then gave her his own version of how he came to be here." Well, I am originally from Bath but have been living in Nottingham for a while and decided to come to London as I have never been here before".

"I thought there was a West Country accent there. So where do you work?" "I work at the garden on the flower stall, so I am up early and early to bed, but the rest of the day is my own". "I hope you don't mind me asking you questions but I find you intriguing". "Not at all it's nice to talk to someone when you are in a strange town" Harold said. Just then customers began to come in, so she had to leave, but gave him a big smile. As usual the new waitress arrived, and the place was very busy, so Harold had to leave without seeing Diane again.

Most of his days followed the same pattern, working at the market, sleeping, going to the restaurant and then back home to bed. He was becoming more and more obsessed with Diane but was still too nervous to ask her for a date, he had found out that she owned the restaurant that had been left to her by her father and she didn't have any boyfriends.

One evening after his meal he decided to ask her for a date, now never having been on a date he wasn't sure what he was supposed to do, in fact if you asked him he probably wouldn't even understand the word. So that evening he waited for his bill and then asked the waitress, whose name was a Sally, if he could speak to Diane when she wasn't busy.

He had to wait about half an hour before she appeared, smiling and laughing. "What can I do for you? Do you have a complaint?" she laughingly asked. Flustered he looked at her and then gasped out "Can we go out?" for a moment she looked at him and then said with a pleasant voice "Sure, I can take an evening off, I will get another cook to come in. when would you like us to go out"

Harold hadn't thought that far ahead so he stuttered, "Whenever you are free". "OK" she said, "I will arrange for someone to come in. is that all?"" Yes". Now he was in strange territory he wasn't sure what to do next. "Well I will let you know when I am free. See you later" she said and smiled as she walked back to the kitchen.

All the way home Harold was in a daze, she had said yes, wow! What do I do now? Where do people go on an outing? The next day he casually, as he could, said to Sid "Where is a good place to go out with a girl?" "Well it's about time you got a girlfriend and I am glad about that. Well a good place is to a meal" "No she runs a restaurant, so I don't think so"." Well, then it must be the cinema. Go down to Leicester square and there are two cinemas there, you could ask her which one she would like".

"Great" said Harold and after he finished work, he wandered down to Leicester Square and looked at the board outside the cinema. He had never been inside a cinema; the only place he ever went in Bristol was to the pub, so this was another new experience. He looked at the prices and was surprised how expensive it was, but this was London and she was worth it.

It was three days before he got his answer. "I have arranged for someone to come in on Wednesday next week, is that OK?" "Yes" said Harold "But we need to go to the early show as I have to get up early"." No problem we can go at about 2 pm, is that OK? "Yes, the show starts at 2.30. I checked" "Oh we are going to the pictures? What are we going to see?" "I am not sure I wanted you to choose as I am not a great picture person" "Wonderful I think there is a love story on, I love romance. Do you?" thinking for a moment Harold decided that romance sounded good whatever it was. "Oh yes, I do".

He couldn't wait until Wednesday, but he did see here every night in the restaurant, so it wasn't all bad. Come the day he couldn't wait to finish work. "So, this is the day!" said Sid. Harold nodded. "What are you going to wear?" Wear! Harold hadn't considered that. "What should I wear" he asked anxiously. "Well go and buy yourself new shirt and trousers, a pair of black socks and black shoes. Then buy her a bouquet of flowers, you won't have far too look we sell them every day" he laughed at his own joke.

Harold was more serious, this was becoming expensive, still Sid must know what to do so he looked for a men's shop and cautiously walked in. "Sir!" an assistant looked at him as if he was something the cat dragged in. "Can we do anything for you?" he said sarcastically. "Well I need a shirt, pants, socks and shoes" instantly his demeanour changed. "Of course, sir, come this way' Harold allowed himself to be led to the back of the store and the man found him a white shirt, black pants, some black socks and shoes. "Will there be anything else, sir?"

Harold was sure that he already had too much. Shaking his head, he walked to the cash desk. "That will be 10 pounds and 12 shillings, sir" Harold stood and gaped at him. "What! That's a lot of money." "Yes sir, but it will last you for years, so it's worth it" luckily Harold still had his pay in his pocket so was able to pay the man.

Walking out he felt that he had been robbed but then thinking of Diane he decided she was worth it. Getting home he saw it was already 11 am so decided to have a wash and shave. Then he got dressed in his new clothes, looking in the murky mirror on his wardrobe he was surprised at what he saw. This was a new man and on reflection he quite liked him, he hoped Diane would.

He waited impatiently until 1.30 and then walked down to the restaurant. As he approached, he saw that it was closed, that was unusual, he knocked on the door and Diane came hurriedly out from the kitchen. Opening the door with a smile Diane said "Sorry, I am a bit late. Come on in and I won't be long." Harold came in and sat down. Diane appeared in about 30 minutes and said "you look really handsome, much better than your work clothes. Harold smiled and nodded he looked at her and said "you look much prettier than in your work clothes" they both laughed. and she took his arm and guided him out into the street.

As they walked along, they must have seemed an odd couple, Diane was only 5 ft 4 in slim and weighed about 7 stone and Harold was 6 ft 2 in and well-built weighing about 15 stone with all his hard work at the market. Diane kept up a constant chatter, Harold had nothing to say so he just listened to her and it made him feel very happy, he couldn't remember the last time he was so happy.

When they arrived at the cinema they looked at the films on show and Diane said "Let's see this one, it looks romantic" Harold nodded and they went in to the box office, now Harold had never been inside a cinema so wasn't sure what to do, luckily Diane took the lead and booked two seats in the balcony "I like the balcony you are higher up and more level with the screen" she explained.

Harold looked around and saw there were various things on sale, so he asked Diane if she wanted anything. "Hmm. Well I would like some popcorn and lemonade. Is that alright?" "Yes". He bought them each a bag of popcorn and a lemonade then they went up the stairs to the balcony, where the lady ripped their tickets in half and guided them into the auditorium. Harold was bemused he had never been in so magnificent a place before, with plush seats and wonderful decorations.

They sat down in the front row and Harold took in the view below, Diane touched his arm and said "Thanks for asking me out,

I haven't been out since my dad died. I have been so busy with the restaurant and of course nobody has asked me." She smiled up into his face and he felt so happy that he smiled back and wasn't sure if he should do anything like putting his arm around her. The moment passed and they settled back to watch the adverts, then the newsreel and finally the coming events trailers.

Harold wondered when they would get to the film. Finally, a film started but this wasn't the one he was expecting, he was about to say something to Diane when she said, "We will have to sit through this B film before we get to the one we want." He sat and watched some film about bank robbers who made a mess of the job and got caught, he was transfixed, he had never seen a moving picture before and loved it.

He was like a schoolboy at his first picture outing, which of course he was. By the end he thought I could do a better job than that. Then the lights went up and he looked around in wonder, now what? It was the interval and there was a lady with a large tray standing near him. "I wouldn't mind an ice cream, if that's alright". Of course, anything she wanted was alright, so he got up and went to join the queue and bought two ice creams. They came in a round tub with a wooden spoon stuck to the top. Diane quickly opened hers and Harold followed her example.

Then the main feature started. Harold was fascinated as he watched the film forgetting for a while who was with him, until she put her hand on his arm. Alarmed he jumped then came back to reality and smiled at her and put his hand on hers. She smiled at him and then laid her head on his shoulder; Harold didn't know what to do so he just enjoyed the feeling of her head on his shoulder.

From then on Harold didn't really watch much of the picture he just loved the feeling of her head to close to his. When the film finished, and the lights went up he was disappointed he wanted to stay this way for ever.

They got up and joined the queue to get out, slowly moving up the steps and then down the main stairs to the concourse. Out in the street the lights were on as it was 9 o'clock and normally Harold was in bed by now but there were no thoughts of sleep. As they walked home, she put her arm in his and he felt so proud and stood at least another foot higher.

When they got to her restaurant and saw it was busy so she said "Thanks for a lovely time, I must go in and help. See you tomorrow for dinner?" then she gave him a quick kiss on the cheek and was gone.

For a moment Harold stood there watching her run into the restaurant and into the kitchen, and then he turned and slowly made his way back home. His thoughts were racing; his emotions were in turmoil he didn't know what was happening. She kissed me! He thought nobody had ever kissed me before so that is how it feels. I want her to kiss me again and soon. Eventually he got home and realized he was exhausted so fell into bed. He overslept and didn't get to work until 4.30.

Sid was unhappy but said "I guess you had a late night, but don't be late again there is work to do". Harold worked extra hard to catch up and it drove the thoughts of the night before from his mind. When he finally finished, he went to the pub for his breakfast and a pint, halfway through he suddenly remembered all that had happened. It was like a dream; he went through every detail and especially the kiss!

He wondered how Diane would be when he went for his dinner and couldn't wait until then, but he was very tired, so he went home and had a good sleep. When he awoke it was 5 pm so he washed and shaved and put on his shirt and trousers, they were a bit rumpled, but he didn't notice anyway he didn't have any others. Then he rushed to the restaurant until he got to the corner when he slowed down and cautiously crept around the corner looking for Diane.

The restaurant only had one client so Harold slowly came through the door, but it had a tinkling bell, so Diane came out of the kitchen. Seeing it was him she smiled a big smile and almost ran to him and seemed to be about to hug him when she stopped. He wanted to hug her but as she had stopped, he didn't.

"John lovely to see you again. Had a good day?" "Yes, not bad" muttered still in awe of her and not sure what to do. "Well come on then, here is your usual table. And the soup tonight is mush- room. Shall I come back in a minute to get your order?" but she seemed reluctant to go and leant on the chair next to Harold. "I really enjoyed our outing, did you?" "Yes, it was very good, can we do it again?" "Why yes I thought you would never ask. How about next Wednesday?"

Next Wednesday! Harold didn't want to wait that long. Couldn't you make it a bit sooner?" he cautiously asked. "Well yes, I don't open on Sunday so how about that?" "Yes. I don't work on Sunday so that would be great" now happily relieved Harold smiled broadly and said, "I will have the beef dinner and apple pie with custard."

Diane smiled and touched him on the shoulder; "I am yours to command sir" she said jokingly and left to get his dinner.

That dinner was the best he had ever tasted he thought as he dwelt on her wonderful smile and happy personality. Sunday would be great, what should they do? So that night he went home a happy man and slept well and wasn't late for work.

His life followed the usual pattern but now Harold had something to look forward too. Each night he went to Diane's restaurant and managed to get some conversation before it filled up. It really was very popular, and it probably wasn't the food or the prices, though they were very good, but probably the presence of Diane who lit up the place and seemed to know everybody who came in.

Most of the patrons were couples but there were several single men and women who came in regularly for their evening meals. Harold had never felt happier in his life and Saturday evening he said to Diane "What time shall I call for your tomorrow?" for a moment she stopped smiling "Well I have to go to church first so I won't be home until 12.30. I can be ready by 2 pm is that O.K.?" he was relieved because Harold had been expecting something worse, he said "Of course not, I will see you then".

Sunday morning and Harold couldn't wait until the time came to go and get Diane, he had bought himself another shirt, a blue one this time and the assistant in the store was glad to see him again and fussed around getting the best shirt, he persuaded Harold to buy 3 with the promise that he would give him a 10 % discount. Harold by now was used to London prices and his wages at the garden were good enough to let him buy what he wanted.

Walking happily down the road he even tried to whistle, he never had before, and still couldn't. Arriving at the restaurant he saw the Diane was waiting outside, quickening his step he arrived. "Sorry, am I late?", "No I was finished early so I came out to wait for you" smiling Harold said, "Well where would you like to go today?" "Well it's a lovely day why don't we go to Hyde Park?" this was new to Harold, so he asked, "How do we get there?" "Oh, we take the Piccadilly line from Leicester square and get off at Hyde Park Corner".

Another new experience for Harold he hadn't yet used the tube as he walked everywhere. When they got to the station, they went down the steps to the concourse and he looked around. He saw that there was a ticket office in the middle leading to some escalators, he followed Diane as she bought two tickets and then to the escalator.

He stopped as he had never been on one before. Diane looked at him quizzically, "Is there a problem?" "Well" he admitted "I have never been on one of these before". "Well that's O.K., here take my arm and as I step on you do the same" nervously he took her arm and stepped on the moving stair, he grabbed the rail as he saw how far down it went. Diane held on to him and smiled, he always loved that smile, he gradually got used to the sensation but then came getting off. Diane held on to his hand and said "Just step off when I do, don't jump" so following her lead he managed to get off without any great problem.

A feeling of relief came over him and for a moment he felt a little faint so leaned against the wall. Diane looked anxiously at him, and then he recovered and gave her a weak smile. She smiled back and took his arm again as they walked through the tunnels to get to the Piccadilly Line. Harold could hear trains coming and going but couldn't see where. When they arrived on the platform, it was fairly crowded, and he looked around.

There was a destination board saying the next train was to London Heathrow, well we aren't going there he thought, but when the train pulled in Diane pulled him into the train. "We aren't going to Heathrow, are we? "No, that's where the train terminates, we get off in two stops".

By the time they got there Harold was feeling more comfortable with the doors opening and closing and the noise going through the tunnels. With Diane pulling he jumped of the train and followed her and the crowds up the stairs and then another escalator, he didn't find this one so bad because it was going up and he just stared ahead, waiting for the top. He found that much easier this time and they walked up the stairs into the sunshine.

The roads were very busy and there were lots of people around, Diane guided him to the park entrance. There were lots of people there as it was a lovely day, so they walked along the path looking at the people lying on the grass, some were eating and drinking, children were running around screaming and laughing, some were playing with a ball. All in all, it was a great scene and Harold felt wonderful, looking at Diane she was smiling too.

"How about sitting down for a while?" She asked. "Sounds a great idea" so they sat down under the shade of a tree. Harold lay alongside her and although he didn't touch her, he could feel her body close to his. He half turned and saw she was lying back with her eyes closed, he looked and wasn't sure what to do then he moved his arm across her waist. She looked down and smiled, Harold thought that was a good sign, so he moved closer and put his head near hers. She also moved her head and touched his forehead, Harold liked that and looked into her face, it was a lovely face and she was always smiling.

Then he reached down and kissed her, she moved her head away and wasn't smiling. "Sorry she said I haven't had a boyfriend for a long time, so I was a little surprised". Harold was glad that everything was going well so a little later he kissed her again and she responded. His emotions were high, and he wanted to have sex with her but obviously couldn't, not here in the middle of the park.

They lay there and nothing was said, it was one of those companionable silences that two people can have when they of the same mind.

After a while Harold fell asleep, the sun, the occasion and the emotions overcame him. When he woke up, she was looking at him smiling again, "Sorry I usually have a nap this time of day". "Don't worry I was just looking at you, you are very handsome when you are asleep" "Let's go and get an ice cream" she said, and Harold agreed. They walked along looking for the ice cream cart. They found one near the lake and sat down on a seat to eat their ice creams. "Tell me more about yourself" said Diane. Harold had always been worried about this question so for a moment he didn't answer, then he said" I am not interesting, you are much more interesting. Tell me about your father?"

"Well my mother died when I was only 12 so he brought me up by himself, I don't have any brothers or sisters. He was wonderful loving and taught me a lot. I started helping in the restaurant when I was 16. Then he suggested I go to catering college and learn how to cook properly. I did, I passed my exams and then came to work here full time 3 years ago. Dad loved my ideas on food and together we created some good meals and they were very popular with our customers.

Then 6 months ago he died, heart attack, there was no warning no signs or anything. His death really shook me up and I wanted to leave because his memory was everywhere. Sally, my waitress and best friend persuaded me that dad would want me to keep the place going. She was right, working gave me something to take my mind off his death and the customers were so encouraging as well. There we are. O.K. now it's your turn". "It's getting late, so we ought to be getting back. How about getting something to eat, I didn't have any dinner today." "What! No dinner! You're coming back to my place and I will cook you a meal myself"

Relieved Harold walked back to the station and home, now he quite enjoyed the underground but still wasn't sure about the tunnels.

When they got back, she said "take a seat I won't be long. Would you like something to drink?" "Yes, please. Would you have a pint of beer? "Sorry I don't have a drinks licence, how about some tea or lemonade?"." OK I will have some tea." she came back quickly and put down a white pottery teapot, white cup and saucer. Smiling she said, "Won't be too long, enjoy your tea". Then she was gone again. Soon she re-appeared with a plate with two pieces of crispy cod fillets and a huge pile of chips and 2 pieces of bread and butter. "Thought you would probably like your favourite dish"

"Yes, I sure am hungry. Aren't you eating?". "I have made a sandwich I'll be back in a jiffy". When she returned Harold was well into his meal, so she sat down opposite him and started on her sandwich. Harold having got well into his food before he slowed down and looked across at her. He saw that she was very pretty, probably beautiful but he had nothing to compare her to.

Finishing up he was well satisfied and leant back in his chair feeling very happy, looking at Diane he smiled and said, "Well you have certainly satisfied the inner man". She smiled and put her hand on his, it was like an ant sitting on an elephant's foot.

Harold smiled he loved he touch, and emotions began to stir in him, so he stood up and walked around to her chair. Taking her head in his hands he bent down to kiss her, she did not resist and so he picked her up and began kissing her more violently. "No!" she pulled away from him and was no longer smiling. Then she said "Sorry, I haven't had a boyfriend for a long time, so I am not used to being kissed like that".

Harold just stood there; thoughts raced through his mind; well he hadn't been kissed ever like that, so he knew what she said. "Sorry, Diane. I haven't had a girlfriend for a long time either. Let's call it a day and I will see you tomorrow". Diane moved back to him and kissed him on the cheek, "Thank you, I do like you a lot so let's do things slowly, O.K.?" "Yes, that would be a good idea. When could we go out again?"

"Well, I had made arrangement for Wednesday as it is my quiet day. Would that be fine?" Eagerly Harold smiled and said with great joy "Yes that would be great. I'll see you tomorrow anyway for dinner". "Yes, that will be good; I will do you something special. What would you like?" thinking Harold remembered in the pub in Bristol they did a great steak and kidney pie. "I used to have a wonderful steak and kidney pie, could you make me one of those?" smiling she said "Yes of course, with potato, cabbage and carrots",

Harold smiled he could already taste it and said "wonderful, I will see you tomorrow" they walked to the door and as he went to leave she jumped up and held him around the neck and gave him a kiss on the lips, in an instant she was gone and Harold stood on the step gazing back into the restaurant.

He was in ecstasy and all the way home he could have run, hopped and skipped. In fact, he probably did but didn't realize. As he lay on his bed, he was so happy he had never been this happy before, no one had ever loved him as he thought Diane did, no one had kissed him like that goodbye kiss. Eventually his mind was overcome with bodily exhaustion and he slept.

CHAPTER 7

Arrested

When he got home, he began to pack his few belongings and his stash of money, thinking perhaps he could escape again as he did before. As he was still thinking what to do there came a loud knocking on the door and it was the police. He didn't put up any struggle because he knew it would only cause him more trouble.

He was taken to the police station at Leicester Square and charged with rape and assault causing bodily harm.

"I need to take down some details, OK?" said the policeman.

Harold nodded his head.

"Name", Harold paused for a moment and then said "King, John King"

"Address" "Unity Mansions, Mercer Street, London". "Where do you work?", "Convent Garden Market". "Age", "24".

"Date of Birth?", "January 21, 1940".

"Where were you born?", Harold thought a minute, then he said "Bristol". He wasn't sure if that was a good idea or not. Anyway, he had said it now.

"Next of kin",

"I don't have any relations".

The officer looks at him questioningly, "Are you sure you don't have anyone living, or someone who knows you?" "No, they are all dead". He didn't know but wished it was so.

"Who can we contact?"

"I don't have anyone you can contact; I am not sure if my boss at the market would want to know."

"O.K. that s all for now". "John King I am formally charging you with Rape, Causing Bodily Harm, Fleeing the site of a crime. Do you have anything to say. "You do not have to say anything. But it may harm your defence if you do not mention when questioned something which you later rely on in court. Anything you do say may be given in evidence."

"Do you have a solicitor?"

"No".

"Do you have the money to pay for one or do you want a court appointed solicitor?",

"I don't have money for a solicitor".

"Right, I will pass your name to the court. You will appear before the magistrate tomorrow morning. As you say there is no one to tell. You will now go to the cells".

Saying nothing, Harold is led away by two officers, taken down to the cells and locked up for the night. This was a new experience for Harold his life seemed to be full of new experiences now and he didn't like this one at all. Lying on the hard-wooden bed he eventually fell asleep.

The next morning the policeman brought him breakfast of toast, egg, bacon and a large mug of tea. Harold was hungry and soon wolfed it down. When the policeman came back, he took him to the toilet to pour out his slops and then back to the cell. "You are due in court at 11 am, I will come and get you at 10 am, so be ready". Harold nodded his head. He wasn't afraid just unsure of the situation as he had never been in trouble with the law before, and he was a little worried about the lies he had told.

Come 10 am the policeman was back, Harold was handcuffed and taken to the van in the back yard, there was two other men with him. They looked as if they had a good night, or bad depending on your situation so they were probably up for breaking the peace, fighting or being drunk and disorderly. It only took 5 minutes to get to the courts on the Strand and he was taken from the van and with the others put into a holding cell underneath the court.

Waiting was the worst of it, as the time went by, he began to get more worried. The time dragged on he didn't know what the time was as he had no watch. Slowly the time seemed to pass, and he thought it must be 11 by now, eventually a warder appeared and said the cases were running late so the magistrate had adjourned for lunch. "I will go and get you something to eat from the canteen, see you in a little while".

Sometime later he re-appeared with a meat pie, potatoes and peas, apple pie and mug of tea. Harold was happy that he was getting fed and enjoyed his food. Then a man appeared at the door. He was young, Harold guessed about 26, and asked for Harold. Harold rose and he motioned for him to follow him. They went to an interview room and sat down.

The man spoke, "I am David Jenkins and the court has appointed me as your solicitor because I believe you don't have one, is that right?". Harold nodded; he didn't know what to say. "Right so first let us look at the charges. It says you raped a waitress, hit her and left. What do you have to say?"

"Well she was my girlfriend and wouldn't let me have sex, so I got angry and had sex. I'm sorry I hurt her, I didn't intend to, but I just lost my mind for a while. I love her and would normally never hurt her. It was just the heat of the moment".

"O.K. So it looks like a crime of passion, in the heat of the moment. So how long have you been friends?"

"About 3 months, I think".

"And did you try and have sex before?"

"Yes, on several times but she always stopped me, and I did".

"So why not this time?".

"Did she try and stop you?".

"Yes. I should have listened to her. I am so sorry I wish I could talk to her and apologize. I do love her so much".

"Well, I could try and get the magistrate to believe it was just a momentary loss of temper. With you being in a fairly long relationship I think he will agree, and you might get a suspended sentence or possibly even probation. Let's hope he sees that you are not a violent man and is lenient".

Harold felt relieved that he wouldn't go to prison, so felt much happier. He was escorted back to the cell and waited for his appearance in court. Eventually the warder came and collected him and took him up the stairs that led to the dock, coming out Harold looked around.

He was not able to recognize anyone. "Will the accused stand up" Harold looked around then realized it was him, so he stood up. The man gave him a bible and said repeat after me." I will tell the truth and nothing but the truth, so help me God". Harold repeated the words and went to sit down but the warder pulled him up. The man held up a piece of paper and said, "Is your name John King?" "Yes" "Do you reside at Unity Mansions, Mercer Street, London?" The warder seeing, he didn't understand the question, whispered "Is that where you live?"

"Yes Sir"

"You don't call me sir. You are charged that on the night of August 2nd at the Rose Restaurant you attacked and raped Diane Forrest, causing actual bodily harm and that you left the scene without informing the police. How do you plead?"

Harold didn't know Diane's name so was a little surprised, the warder nudged him. "Not Guilty"

"Do you have a solicitor?"

"David Jenkins". His solicitor rose.

"Sir, I have been appointed by the court as Mr. King does not have a solicitor".

"And have you consulted with him on these matters?" said the Magistrate.

"Yes, Sir and I have agreed his plea".

"Good, then let's start we are already running late".

Another man in a wig stood up and announced he was the prosecutor. "Sir, the case is quite straightforward. Mr. King was dating Miss Diane Forrester and they had dinner and after he attacked her, raped her causing bodily harm and then ran away. The police found him at his lodging packing up and preparing to leave town. I submit that the case is quite straightforward and submit that Mr. King be found guilty and given a 2-year prison sentence."

"Please call your first witness". "I call Diane Forrester"

Harold went to stand but the warder pushed him back. Diane came in slowly and Harold saw that she had a big bruise on her face. She looked down at the floor. He wanted to jump up and tell her how much he was sorry, but the warder guessed and held him down and said, "Don't speak unless you are asked to".

Harold felt so miserable and his heart was breaking but he had to sit and listen.

"Miss Forrester, would you please relate the happenings of yesterday evening.". She began to speak very softly, "Miss I understand the pressures but please speak up so we can all hear what you are saying" said the magistrate. Diane looked at him briefly and began again. "We had been out to Hyde Park and I invited Roger to come back for a meal. We had had many meals before and had got on so well I had no thoughts of violence. I cooked him his favourite meal and we had some wine and then after he tried to have sex, but I tried to stop him. Usually he does but this time he just wouldn't." She began to cry softly and got out her handkerchief.

"Take your time Miss Forrester, I appreciate that it is an ordeal for you, but we must see justice done". Said the magistrate.

"Please sir I don't want Roger to be punished, I forgive him, and I know he didn't mean to hurt me. Because I know he loves me, and I love him. Its, just that I haven't been in a relationship since my father died. Can he just be let off with a caution?"

The court was in a murmur, the magistrate leant back in his chair and looked at her and at Harold. "Well Miss Forrester, I am surprised at your plea, can I ask if the police asked you if you wanted to have charges brought?"

"No, sir no policeman has spoken to me".

"Well it looks as if the police have not followed correct procedure and will need to investigate why they did not. Regarding your pleas according to the law if the victim refuses to press charges then there is no charge. So as a result, I have no option to find Mr. King not guilty of Rape or Actual Bodily Harm.

There is the third charge of leaving the scene of a crime. In the circumstances I have to find him guilty and I sentence him to 6 months' probation".

"The case is now closed".

"All rise". Everyone rose, as the magistrate left the court. Harold sat amazed at what had happened and then he rose to see Diane, but she was gone!

He was taken back to the cell and given his property back and released. He stood on the pavement in the sunshine not sure what had happened or what to do next. He wanted to go and see Diane but wasn't sure of his reception. He wandered around the streets for several hours and then decided to go and see her.

Approaching the restaurant, he saw that it was not open, he went to the door and saw no-one inside, but he knocked several times. No-one came, Harold found a piece of paper in his pocket and a pencil stub. He wrote a short note. "Dearest Diane, I am so unhappy with what happened, if you can please forgive me and I promise that I will never hurt you again. I love you" Those three words were what he had never heard until Diane said it in court and he had never said them before to anybody. Pushing the note under the door he took one last look and then turned and left.

That evening he had his meal at another restaurant and then slowly made his way back to his room. He had never been so unhappy in his life, even as a small boy, because then he never knew love but now, he did, and he hoped he hadn't lost Diane altogether.

Tossing and turning in his bed he didn't get much sleep but come the morning he got up to go to work. Arriving at the market he was met with glares and some called out "Go away, you rapist". He tried to ignore them, but it was difficult. Coming to his pitch he found that his boss looked at him and said "Well, Roger, I always thought of you as a decent law-abiding man. But now that you have done this, I am not sure I can keep you on, especially as the traders don't want you here. You have been a good worker and certainly helped me, but I am forced to let you go".

Harold stood open-mouthed he couldn't believe what he was hearing. He had done wrong but had been forgiven now the workers didn't want him here. "I must let you go. Because you have been such a help, I am giving you a month's wages to help you until you find a new job. I am so sorry". He gave Harold the money and shook his hand and then turned away.

Harold felt like crying, his temper had lost him not only his love but his great job. Slowly he made his way out of the market and went to the pub to get drunk, which he did in the next 3 hours.

Finally, he staggered out of the pub and slowly made his way back to his apartment. It had been raining so it was slippery, and he fell over twice, some kind people helped him to his feet but when they smelt his breathe, they walked away muttering "Just another drunk".

Arriving back at his flat he fell on his bed and morosely looked at the ceiling, he couldn't believe all that had happened to him in the last 24 hours. Thinking of Diane, he wondered if he should try and see her again. He wasn't sure of her reaction, but she did say in court that she loved him, did she still? He had never been very good with relationships and this was his first serious one.

Eventually he got up washed his face and combed his hair with his hand, he didn't have a proper comb. Then started out to the restaurant, it had stopped raining and being mid-afternoon not too many people were around. He came to the restaurant and saw that the closed sign was still there and there was another hand-written sign it said "Sorry I am closed for the next week while I sort out my problems. I will re-open on the 24th, Diane".

Looking at the note he wondered if she was still here or had gone away, he hadn't had an answer to his note so perhaps she had gone away. Looking through door he tried to see the floor and saw that his note had gone, so perhaps she had seen it. Just in case he knocked on the door loudly several times and waited, but she did not appear, how he yearned to see that smiling face and happy laugh, but she was not there. Writing another short note, he was not too good at writing, he pushed it under the door. It pleaded with her to talk to him and begged her forgiveness and told her he was waiting to see her again.

Disconsolately he turned and walked back towards his flat and wasn't aware of his surroundings until he turned the corner and saw a police car outside his block. Stopping to take in the scene he wondered why they were there, perhaps the magistrate had made a mistake and he was being arrested again. Or perhaps it was someone else they were looking for, there were several undesirables in the building. While he stood there thinking, one of the policemen saw him, "There he is". He shouted and began to run towards Harold.

Shocked Harold stood for a second then turned and ran as fast as he could. Down Mercer Street he ran and towards the Seven Dials, there were some narrow lanes here where he might hide for a while. The policeman ran by not seeing him and stopped at the seven dials looking in all directions but couldn't see him. Then coming slowly back he paused by the lane and looked in but couldn't see Harold, then continued his way.

Relieved Harold slumped to the ground. What was he going to do now? He didn't have much money and all his possessions were in the flat, which the police were obviously watching. As it got dark, he had an idea, he walked slowly back to his flat watching out for any policemen. In the street he saw that the police car was gone but he noticed another man on the other side of the road who looked suspicious. A young lad came by and Harold caught him by the shoulder, "Oye, let me go. I ain't done nothing to you!".

"Quiet. Would you like to earn a shilling?".

"Doing what?" said the boy inquisitively.

"Well I need you to go into that building there, to the second floor room 12 and take a sack and put into all you can find and bring it back here".

"Why don't you do it yourself?"

"Because I owe the rent and don't want the doorman to see me, alright?"

"O.K where's my shilling?"

"Here's sixpence the rest when you get back. If anyone asks what you are doing say that your uncle had died, and you are collecting his things".

The boy took off and Harold watched as he entered the building, it seemed ages before he re-appeared carrying his sack. Harold was elated as the boy came up to him and handed over the sack. "Thanks, here's a shilling"' the boy looked amazed, smiled and ran off.

Now Harold had his belongings he walked down to Charing Cross station sat on a bench and sorted through the contents of the sack. Having done that and discarded some items and found his money hidden in a sock he felt much happier. But now what he didn't have a place to stay or a job, so he went into the café and had a cup of tea and a cheese sandwich to think about it.

Coming out he walked into a burly policeman who was about to apologize when he recognized him and grabbed him quickly hand-cuffing him he marched him of the police station.

He was now familiar with the procedure having gone through it only 5 days before, so he knew what was going to happen.

"Well here we are again. I need to clarify some of the answers you gave before just to make sure we have them correct. Anything to say?"

Harold just hung his head, he guessed that something he had said before had been questioned, so just waited for the questions.

"Sergeant Wilson and Constable Kennedy are here and will take down everything you say and at the end we will ask you to read it and confirm that it is a true record. You will sign it and it will be submitted as evidence if you must go to court. Any questions? Do you understand?"

Harold nodded, "Please answer for the constable to write down what you said".

"I have nothing to say".

"O.K. So let us start by going through what you said at your last interview. The name you gave us was John King. Is that your proper name?"

Harold now began to understand what was going to happen. For a moment he thought to lie again, but instead said nothing.

"You said that you are aged 24 and your date of birth was January 21st, 1940, and you were born in Bristol. Do you wish to change any of those details?".

He knew that he should, but he said nothing.

"We have checked the birth records in Bristol for 1939 and 1940 and could not find anyone with the name of John Kingdom, in fact there were no Kingdoms' registered during that period. So, we believed that you told lies. What do you say?"

Now knowing that the truth must come out Harold muttered "I am sorry I lied".

"Well that is good, so now let's get the facts, the correct one this time"

"What is your birth name?"

"Harold Wilson".

And when is your date of birth?"

"10th of November 1945".

"Were you born in Bristol?"

"Yes".

"Do you have any relatives?",

"I don't know I haven't spoken to them for years".

"What family did you have?"

"Father, Mother and sister".

"Who can we contact?",

"I don't want them to be contacted. I left them years ago and I am sure they don't want to be reminded of me".

"O.K. that s all for now. As you have admitted that you lied in court, that is called Perjury, so you will be charged and taken before the magistrate tomorrow morning. Harold Wilson I am formally charging you with Perjury and perverting the course of justice. Do you have anything to say. "You do not have to say anything. But it may harm your defence if you do not mention when questioned something which you later rely on in court. Anything you do say may be given in evidence."

"I remember you did not have a solicitor, is that correct? I will contact the court and get you one for tomorrow".

Harold was led to the cells and locked up for the night. It was not the same cell as last time, but it might have been as it was identical to the other one. An officer brought him a meal of fish and chips and rhubarb pudding with custard and a large mug of tea.

Harold realized he had not eaten so rapidly downed the lot then lay back on the hard-wooden cot to think about his situation.

Now that they knew his real name would they connect him to the murder of the girl. As far as he knew nobody had seen him before or after so he hoped that he would not be found out. He didn't know what the sentence was for perjury, he had never heard of it so hoped it might only be a light sentence. Eventually he dropped off to sleep and tossed and turned all night as he had nightmares about what the police might find out.

CHAPTER 8

The Interview

He was roused by a police man and escorted to the toilets to get rid of the contents of his pot, then he had a quick wash and a shave with a razor the policeman gave him, but he stood and watched and took it away as soon as Harold was finished. Breakfast arrived, today it was porridge, toast, marmalade and a mug of tea. Harold eagerly ate it and then waited to be taken to the court. Into the van with 1 other man and they drove into the back of the court.

He sat in his cell and wondered how long it would be today, after the last time. He was surprised when the warden came and took him upstairs to the dock. This was a lady magistrate, but he didn't think there was much pity here she looked really stern.

"Madam, Harold Wilson appeared before this court 6 days ago on another charge and was acquitted by the victim withdrawing all charges. But he gave the police a false name, date of birth and place of birth. As the police could not find the evidence, he had given he was questioned further and admitted he had lied. Madam, he has been charged with Perjury and perverting the course of justice"

"How do you plead?" asked the Magistrate. "Guilty, your honour".

"I am not your honour, I am not a judge, address me as Madam. As you have pleaded guilty and this is your first offence, I am going to be lenient. But if you do this again the penalty will be severe. Do you understand?"

"Yes, Madam".

"Good, I am sentencing you to 12 months' probation. Do you understand what that means?"

"I am not sure, Madam".

"Well, it means that you must not get into any trouble in the next year or you will be brought back, and you could go to prison".

"Thank you, Madam". "Case closed".

"All stand" called the usher, everyone rose, and the warder took Harold downstairs. There he was shown the probation order and had it explained again. He signed it and to his relief he was outside the court, a free man again!

He stopped and thought what to do now. He had no job, little money, and he wanted to see Diane again. Taking action, he strode of in the direction of Diane's restaurant, as he approached, he slowed and looked carefully at the door. It looked like it was open, so he cautiously approached on the other side of the road.

Now he could see that it was open and there were a few people inside, he hesitated not knowing how Diane would greet him. He walked up and down keeping an eye open on the door, he just couldn't decide. Then he saw that the customers had left, and he couldn't see anyone inside so taking courage he walked across the road, but on approaching the door he hesitated. He peered in and couldn't see anyone, so he cautiously pushed open the door, forgetting that there was a bell to announce a new customer.

He stopped just inside the door and then his heart leaped as she came out with a smile, that disappeared as soon as she saw him. Standing there neither spoke for a moment then Harold hesitantly said "Dearest Diane, I am so sorry about what happened, and I am so grateful that you did not press charges. I love you and will never hurt you again, I promise". Tears welled into his eyes as he spoke and looked anxiously at her to see her reaction.

"I cannot forgive what you did, although I think I love you I cannot forget the hurt you caused. I never want to see you again, the very sight of you brings back painful memories. Please leave and never try to see me again. I am so sorry, but I just cannot accept you back. Goodbye". With that she turned and ran back into the kitchen.

Harold stood there in deepest sorrow, he expected her to be angry but had a hope in his heart that she would not reject him entirely. Now he had no-one again, his love had been rejected once more and his anger began to well up in his chest, he wanted to break something, hurt someone, release his anger. He looked around then kicked at a table and sent it flying with the tablecloth and cutlery falling on the floor. The door opened and Diane looked then shut the door again.

Harold turned and ran out of the restaurant, down the street and towards the Seven Dials where he found a place to sit. His head in his hands he started to cry, and he did just like he did all those years ago when he ran away from home having had one beating too many from his brutal father.

People passed by and gave him a wide berth, but one elderly lady touched his arm "Can I do anything to help you?". Harold shook his head and buried it into his two hands. Eventually he stopped and sat there the perfect picture of misery. His mind was a blank, he had no feelings, he had no thoughts, he had no way to plan what to do next. He sat there for hours and it got dark and started to rain which roused him a little.

He morosely looked around and then got up and started to walk back to his flat and realizing he hadn't eaten since breakfast stopped at a café and had a beef pie, potatoes and peas, with a large mug of tea. Feeling a bit more human he paid and set off again.

Arriving home, he lay on the bed trying to make some sense of his situation, he needed to find a job as he had little money left. Eventually he dozed off and had dreams of Diane calling him back.

He was woken by a banging on the door and a voice calling "Harold Wilson, open the door it is the Metropolitan Police".

Startled Harold jumped up and looked around, but there was no way out, so he slowly walked to the door and went to open it when it burst open and two large policemen ran in and grabbed him. "What have I done now?"

"We need you to come down the station and explain a few more things wrong with your story".

Harold ceased to struggle and went quietly with the officers down the stairs and along the street to the police station.

Entering he was met by Sergeant Wilson, who escorted him to the interview room. Once they were seated, he looked at Harold for some time seemingly trying to put into words his thoughts. "Well, Mr. Wilson you certainly have me puzzled. I can't get a grip on who you are or what you may have done. I have investigated your record and I see that you never were in trouble in Bristol although you did have a few fights over some prostitute. Can you tell me why you came to London?"

"I wanted a new place to be after the fight in the pub and my friend Jim had died so I had no need to stay in Bristol, so I came to London".

"Did you leave in a hurry?".

"Well just a bit, I had no need to hang around".

"Did you come by Queen Square on your way to the station?". "No, I went to a café and then walked to the station".

"About what time was that?" "I think it was about 11".

"What time train did you catch?" "It was the 12.20 to Paddington".

"And you didn't go near Queen Square?".

"No why should I? I lived the other side of the Centre".

"Well the thing is a young woman was raped and killed in Queen Square that evening just about the time you were walking to the station. A young man about your age and build was seen in the Centre about the same time, were you that young man?".

"I could have been I am not sure where I walked because I was upset and was not really thinking straight".

"Yes, I see that you might be upset as you had the fight over the prostitute, were you looking for someone to have sex with?".

"No, I had not thought of having sex, I was too upset".

"Well I think that you were that man and you did rape the young woman and killed her, so I am arresting you and sending you to Bristol for the local police to question you."

"But I didn't do it, I was too upset to have sex with anybody and I would never kill someone" Harold exploded with rage but really on the inside he knew he had been caught out and was anxious about what was going to happen.

"I am sending you back to Bristol with an escort on the 9.15 train from Paddington and on arrival in Temple Meads you will be handed over to the local police. If you are innocent, they will find out and if not, they will make sure that justice is done".

Harold quietly followed the policeman back to the cell; his world was rapidly disappearing. How happy he had been just a few short days ago and now he was headed back to his hometown and probably prison for an act that he had not pre-meditated.

Sitting on the hard-wooden bed his mind was in a whirl as he contemplated his future that he could only see as being bleak.

The policemen arrived to escort him to the railway station. There were two of them as big as Harold and he was handcuffed to both, so he had no chance of escaping, not that he had even thought about such an act. The journey to the station in the police car was quiet, no-one spoke, and he was glad in a way when they arrived.

Entering the station, they proceeded to the train, showing their police passes they entered the platform. Being the middle of the day, it was not too busy. They found their apartment labelled "Metropolitan Police use only". As was normal it was a non-corridor train so there was no chance of anyone entering or leaving unnoticed. Settling down the handcuffs were removed, and Harold was seated opposite the two officers.

They produced some sandwiches and gave Harold one of Cheese and Ham. He wasn't really hungry, but he ate it slowly anyway. He was given a carton of apple juice and he drank that as well, he felt better with some food inside him.

All the way to Bristol, three hours, the officers talked to each other but not to Harold, he looked out of the window as the countryside sped by thinking he would not be seeing it for a while now. The train only stopped at Maidenhead, Swindon and Bath before pulling into Temple Meads. As they approached the station he was handcuffed again.

The officers waited in the compartment until two policemen arrived from the Bristol Division, "Thanks, we can take him from here, have a good journey back". Harold was transferred to the new policemen and escorted out of the station to a waiting police car and taken to the main police station in Broadmead. Arriving he was hustled into the room and sat down at the table. His handcuffs were removed, and he waited to see what happened next.

In walked a plain clothes detective with a brown folder, which he placed on the table and before he sat down, he looked at Harold.

"My name is Detective James, and I need to ask you some questions. Well young man, it seems you are in some trouble".

Harold said nothing, he decided it was best not to speak unless he had to.

"From your file it appears that you assaulted a young woman and killed her and then ran off to London where you have been living under an assumed name. You then assaulted your girlfriend, but she refused to press charges, so you got off. But it was discovered you had given false information and were arraigned on a murder charge and brought back here for trial. Is that correct so far?"

Harold realized that he didn't have much chance of escaping, so he nodded his head. "Good, so let's get some more facts from your point of view. So, tell me what happened that evening?"

"Well I had been to the pub as usual and had an argument with a prostitute and her customer hit me, so I left".

"I expect you were angry!".

"Yes, I hadn't had much to do with women and didn't understand how it was".

"Good. What happened next?".

"Well I walked around and then found somewhere to eat. I decided that I had no hope of getting on in Bristol so decided that I would go to London and try there. Then I walked to my flat and then to the station to get the train".

"When did you see the young woman?".

"I never saw any young woman and I wasn't anywhere near Queen Square".

"I never mentioned Queen Square, why did you?". "Because they said that in London".

"Oh! Well you never went near to Queen Square?".

"No. My flat is over by the market and I walked down the road to the station from there, it is only a five-minute walk".

"Did you see anyone on your walk?".

"I don't recall seeing anyone, but I wasn't really looking just intent on leaving this town".

"Nobody you know can vouch for your story?". "No".

"Did anyone see you at the station?".

"I expect so although I can't remember as it was late there weren't many people around".

"What about the booking clerk? Do you remember what he looked like?".

"Not really I wasn't paying much attention".

"Surely you can remember something about him. Was he old, young, middle aged? Did he have a beard or moustache? What did he say to you?".

"I can't remember, I just asked him when the next train was and paid him the money. I wasn't taking any notice of him".

"What about when you got to the barrier, what did the ticket collector look like?".

"I think he was older, about 50 with grey hair". "How tall was he?'.

"Shorter than me, maybe about 5 ft 8 in". "Did he say anything to you?".

"No. just clipped my ticket".

"When you were on the platform who else was there?".

"I can't remember if there was anybody. I just sat on a seat and waited for the train to come".

"When you got on the train do you remember anybody who got off?".

"Nobody got off near where I was".

"And you got into an empty compartment and nobody got on?".

"It seems you can't remember anyone, who saw you, you can't describe the booking clerk and only vaguely the ticket collector. Seems to me that you walk around not noticing anything or anybody".

Harold said nothing.

"OK that will do for now". "I need a solicitor".

"The court will provide you with one if you can't pay". "I have no money".

With that detective James left. A policeman escorted him to the cells and said he would be back with some lunch. The cell was similar to the one in London. But it had a hang-down bed that could be drawn up against the wall. There was the usual bucket in the corner, no table or chair and had one window high up that let in some sunlight.

Harold sat on the bed with his head in his hands full of unhappiness and fear of what his future held for him.

Later his lunch was delivered, a sandwich of cheese and ham with a lettuce leaf. A small bun and a mug of tea. This seemed to be the staple meal as it was the same as in London, there was no choice. Harold ate it up and lay down on the hard bed.

Eventually he drifted off to sleep to dream of nightmares in prison. He was woken by the cell door being opened and the policeman said he had a visitor. Harold wondered who his visitor was as he followed the policeman to the interview room, as he entered, he was a youngish man sitting at the table. He rose and offered his hand to Harold "Hi, my name is Charles Goodworth and I have been appointed your solicitor".

Harold took his hand and shook it, he liked this man and hoped that he could help him in his trouble.

"Well, let me get the facts and then we can decide what action to take to get you out of this situation. I have read your statement to the police and on first glance there seems to be a chance we can get you out of this. I say a chance because you never know what witnesses the police may be able to find. Now as it was late at night it is possible that they can't find anyone, but they will obviously bring in the station staff to identify you and place the time you were there.

Whether they can find anyone who saw you before that I am not sure.

Let's go over your statement and see if you have missed anything out or want to change anything. In your own words tell me what happened after you left the pub".

"Well when I left the pub, I was angry and didn't know where to go, in fact I was not thinking about anything except my anger at her and how I could get back for her treatment of me. I don't know really where I walked but I found myself at the Centre and saw this café. I hadn't eaten for a while, so I decided to go in and get something to eat".

"Just a moment you never mentioned the café in your statement. This could be a vital piece of information establishing where you were and who saw you. Can you tell me if there were any other customers, describe the waitress and what was said"?

"I ordered a cup of tea and a sandwich. Then I realized I was hungry, so I ordered some fish and chips. I noticed that she was about my age and quite pretty and had a lovely smile. She said her name was Emily, when she came back with the plate of fish and chips, I asked her if she would sit and talk and she said yes. I asked her if she had a boyfriend and she said "No, not at the moment. Working here I don't have much time to go out". I asked her if she got any time off, she said as she worked until 1 am and started work again at 5 o'clock. She was sleeping late, and she couldn't have a date because I am working, but I do have Monday of. I said to her that we had similar lives as I worked in the vegetable market and start at 4 in the morning, finishing about 10. then I asked her if she would like a date and she got up and was angry and said No, thank you"

I was a bit upset at her attitude and paid and left"

"Well, I am sure the waitress, Emily, will be a witness to where you were at that time. So how far is it to Queen Square from there?" "I think about a 10-minute walk, but I didn't go that way!"

"Yes, I know but the prosecutor will make a case about where you were and how far it was to Queen Square and we need to have an answer ready. Carry on".

"When I left, I went back to my flat near Old Market and packed my things as I had decided that I was leaving to find a better place to live and work. Then I walked to the station, about 6 minutes and bought a ticket and then waited for the train".

"Right so let's get the times right. You left the pub at 9.23 according to witnesses, what time did you get to the café?"

"It was about 9.45, I noticed the time on the clock in the Centre". "And what time did you leave the café?" "Well I think I was there about 30 minutes". "That makes it about 10.10. How long does it take to get back to your flat?" "I would say about 15 minutes".

"You arrived at the station at 11.33 and waited for the 12.00 train to London. You were at your flat for about 55 minutes, is that, about right?".

"Yes. I would say so".

"Good. The times could be crucial so we will check them again later.

Now if we can prove these times the prosecution needs to prove how long it would be for a man to walk from the café to Queens Square, back to your flat and then to get to the station by 11.33".

"If no further witnesses are found then the prosecution case is not very strong and based on assumptions that may be wrong. I can see that they will have a hard time proving beyond any doubt that you were the person who did the attack. Now are you sure that there is nothing else you have missed out? If the prosecution catches, you out in a lie then that won't be good for you. Understand?"

"Yes, I haven't missed anything but if anything comes to mind, I will let you know. What happens now?"

"You will appear before the magistrate tomorrow and I will attempt to get the charges dropped. If the magistrate agrees it will be all over but if he doesn't you will be remanded in prison until the trial which could be several months away. Let's hope we can convince him you are not the assailant. I will see you in court tomorrow".

Harold was led back to his cell feeling a lot happier after his talk, he had a glimmer of hope that the police could not find evidence to convict him.

CHAPTER 9

Magistrates Court

The next morning the policeman came and handcuffed him and led him to the van with six others who were also going on trial. Nobody spokes, during the short ride to the courthouse. They were driven inside and pulled out of the van then led into the court and to the holding cells. They were all placed in the same cell as there was no room elsewhere. Having experienced previous visits, he expected a long wait, everything seemed to take forever in the court.

After about an hour the policeman called his name. He went out escorted by a policeman to the interview room, there he found his solicitor, Charles Goodworth, waiting for him. Shaking hands Charles said,

"How are you doing?"

"Pretty good, considering I wish it was all over".

"Well if we get the wrong verdict then you could be in prison for months waiting for a trial date, so let's hope we get the verdict we want. I am hopeful. But we need to wait for the prosecution's case. So far from the evidence the case against you seems to be weak, so let's hope they have no shocks today". They shook hands and Harold was escorted back to the cell.

There was another long wait, lunch was served. Again, the usual sandwich and tea. Nobody seemed inclined to talk and Harold didn't want to either so there was silence. Eventually one man said

"What the hell is going on! We have been here all day, and nothing has happened. Hey! You policeman, what is happening here?" the policeman came over, "No point in shouting, we all must wait for the magistrate to get to you. It's a busy day today so just keep quiet and wait".

The man continued to mutter under his breath, but nobody was interested in his thoughts, so they kept quiet.

"Harold Wilson!" He walked to the door and a policeman took his arm and let him up the stairs to the dock. Looking around he was surprised to see so many people then the clerk rose and came to him with the bible. Harold had never seen a bible before, so it didn't mean much to him, just a book.

"Please place your hand on the bible and read the words on the card".

"I swear by almighty God that I will tell the truth, the whole truth, and nothing but the truth. So, help me God".

"Please state your name" said the clerk. "Harold Wilson".

"Harold Wilson you are charged that on or about the third day of August 1960 you did rape and kill Suzanne Johnson. How do you plead?"

"Not guilty".

"Do you have a solicitor?" the magistrate asked.

Charles rose "I am representing the accused. Sir".

"Does he understand the charges laid against him?" "Yes, Sir".

"Right. Let's proceed. Prosecution please call your first witness". "I call Jim Smith"

Jim Smith took the oath he was about 50 small man with greying hair and looked very uncomfortable.

"What is your name and occupation?"

"My name is Jim Smith and I work as a Booking Clerk at Temple Meads station".

"Do you recognize anyone here today?".

Nervously looking around the court he hesitated then pointed at Harold he said "Him".

"How do you know him?"

"He bought a ticket to London"

"Can you confirm the date and time?"

"It was about 6 months ago, and he bought a ticket to London at about 11.30 at night"

"Was there anything about him that causes you to remember him from that long ago?"

Not really, but at that time of night you don't get many passengers"

"Do you have any evidence to prove your story?"

"According to my log I sold a ticket to London at 11.29 on 3rd August 1960".

"No more questions. Your witness"

"How many tickets do you sell in a typical shift?" "About two hundred"

"Two hundred! A day and this was 6 months ago, how can you possibly remember that this was the man you have identified?"

"He seemed shifty to me" "Shifty! What does that mean?"

"Well he looked a bit upset and anxious"

"I see so you don't get many 'shifty' people in the 6 months since you saw my client"

"I remember him distinctly" the booking clerk looked a little desperate and glanced at the prosecuting counsel.

"Let me tell you that I have difficulty remembering people I met 6 months ago. Please tell the court again why he was distinctive?" "Well, I am not sure now. But he definitely was different" he finished lamely, seemingly now not sure of his ground.

"That is all for now, but may I reserve the right to recall this witness if necessary?"

"Yes, that seems alright". "Call Albert Stevenson"

"Place your right hand on the bible and read the words on the card".

"I swear to tell the truth the whole truth and nothing but the truth so help me God"

"Please state your name."

"Albert Stevenson?"

The prosecutor stands and comes towards the witness box,

"Please state your occupation and where you work"

"I work for British Rail as a ticket collector at Temple Meads Station".

"Thank you. Would you please look around the court and tell me if there is anyone here you recognize"?

He looks around the court and when he comes to the dock he points at Harold and says "Him".

"Are you sure? And where have you seen him before?"

"He came to the station late at night to catch the London train about 6 months ago".

"How can you be sure it is the same man, after all 6 months is a long time and you must see hundreds of people everyday"

"I remember him because he was young and had blood on his cheek".

The court gasps, Harold looks startled. "How do you know it was blood?"

"I fought in the war and I know blood when I see it, I saw enough then, so I am not mistaken"

"You saw some blood; did you do anything about it?" "No, at the time I didn't think it was important"

"But now you do?"

"Yes, he is charged with murder so having blood on him means he did it, doesn't it?"

"You can't say that Mr. Stevenson you can only answer the question do not draw your own conclusions". It was the magistrate who intervened at this point.

"Thank you, Mr. Stevenson, that is all"

He went to leave the box when the magistrate said, "You haven't been questioned by the defence yet so please stay where you are".

"Mr. Stevenson, why are you certain that this is the man you saw 6 months ago? As the prosecution has said you have seen hundreds of people since then so how come you recognize him?"

"Well in the war I was in intelligence and had to look at hundreds of possible spies faces so you get to know faces and remember them".

"I see, so you remember everybody you see?"

"Oh no, only those who are different or odd or out of place" "And this man was one of those things?"

"Yes, he sort of rang a bell in my mind as having something different about him, and the blood also helped."

"Yes, you mentioned that previously. Whereabouts did you see the blood?"

"It was on his cheek just below the ear". "And how much blood was there?"

"I would say about an inch"

"From where the blood was it could have been caused by cutting himself with a razor if he was in a hurry, don't you think?"

"No, it wasn't a cut just a smear".

"If you were suspicious why didn't you report it to the police?"

"Well, I did think to especially as Constable Vernon came by a bit later as he usually does". "Why didn't you?"

"To be frank I had forgotten about him as I was thinking of other things".

"If you had forgotten about him in 10 minutes how come you can remember him in 6 months?"

"It just slipped my mind"

"But you still maintain this is the same man?" "Yes, sir definitely".

"No more questions".

The defence lawyer sits down not happy with the situation.

"Do you have any other witnesses to call?" asked the magistrate. "Yes, Madam. Please call Emily Woodhead"

"Call Emily Woodhead"

Emily enters a little nervously and looks around when she sees Harold, she grimaces a little.

"Place your right hand on the bible and read the words on the card".

"I swear to tell the truth the whole truth and nothing but the truth so help me God"

"Is your name Emily Woodhead?" "Yes" she answers a little timidly.

"Miss Woodhead, please speak up so the court can hear your answers" said the magistrate. Emily nods her head.

The prosecutor stands and comes towards the witness box, "Please state your occupation and where you work"

"I work as a waitress at the Centre café".

"Thank you. Would you please look around the court and tell me if there is anyone here you recognize"?

"Yes, him in the dock" "How do you know him?"

"He came into the café one night, late and had some food and then we chatted, and he asked me on a date. Honestly I only knew him for about half an hour and here he was asking for a date!" she was contemptuous and glared at Harold.

"And about what time did he leave?" "It was about ten thirty".

"Did you see him again?" "No, never did".

"Your witness".

"Miss Woodhead, how did my client act while you were talking to him?"

"He seemed quite a nice bloke and I quite liked him". "Good and what else happened?"

"Well he was O.k. until he asked me for a date, then I was a but upset him being so forward. He jumped up put some money on the table and rushed out the door. He left too much as it happened."

"Did he in anyway threaten you?" "No. just left"

"Thank you. Miss Woodhead you have been most helpful". "Before you call your next witness it is 12.30, so we will have a lunch break. Court will resume at 2 pm" said the magistrate, rising and leaving his seat.

Harold was led down to the cells and given his lunch of a Ham and Tomato Sandwich, a bag of Crisps and a mug of tea.

He ate it slowly his mind going over what had happened, he felt that it was going O.K. But wasn't sure if the magistrate would believe the story the solicitor was going to tell. The warden came and told him his solicitor wanted to talk to him, so they went to the interview room.

"Well, I thought it went reasonably well it all depends on if we can prove the timings we spoke about. It seems they don't have any other witnesses so their case is very weak, and I can't see the magistrate agreeing with their arguments. Let's hope that all goes well after lunch".

"Thanks" said Harold "Let's hope all goes well".

The warder came and took him upstairs to the dock. The court-room seemed fuller than before lunch, perhaps they had heard about the trial and had come to look.

"Does the prosecution rest?" asked the magistrate.

"We have one more witness, sir".

"Right, call him".

"Call Martin Rush!"

Harold wondered who this new witness was, then in walked an elderly man who was dressed in a jacket that looked black, it was dirty and crumpled, he wore a pair of oversize trousers, boots that had seen much better days and probably leaked when it rained and a black overcoat. He looked a complete mess and most people would have given him a wide berth if they saw him on the street.

As he walked in, he looked nervously around the court and hung on to a large sack. His solicitor looked a little worried and so did Harold. What could this person know about the case?

"What has the witness got in his sack?" the magistrate asked.

The Bailiff conferred with the man, shook his head and said, "He says it's his life savings and won't let them go".

"Sir, I cannot allow you to bring that sack into my court. Give it to a police constable and he will guard it for you"

The man began to protest but gave up the sack to a policeman. "Proceed" said the magistrate.

"Place your right hand on the bible and read the words on the card".

"I swear to tell the truth the whole truth and nothing but the truth so help me God"

"Is your name Martin Rush?"

"Yes"

"What can you tell us about what you saw on the night of 3rd August 1960?".

"Well I usually sleep around the dock area as its quiet there and on that night, I was sleeping in the Queens Square garden".

Harold froze and his solicitor looked worried.

"Yes, go on".

"Well I had just dropped off when I heard a bit of a commotion in the bushes, I didn't take much notice at first as I thought it might be some animal. Then I heard a scream and kneeling and looking over I saw a couple. I suspected they were having sex, so I didn't bother just went back to sleep".

"Do you recognize anyone in the court?"

Looking around Martin stared at Harold for some time, then he said,

"Well it was dark, but I am pretty sure it was the man in the dock".

"How sure are you?"

"Well not 100% but sure enough".

"What happened next?"

"Well I was woken by Police siren, not the nicest sound to me I have been arrested to many times. I sneaked away down to the Centre".

"How come you are here today?"

"Well, I heard about the trial and I remembered what had happened that night".

"Your witness".

Harold's solicitor rose slowly, obviously thinking how he was going to deal with this unexpected witness.

"Mr. Rush. You stated that you were asleep when you heard the commotion. Are you sure you really woke up or could you have imagined the whole episode"?

"I don't know what an episode is, but I was awake when I saw them having sex. I did go back to sleep again it's true, but I was woken by the police siren".

"Now, it was dark. Are there any streetlights nearby?"

"Well, it's not far from the Centre which is very bright and there are streetlights around the square".

"Are there any lights in the square itself?"

"No, sir".

"How did you hear about the trial?"

"It was all over the newspaper and I remembered what had happened, so I went to the police".

"You could have made up the story from what you read in the newspaper, were you hoping for a reward?"

"No! I didn't make it up and the paper never mentioned a reward. Is there a reward?"

"No, there isn't"

"Thank you, no more questions".

The solicitor sat down, not happy with what had happened and suspected the police were.

"Please sum up, Mr. Wilson".

The prosecutor stood up with a smile, he started

"We have proved that the accused was in Queen Square at the relevant time. We have the evidence of the Ticket Collector that he had blood on his face and that he appeared to be worried. He left on the 12.33 train for London. He was apprehended because he had perjured himself in another trial in London and was identified as coming from Bristol and he was using an alias. I submit that he should be sent for trial at the Assize Court".

"Has the defence anything to say?"

"Yes, sir. The accused did not go to Queen Square that night. After he had left the café he went home and decided to leave because of his troubles at the pub. He walked to the Station and arrived at

11.15. He did not have time to go to the Square and assault anyone so I would say that it is a case of mistaken identity by Mr. Rush. I submit that there is no evidence that my client assaulted this person so should be acquitted".

Sitting down he didn't look too confident, the magistrate said, "I will consider the evidence and return in 30 minutes with my decision".

Harold was escorted back to the cell, the warden said, "Looks like your, in for a long time in prison". Harold said nothing, although he believed that the warder was right. They were called back to the court.

"Accused please stand"

"Mr. Harold Wilson, I have looked over the evidence and although it is not solid, I think that it is strong enough for you to go to the Assize court. I remand you in custody for trial".

The magistrate stood and left the court.

Harold was dazed, he looked at his solicitor who motioned that he would see him later. He went down to the cell and was left alone to think about his situation. If only the tramp had not been there, he would be a free man but with his evidence, although shaky might be enough to convict him.

His solicitor came down to see him and decide what to do next. "Unfortunate, about that tramp. Although his evidence is not so strong, I am sure we can rattle him and get the jury to believe he dreamt it all. For now you will have to stay in prison, I would ask for bail but you do not have a fixed place of residence or a job or someone to vouch for you I am sure it will be a waste of time.

At least in prison you will be fed and housed, as a remand prisoner the conditions won't be too bad. Do you agree?"

"Yes, I think your right my situation is not too good, although I don't like the thought of being in jail as you say it is probably better than being out. How long do you think it will be before my trial"?

"Well, the next assize sessions does, not start until September 2nd, and then you have to be found a slot with a judge available. At the best we can hope for is sometime in September and maybe not until next year. In the meantime, I will try and find you a Q.C. To lead your defence. Now as you don't have any money or assets, I will have to go the Board and ask them to fund your defence and then to find a Q.C. who will accept their fees, not usually very high so it could be difficult.

Probably a young man under training will do the job, but I will do my best. I will come and see you in Prison once I have any news to tell you. Don't fret if it is a while there is lots of time and I want to make sure you get the best I can".

"Thanks, you are doing a good job. I will just be patient and wait to see you again".

He had to wait until the end of the day then along with the others he was put in handcuffs and taken to the wagon for transport to Horfield Jail. Arriving there he was taken to the remand wing, here the warder gave him his instructions.

"You will obey all warders at all times, no fighting, keep your cell tidy, you may use the library between the hours of 10 and 2, your exercise time is 2 to 4. after dinner you will be locked in your cell, lights out is 8 pm. Waking up time is 6 am, when you will slop out, have a wash and shave and then go to breakfast from 7 to 8. You are allowed one visitor a week, Your legal representative any day. You can wear your own clothes with an overband of yellow to show you are a remand prisoner. Any complaints speak to your warder, if you have a problem, he cannot solve then you may be referred to the governor. Any questions now?"

Nobody spoke, so they were escorted to their cells. There were two people to a cell and Harold had an older man whose name he found out was mike and was on remand for fraud, he had tried to defraud an insurance company. He was quite a pleasant man and he and Harold got along well.

Jim had taught Harold how to read so to pass the time he went to the library and discovered the world of books. He loved the adventure books like Treasure Island and Rob Roy so he passed the time quite well, he could take out one book at a time so he could continue reading in his cell.

Every day was the same and without his new love of books he would have been bored out of his mind, so time passed, and he waited for his solicitor to return with some news.

CHAPTER 10

Penny at College

Everyone who has ever moved to a new house, school started a new job knows the feelings you get as the day draws closer moving to college was worse than any of those events. To start with I was only just 18, I had never been away from home for more than a couple of days before and now I was going away for months. There would be no flying home to mother because I was going to Manchester and the connections between Ipswich and Manchester were not easy.

I had been to Manchester University for my interview and then for a visit to see how the place was laid out and where I would room, first year students were allowed to room on the campus where we share rooms with another person. The University is called the Victoria University of Manchester and was founded in 1851, so the buildings were of Victorian origin, built right in the middle of Manchester.

I arrived the evening before with my mother and father who had loaded the car up with everything I might need to survive a term, or it seemed to me I had so much stuff I was moving out permanently. My room was on the first floor and my roommate had not arrived, so I was able to get all my things in and safely stored. The room had two beds and a small bathroom with a tiny kitchen area that was obviously only for making a cup of tea, as most meals would be taken in the refectory or if money allowed in the city.

My parents being reasonably well off had not got much of a grant and were expected to pay nearly all my living expenses, so I was careful not to appear to be extravagant in my plans. I said goodbye to them and was a little surprised by my parent's emotional reaction, not something I expected of them. After they had gone, I wondered if I had misunderstood them all these years but probably many children sometimes wonder as such once, they actually leave home.

Suddenly the door flew open and in rushed a red headed girl wearing baggy blue jumper and black trousers and carrying two suitcases. "Hi" she said banging the cases on the floor.

"I'm Henrietta, and you are?"

"I'm Penny"

"Well great to see you, could you be a darling and go and get some of my cases I am absolutely petered out".

"Well, yes, OK" I stammered out taken by complete surprise at this gust of energy. I walked down the stairs and there was a Rolls Royce sitting there with an elderly lady standing surrounded by bags, boxes and suitcases. "Henrietta asked me to help her with her belongings," I politely said. "I'm her Aunt Mary," the lady said proffering her gloved hand. I wasn't sure whether to kiss it or shake it, so I took the fingers and gently shook them. "She's brought a few things with her I will have the rest sent on" she said. Amazed I looked at the pile of luggage thinking where she was going to put this lot let alone more.

Eventually I managed to get the luggage up to our room; Henrietta mentioned she was too exhausted to move so I did it all. Once everything was in the room Henrietta left saying "I'm just off for some dinner with my aunt, see you later and be a dear and put this stuff somewhere out of the way", without waiting for an answer she left. I stood there dumbfounded, who did she think I was her servant. Well obviously, that was exactly what she thought and I dutifully tried to find some hole to put all these things in. In doing so some of my carefully stored items had to come out and be stuffed somewhere else.

Even with the best will in the world there was no way I could find a home for everything and when Henrietta eventually returned at about 11 o'clock she immediately started re-arranging the things I had already spent hours sorting out. With no thought of what I might want she turfed my clothes out and left them in a pile on the floor." Look" I said a bit weakly "those are my things and I need somewhere to put them", "Oh, well I'm sure that you can squeeze them in somewhere, but I must have my clothes hung up or they will get all creased otherwise. I'm sure you understand" smiling sweetly she carried on regardless.

Eventually I managed to find enough places to put most of my clothes but my dresses, the few I had, were hung over the door to the bathroom. Henrietta had decided she needed a bath now and had ensconced herself in the bath and then when she came out an hour later slipped into bed with a quick "goodnight" she was asleep. Leaving me to get ready for bed and wondering what I had got as a roommate. Eventually I got to bed and was so exhausted I fell asleep almost immediately.

I was woken the next morning by the loud singing from the shower, it was Henrietta. Looking at the clock it was 7 am, I never got up this early at home but as I was awake, I got out of bed. The room was a mess, her clothes were strewn all over the floor and her bed, I was shocked being a neat and tidy person myself I hated untidiness. Eventually she came out of the shower "Well, morning. Isn't it a wonderful day?".

"Well, I am not so sure, got to get registered and have the welcome meeting. Not sure what goes on, so I am a little nervous".

"You will have to tell me later because I am going shopping and might not be back in time".

"But you have to register, or you can't attend any lectures!"

"Can't you do that for me?" she simpered.

"No, I can't you need to be there yourself"

"How can I do my shopping and go to the meeting? I must get myself a new pair of jeans, these old ones are months old".

"Sorry, but rules are rules. And before you go tidy up the room, I don't want to live in a pig sty" I shocked myself with my belligerence, but I was really upset at her attitude.

She looked at me for a long while then said, "If you are not going to a friend then you had better find another room".

"If anyone is moving out it's you, I was here first, and you intruded with all your clothes and took all the cupboard space. You find somewhere else".

"Do you know who I am?" she demanded.

"I have no idea and frankly I don't want to know anything about you. You are already a nuisance and trouble and I can see you will be nothing but a hindrance to my studying".

By now I was really angry, I don't get angry very often but her whole attitude since she arrived had really riled me up.

"Let me tell you I am the daughter of Lord Evesham and he has well-endowed this university so if I tell him he will have you out, double-quick".

"Just you try and see what happens to you. I don't care if your father is the King, I have my rights here".

She made some sound then dressed quickly and left.

I had my shower, got dressed and went down to breakfast leaving her clothes all over the floor.

The refectory was big and lots of noise with people all talking at once. I made my way to the server y and got myself a breakfast. I was very hungry, so I had Corn Flakes, Bacon, Eggs, 2 pieces of Toast, Coffee and Milk. I found a table that was empty and sat down to eat. As I was eating a young man came along with his tray and said, "Do you mind if I sit with you?"

"No, that's fine" he seemed a pleasant man, blonde hair down to his collar, fresh complexion, brown jacket, white shirt, black trousers and shoes.

"My name is Robert Humphries, what's yours?"

"My name is Penny Kent".

"Glad to meet you. Interesting day getting to know people and finding out how to live here. Is this your first time away from home?"

"Yes. It's a bit frightening. But I expect I will get used to it".

"That's true. What course are you doing? I am doing History and English".

"Yes, I am doing English as well but with Geography".

"Well at least we know one other person on our course, that's a good start. I come from Worcester, where are you from?"

"I am from Ipswich in Suffolk".

"I have never been there, is it a very big place?"

"No, quite small. Is Worcester a big place?"

"Not really but has a wonderful Cathedral and the river gives us plenty of things to do".

After breakfast they started off to the lecture theatre for their induction training. Nothing very special was mentioned just rules and regulations, attendance registration, lectures etc. After that off to the registration section to fill in more forms, get a pass, lecture timetable, and payment of the fees.

Coming out of the section they passed into a large room where there were many tables set up offering non-academic activities to do. There were many things you could do, and I wondered if anyone did any studying with all these other things on offer. I was not really interested in any of these but Robert doing History joined the archaeology club and urged me to join as I was doing Geography, so I did.

The next stop was the student union table, my father had told me I must join, and I never argued so I did. The young man doing the registration was a quiet person wearing a dark suit, white shirt and a tie. I noticed that not many people wore ties, so he stood out. I thought he was quite nice but a bit quiet, a bit like me.

After that we went into Manchester and had a sandwich at a nearby café, with a glass of milk. We had a list of books to buy so went to the suggested bookstore and of course it was full of new students.

Struggling through the crowds I managed to find nearly all my books but was worried about the cost, I knew that my parents would pay for my education, but I didn't want the be frivolous with their money.

Robert and I made our way back to the Campus and parted as he went to his room and I made my way back to my room. I quite liked Robert and he never made any unwelcome advances; I was not into having a boyfriend I just wanted to study and get good marks. But we enjoyed each other's company and I was feeling very happy.

The Christmas recess was approaching, and I was thinking about going home but somehow, I did not feel happy about it. What was there for me? My parents were pretty boring and always did the same things every year, I didn't really have any friends they had all turned on me in my last year at school, so I had no great reason to go home. Then Robert suggested I might like to have a Christmas in the country at his house.

Well I was taken aback but I thought it would be a great idea, so I said yes, but I did ask him if we were to be treated as boyfriend and girlfriend and he said no just friends. Having that out of the way I felt much happier and looked forward to our visit.

When I told my parents of my decision, they were most upset and complained that they were looking forward to me coming home and having a family party. Knowing how boring a family party would be I was not unhappy with my choice. I promised I would come home for Easter, and that seemed to appease them. I wished them a merry Christmas and rang off.

We took the train to Worcester; the train was a newer one with corridors and even had a buffet cart that came along. The journey was 3 hours and it soon passed as we talked and looked at the countryside. Arriving at Worcester station I thought we would get a taxi or bus but no, as we left the station this glamorous middle-aged lady ran forward and hugged Robert. "Welcome home, we have missed you so much and so has Geraldine she can't wait to see you". She spoke with an upper-class accent and I began to realize that Robert was no ordinary man, we had never discussed our family backgrounds, so it was a bit of a surprise. "Mother this is Penny a friend from University she has come for a visit".

Looking at me his mother quickly eyed me up and down then said "Welcome. I am glad that Robert has made a nice friend, I was so worried he might get into the wrong crowd".

A chauffeur appeared and took the luggage to a large limousine. Now I could see that I may be a bit out of place here, after all I was only the daughter of two teachers and maybe middle class, now here

I was with an upper-class family. The drive was quite good, I was ignored by his mother and she only wanted to talk to him, he did try to get me in the conversation, but his mother would have none of it.

After a drive of about 30 minutes we pulled into an entrance with high walls and large iron gates. Then before us was a drive of about half a mile and at the end was this huge building with tall columns and a huge entrance door. We got out of the car and Robert took my hand and drew me into the house. "What about my luggage?" "Don't worry William will look after that".

As we entered the house it was a huge atrium with two staircases on both sides leading up to the second floor. We went into another room with a huge fireplace and a number of comfortable sofas and coffee tables. We sat down with Robert next to me and a maid brought in tea and cakes.

"Well dear, tell me something about yourself, Robert hasn't mentioned you in his letters" said his mother.

"I am from Ipswich and my parents are both teachers. Robert and I are doing the same course and it was only on the spur of the moment that Robert asked me if I would like Christmas in the country".

"What are your plans for the future?"

"I hadn't really decided but I will probably become a teacher like my parents".

"And what about marriage?"

I was beginning to get a little embarrassed by these questions, but I replied. "I expect I will get married but not for a while, I am still too young"

"So, you and Robert are not courting?"

Courting? What a quaint word for a moment I stopped and looked at Robert, he just smiled.

"No, we are just good friends. We like the same things and of course we are studying the same subject so that helps. But definitely not boyfriend land girlfriend".

My answer seemed to please her, and I got the impression she did not consider me a suitable mate for her favourite son. From then on, she treated me very well as if I was no longer a problem.

A maid took me up to my room and said, "My name is Emma and I will be looking after you during your stay".

"Thank you. I did not realize who Robert was he never mentioned his family. I am a little out of my depth here".

"Don't worry I will help you and advise you what you need to do. In this house you should dress for dinner. I see you only brought one dress".

"I didn't know what to expect. We don't dress up in my house. What shall I do?".

"Let me see what I can do with this dress and tomorrow perhaps you could go to Worcester and get another one".

"Well I don't have any transport or much money".

"Oh, don't worry William will take you and bring you back. I will mention to Mary, she is the House Mistress and I am sure she will find you some money".

"Really! How will I pay her back?"

"Nothing to pay back. This family is loaded and won't miss a hundred pounds".

"A hundred pounds! I have never had that much money before".

"Well we will sort it out tomorrow. Meanwhile let's get you dressed."

I watched as she got to work on my dress. It was pink with a scalloped top, fluffy sleeves and a pink bow around the waist. Not a particularly great dress but I had not expected to be invited to a great dinner. Emma worked on it and added blue material around the bottom of the sleeves and at the bottom of the dress. Took away the bow and replaced it with a blue cummerbund. Then to finish she added yellow flower on my left shoulder. I was amazed at the transformation.

"Wonderful! Thank you so much it doesn't look the same dress".

"I am so glad you like it. Now you will remember that no-one starts eating until the master does and when he finishes everyone does. Have you had wine before?".

"No"

"Right, you will see there are 3 glasses on the table, one is for water, one for Red wine and one for white wine. Red is for the meat course and white is for the fish".

"How many courses are there?"

"Usually four, appetiser, fish, meat and dessert. You don't need to eat everything, just some of each course. There will be supper at about ten before you go to bed so leave room for more".

"Thanks. I hope I don't embarrass Robert".

"I am sure you won't, just follow the others and you will be fine".

Re-assured I went down to the living room where Robert was already there dressed in white shirt, bow tie and black tails. He looked very handsome and I felt a surge of pride.

"Wow! You look stunning. I have never seen you dressed up before. You are beautiful".

I blushed as I had never been so complimented before.

I noticed there was another young lady there, Robert saw and said, "This is Geraldine, Geraldine this is Penny who is on my course at Uni".

"So nice to meet you" she said in an upper-class voice that seemed to say, "you are not as good as me, so I look down on you".

I could see that she thought that her and Robert were an item, especially as she put her hand in his arm and smiled deprecatingly at me. Robert didn't seem so pleased and gently removed her hand.

"Dinner is served" announced the butler.

CHAPTER 11

Christmas in Worcester

Robert immediately came to me and placed my hand on his arm, much to Geraldines chagrin, screwing up her face she allowed herself to be led in by another young man.

As we entered the dining room, I was amazed at the size of it and the huge table down the Centre laden with plates, cutlery, glasses, flowers and napkins in a silver circlet. Because there were only six of us only one end of the table had been set out.

Roberts' father sat at the end, on his right was his mother and on his left was Robert. I sat next to Robert and Geraldine sat with the young man whose name I did not know. Geraldine showed her displeasure and his mother frowned seeing us sitting together.

"Robert, I think you should sit next to Geraldine, don't you?" Geraldine smiled and started to get up when Robert said, "As my guest Penny should sit next to me, thankyou mother".

Geraldine looked to his mother and seeing that there was no help there sat back down again, scowling at her dismissal. His mother was not pleased either and grimaced at Robert and me.

"I think I should introduce myself; I am Lord Somerset commonly called Geoff; you may call me Geoff as well. I believe your name is Penny, is that correct?"

"Yes, I am on the same course as Robert".

"Welcome to our home and I hope you have an enjoyable time". Motioning to the butler they brought in the soup.

Penny did as Emma had said and watched what the others did before moving, the soup was delicious, and she enjoyed it.

Robert said to her, "How is the soup?"

"Delicious, thank you".

"Have you settled in O.K?"

"Yes. I have a wonderful maid called Emma and she has helped me tremendously; she fixed my dress for me".

"Well she certainly has made you look beautiful, I never noticed before sorry"

blushing I replied "Well I don't dress up at university so that is probably why. I only brought one dress so Emma suggested I go to Worcester tomorrow and get another one but I didn't bring much money with me so I am not sure what I can get".

"No worries just go to Jessops and Smythe and put it on my account. Emma will show you where to go and William will drive you. So that's that settled".

Now embarrassed that I had spoken I said, "Thank you so much, I won't spend too much".

"Don't worry spend as much as you like, I can afford it".

The beef arrived, a huge sirloin, with potatoes, peas, carrots, cabbage, Yorkshire puddings, and gravy. The servant cut off some beef and served starting with Geoffrey.

As we were eating, I said "You should have prepared me for your family. They all seem very nice, but I would have liked to know who you really were".

"I didn't want anyone at university to know my real background, I wanted to know people who liked me not my money. And I am so pleased you did. I think we have had a good time this term and it certainly has made it more pleasant for me".

"Thank you, I have certainly enjoyed our times together and I have certainly enjoyed my studying being happy".

"Robert! Are we going riding tomorrow morning?" it was Geraldine.

"Yes, of course. What time would you like?" said Robert.

"I like to be up early not like students who spend half the day in bed" she looked at me with daggers in her eyes.

"As you never went to University you obviously don't know how much work we have to do, so we cannot spend hours in bed". Robert retorted angrily.

Geraldine realizing her mistake, smiled and said, "I didn't mean to criticize you, I am sure you work hard".

"And so, does Penny!" he was getting angry at Geraldines' behaviour.

"Sorry. Well I will be ready by eight. Shall I meet you at the stables?"

"If I don't over-sleep!" Robert was sarcastic.

"Robert! Don't speak like that to Geraldine". Said his mother.

"Sorry, mother I got a bit upset with her attitude".

Geraldine did not speak for the rest of the meal after her rebuke. The rest of the meal passed of peacefully, Robert and Penny talked with occasional interruption from his mother, his father did not speak he just ate his food.

At the conclusion of the meal he rose and everyone else did, they followed him out of the dining room.

Penny excused herself saying she was tired after the journey and went to her room. There she did not feel like sleep so read some of her study books she had brought.

At ten there was a tap on the door, opening it Penny saw Emma there with a tray of Cocoa and some biscuits.

"Thank you, Emma" "So how did it go?"

"Fine except Geraldine got a bit upset and made Robert angry".

"Yes, she thinks that Robert is going to marry her, but I don't think he will. His mother is friends with her mother, but they are not particularly rich, they just pretend they are. I think her mother is hoping that the marriage will give them some money. If they don't marry both mothers are going to be very unhappy".

"So, that's the situation. Well about tomorrow Robert says to go to Jessops and Smythe and put my purchases on his account".

"Good. I will help you to choose what you need for the rest of your stay. And don't worry about the cost, Robert has lots of money".

"Well I don't want to appear greedy".

"Robert already knows you better than that so don't worry. I will guide you. So, breakfast is 7 am to 9 am. After breakfast William will drive us to Worcester and you can do your shopping".

"Thanks, and good night".

Penny undressed, drank her Cocoa and ate her biscuits and then went to bed, sleeping peacefully.

I awoke as the sunlight streamed through the windows, "Morning Miss, it's a lovely day" said Emma.

I slowly sat up

"Morning Emma"

"Do you want a bath or a shower?"

"Well a shower would be refreshing thanks"

"O.K. Here is a towel and you will find all you need in the shower room".

She indicated where it was "I will be back in 15 minutes to help you get ready"

"Thanks, but I think I can do that myself"

"Well I will come back to talk about what we are doing today, is that alright?"

"Yes, that's wonderful"

I got out of bed and felt the thickness of the carpet, I hadn't noticed last night how thick it was. Walking across the floor I picked up the towel and noticed how thick it was, then went into the shower room. It was magnificent, I had never seen so luxurious a bathroom in her life. There was so much there it could have been a beauty store, so I got to work and had a wonderful shower.

I returned to the bedroom and picked out my clothes for today. I chose a blouse and skirt because I was going to be trying on clothes.

Emma returned and we discussed what to do. "William will be ready for you at nine am to take us to Worcester. He will drop us off and will come back here, so when we are ready, we will phone him, and he will come and get us.

Now don't worry about money, Mrs Watson, the housekeeper has given me 10 pounds to pay for a meal so we can have a leisurely shop and then lunch. Is that OK with you?"

"Yes, I can't believe it. It's like a dream I don't want to awake. "It's not madam, and I will do my best to help you".

"Thank you for all your help. I don' t knows what I would have done without you".

"Thank you, it's nice to be appreciated. Now let's go and get some breakfast". They made their way down to the breakfast room where there was a large table and on the sideboard a number of dishes.

A servant came in and said "If there is anything you want miss, just ring. Would you like coffee, tea or tea, or cocoa?"

"Thanks, I will have some tea"

I selected some bacon, two eggs, a sausage, two pieces of toast and sat down at the table. I was the only one there so all the others must have already eaten.

The servant brought me a china teapot, china cup and saucer, small jug of milk and two slices of lemon. I thanked him and he poured out my tea, as I ate my breakfast, I thought how wonderful this holiday had been already.

Emma came in and told me that William was waiting, so I quickly got up and went to get my coat, but Emma had it already.

I felt so happy as we drove along, Emma was such a help and I liked her attitude to life. It only took about fifteen minutes to get to Worcester. As we came down the hill into town, we passed a large house with the sign Home for Orphans and I thought I knew how they felt, then below we could see the river glistening in the sun.

There were some rowing boats on the water and a large boat was going upriver with passengers obviously sight-seeing. Then the town appeared on the right and over the river was the cricket ground. The streets of Worcester are quite narrow as it is an old town and I thought it was a lot like Ipswich, that thought gave me a little dismay as I thought about my parents at home, but it passed quickly they probably never thought about me anyway.

William dropped us off at the store and made sure Emma had his phone number and then drove off. The store was old and looked Victorian and very stately, Emma guided me to the door where there was a doorman in top hat and tails who opened the door and lifted his hat.

Inside the store was hushed, I thought it was a museum or a library. Emma led me to the upstairs where the lady's garments were, and unlike downstairs where all the assistants were men in suits up here it was ladies only.

We were greeted by a middle-aged lady in a black dress with white collar and cuffs which went down to the floor.

"Welcome to Jessops and Smythe, what can I do for you ladies today". She spoke in a prim voice with precise words and an attitude of "I don't think you should be here".

Emma said, "Lord Robert has asked Penny to purchase some dresses and accessories as she came without much luggage. Is that alright with you?" she spoke in a slightly sarcastic tone.

"Well of course whatever you say any friend of Lord Robert is welcome here. Miss Jones please come and help Penny with her purchases." Her tone was now obsequious and talking to her assistant was commanding.

Emma knew what to do I didn't, so I just followed her directions. She told the assistants what we needed the dresses for, and they left and came back with a selection of dresses on a rolling rack.

I went to rise but Emma touched my arm, so I sat down again. The assistant showed me each dress and asked if I approved. Emma indicated which ones I should try on. I went with the assistant and Emma to the changing rooms and tried on each dress with the help of Emma.

After some time, we decided on three dresses, plus 2 skirts, and 3 blouses, and at the insistence of Emma two hats. I whispered to Emma, "Is this too much?".

"No, they expect you to spend at least 500 pounds". Inwardly I gasped, I had never spent that much on clothes in my entire life. As we left the Senior who had been so deprecating was full of thanks and asked me to come back again. The assistants carried our boxes downstairs and into the lobby where William was waiting with the car.

Emma said that William would take the dresses home while we had lunch and a walk around Worcester. I felt so amazed at the day that I went along with whatever she said.

We walked around looking at the 17/18th century buildings and we entered a restaurant called "Samuels Luncheon". We were met by a Maître D (I found out later) who led us to a table in the corner and a waiter came and gave us the menu.

The wine waiter came along, and Emma ordered a Sauvignon Blanc. When I looked at the menu normally, I would have been shocked, but I was getting used to this life not worrying about money. We had a great lunch and Emma was such an enjoyable person, we had really hit it off and I was so pleased she was my friend and maid.

After lunch we walked down to the river and watched the rowers practising. The sun shone and I was the happiest person in the world, Emma called William from the phone box and he came and picked us up near the bridge and took us back.

Once we got back Emma suggested I have a rest before getting changed for dinner, Christmas Eve dinner was apparently even more formal than the day before.

CHAPTER 12

Christmas Day at Worcester

Emma helped me undress and I lay down, I didn't realize how tired I was and fell asleep almost immediately.

Emma woke me at 5 pm and I had a quick wash and then started to get dressed. Normally that would only take 10 minutes but with all the layers, buttons etc. it took over an hour, then Emma did my face and hair so by 6.45 I was ready to face the family.

Dinner is at Seven, so I walked downstairs in my new blue taffeta dress that had a low neckline showing my big breasts and went all the way to the ground. I would never have chosen to wear such a dress because of my experiences with boys and I was a bit embarrassed about my size. But Emma had convinced me to buy this dress, so I hoped she was right.

As I descended the stairs everyone seemed to be in the ante room, so no-one saw me until I entered the room. Suddenly the conversations stopped. For a moment I was nonplussed and then Robert came forward with a huge smile on his face.

"Wow! You are so beautiful. That dress suits you so well I am glad you took my advice".

Everyone began saying how wonderful I looked, and they were so happy to see me, even Robert's mother had a kind word. The only one who didn't was of course, Geraldine who scowled and said out of the corner of her mouth "Mutton dressed up as Lamb". "How rude", said his mother and Geraldine tried to hide what she said, she could not afford to upset her maybe, future mother-in-law.

When the butler called "Dinner is served" we all went into dinner, I was on Robert's arm again and Geraldine could not hide her displeasure. The room glittered with the fine cutlery, chandeliers and elegant clothes on the table, beautiful plates and three wine glasses per person, I wondered why we had so many glasses. We all waited for Robert's father enter, when he did, he came along to me and said, "You look beautiful, welcome to our Christmas table". Once he had sat down then we all sat down. I looked at the magnificent dresses worn by the women and was glad that I had Emma to advise me what to wear, otherwise I think I would definitely have made a fool of myself. All the men were wearing evening suits and looked very handsome in them. I just loved this scene and drank in everything. At a signal from Roberts' dad the meal began, starting with soup, then chicken slices with beans, then roast beef with Yorkshire puddings, carrots, peas, cabbage, even Brussel sprouts, with lots of delicious gravy, I was already full but we still had a dessert of apples with cream. I found out why there were so many glasses, each course came with a different wine and there was also another glass for water if you wanted it. Because I had never eaten this sort of meal before Emma told me to not clear the plate, that was not ladylike and to start the cutlery from the outside and work inwards. As a last resort just watch what the other ladies did, and all would be well.

Thinking we were finished I prepared to leave but saw that nobody else was so just sat and watched, the table was cleared by the servants and then came the Christmas pudding. WOW I thought what a meal, Roberts dad poured brandy over it and set it on fire, for a moment I thought he had done too much but he had done it many times before so all was well. Now we had a slice with rum flavoured cream or there was also custard.

I was so happy and enjoyed the dinner and Robert's conversation, he hardly spoke to anyone else hand I was quite happy to talk to him. After dinner the men left for a smoke and whisky while the ladies went into the sitting room. There was a huge Christmas Tree covered in decorations and at the base a huge pile of presents. On Enema's recommendation I had only bought presents for Robert and his parents. On the end table was a huge Christmas cake, more like my idea of a wedding cake.

We all chatted away about nothing except Geraldine who sat sullenly in the corner, everybody ignored her. When the men came back in, we re-seated ourselves, I sat next to Robert on a settee.

Robert's father stood up and said "Welcome family and friend" with a nod in my direction "As our usual tradition we give out presents on Christmas Eve so let us start now. Please call in all the servants".

I hadn't realized how many servants there were until they all trooped in, I think there were about 20. They were all given a present and thanked for their work in the previous year.

Then he called on Robert to do the honours. Robert and the servant went to the tree. The servant gave him a present and Robert called out the name of the recipient.

"Mother, Father". The servant carried the parcels to them, and they began to open them, apparently this is the tradition that everyone opens their presents immediately. "Thank you, Son" said his father, "And the same from me" said his mother.

"Penny", Robert smiled as he walked across the room and placed it in my hand. I was surprised but smiled and sat there, "We are all waiting" he said. Embarrassed I opened the flat box and inside was a diamond necklace and earrings. I was so embarrassed "Robert, this is too much", "Not for such a beautiful lady, Merry Christmas". Involuntarily I leaped up and kissed him on the cheek, then looking around I thought I shouldn't have. But the general smiles told me that it was alright.

"Geraldine", Robert was not so happy now but gave the box to the servant. He took it to Geraldine who turned her head away and refused the gift. The servant turned and looked at Robert, he just nodded, and the servant put the present down beside her. She got up and rushed out of the room without a glance at what the present was.

All was silent for a moment then Roberts mother spoke "Well let's get on with the celebration" and the moment was broken. Robert came and sat beside me, "Thank you for the linen hand- kerchiefs, every time I use one, I will be reminded of you". "I wasn't sure what to buy so Emma suggested those, she is so helpful to me I couldn't have a better friend than her". "Yes, she is a treasure and I knew she would help you to get settled in". Some music started up and Robert invited me to dance. Well dancing is not one of my best aspects, but I got up and we walked around the floor. It was so good to feel his arms around me and to be close to his face, I almost forgot where we were.

Later the Christmas cake was cut and passed around with more wine or brandy, but only the men had the brandy, not good for a woman I had been told. Later we all started to leave, as I walked out Robert whispered, "See you later". Puzzled I looked at him, but he just smiled.

I got to my room and Emma was not there, so I sat down at the dressing table and started to undo my hair. I wondered what had happened to Emma when I heard the door open and thinking it was her, I said, "There you are I wondered what had happened". Then I saw Roberts reflection in the mirror and turned quickly around. "I told Emma you wouldn't need her tonight as I was helping you".

Standing up I tried to move past him, but he caught me in his arms and held me tight. "Tonight, we are going to have so much fun". I tried to pull away, but he was too strong. I guessed what was on his mind and was terrified, I was still a virgin and I had not allowed any man to be intimate with me. Despite my protestations he removed my dress in a manner that suggested he had done this before. Although I struggled, he undressed me and pushed me on the bed, I tried to wriggle away but he was on top of me, playing with my breasts, sucking my nipples and running his hands all over me.

Despite my efforts and my resistance I did begin to get some new feelings and as he played with me and soothed my I began to relax, it was quite pleasant too be touched by a man who knew what to do. But then he moved down, and I panicked, but he held me tight and I felt his hand touching me. Slowly at first and then more urgently despite my reluctance I began to enjoy what he was doing then he inserted his penis and I cried out with pain. "Don't worry, the pain is when your hymen is broken so it shows you were a virgin".

He continued to move inside me slowly at first then faster and faster, I felt my passion rising and I felt him climax and then so did I.

What a feeling! I never thought about having sex, but this was delicious and wanted to do it again. We made love three times that night and I was exhausted by morning. Emma came in late as it was the custom, apparently.

"Hope you had a good sleep",

"Not really, but a great night".

Emma looked quizzically at me then understood what had happened. "I am so glad you and Robert are good; I think you make a great couple".

Christmas Day was wonderful, Robert attended to me but not so much to draw a great deal of attention. I was in wonderland and enjoyed every minute, I was beginning to get used to this life and didn't think of the future. In the morning Emma woke me early and said, "We have to go to the hunt". I asked, "What was that" she laughed "Have you never heard of the fox hunt?"

"No" I said

"Well you're going to have a new sensation today".

We went downstairs and everyone was dressed and were eating breakfast. I quickly followed and then we all trooped outside to see the men dressed in Red Jackets and black jodhpurs and a black hat. They were riding beautiful horses of all colours and sizes, even some of the ladies were sat on horses with their large skirts hiding their boots.

The servants came out with a small glass of brandy for everyone and they raised their glasses and toasted "The hunt!". The dogs arrived with the man called the "Whipper in", they were obviously eager for the fray as they pulled at their leashes and barked. Then the huntsman blew his horn and away they went.

Some people climbed onto some carts and went to follow as best they could. I didn't want to go so went back indoors and sat in the library reading some books.

They came back about three hours later, all excited and tired but exclaiming that it had got away, but never mind it had been a "Jolly Wheeze".

The afternoon passed quietly, most people had a nap, and I did as well getting up so early had been tiring. That evening was almost a repeat of the previous. This evening Emma suggested that the pink floral was best suited as people didn't dress up as the previous night. Once again, she was correct, what a gem! Without her the whole week could have been a disaster not the resounding success it had.

The rest of the holiday was so good, we made love every night and enjoyed our company during the day. Geraldine left early on Boxing Day to everyone's gratitude she was such a bore and refused to have anything to do with anyone else.

Then came the time to go back to university, I didn't want to go but I must. The family came to say farewell and his mother whispered, "We so hope you and Robert will come back at Easter. We so like you and think you will be good for him", I smiled in thanks and then got into the car. We travelled back together as a couple and when we got to the college we got out of the cab and Robert gave me a quick peck on the cheek and was gone.

What had happened? He just seemed to ignore me, every day he was not around, he didn't call me, and I was getting more and more depressed. What had happened to my magical romance? Then one day I saw him, he was with a pretty girl and they were laughing and enjoying each other. Robert held her in his arms and kissed her. How I remembered how that felt, I didn't know what to do so just turned around and ran outside to find somewhere to cry.

Oh! The cruelty how could he have done this to me? Took my virginity and my love and then threw it away? I was devastated, I wanted to die, I thought about leaving and going home but I couldn't do that because I would have to tell my parents why.

Next day I ran into him and he couldn't escape me. "What happened? I thought we were having a great romance, even your mother said she hoped we would stay together".

"Well, I can't help what she thinks. Look we had a great time together and I think you are wonderful, but I am not ready for a long- term relationship. Sorry if it hurts but that is how I am. Maybe later we could start again, but for now I want to be free". I stared at him for a long time before he turned and almost ran away. I went outside and sat down under an oak tree and wept softly to myself. As I sat there thinking someone came and sat next to me, at first, I was too absorbed in myself to notice who it was then he spoke. "My name is John; I have wanted to speak to you ever since you came and enrolled at the Union table". He spoke in a soft sympathetic voice and I looked at him and knew he was sincere; this could be my friend to help me through the rest of college.

CHAPTER 13

Preparing for Trial

His daily routine continued, boring and mind blowing but he knew that he needed to show he was a good guy for the trial to come. He enjoyed the garden and learnt quite a lot about growing vegetables and he felt pride when his vegetables were being eaten in the mess hall.

He became friendly with Richard Carlson the trusty and learnt from him about the way prisons are run, he learnt that the guards did not run the prison although they thought they did, it was run by a senior prisoner who decided who did what and if they did not do as they were told he had them punished, usually by a beating.

He controlled all the contraband in the jail, so if anyone brought in some cigarettes. Alcohol or drugs they had to hand it over to him. He gave them back some for themselves but kept the rest. As is well known there is little or no cash in prison, so the contra-brands become the currency. He who controls the currency is the governor.

One day two of Mr Big's associates came to visit him and told him he was wanted. Richard indicated he should go and do what he is told. Now Harold was as big as the two who had come to get him, and he knew in a fight he could beat them both, when the time comes.

Mr. Big, sat in his cell in a comfortable armchair smoking a cigar and with a glass of alcohol by his side, all of which were forbidden to prisoners. He eyed Harold up and down then motioned him to come in. "Well, you are a big boy as I heard. You are on remand for murder, and I see you don't get any visitors. Why is that?"

"I don't know anyone here"

"But I gather you come from Bristol?"

"Yes, but I left years ago and went to London, I haven't seen or heard from my family since"

"So that was after the action? Well don't worry we look after our own. Now as you are on remand, we treat you as a visitor so if you need anything let me know and I will help. O.K.?"

"Yes, thank you"

"Good, see you again later. Oh! By the way as you are on remand you may be able to do me a favour, could you do that?"

"If I can, I will"

"Good I will let you know, bye".

He was led back to the garden and told Richard what had happened. "Hmm, sounds OK but be careful of any request they could cause you trouble in court".

Harold had now been on remand for four months and although he was quite content with his life the threat over him and the coming trial disturbed him. Richard said that sometimes waiting for a trial date could take months. The new session commenced in September so he hoped that he would get some news soon. Then he did.

On a day in July he was called by the guard and taken to the interview room. Harold felt a rising excitement and thought that he might be getting some news. Entering the room, he saw there were two men there, one was his solicitor, Charles Supworthy, and as he entered, they both rose.

"So how are you doing?" Supworthy asked. "Doing O.K. Working in the garden".

"Good, just remember to keep a clean sheet and it will help at the trial. Talking of the trial this is Michael Springsteen Q.C. He has agreed to listen to your side of the story and whether he will take your case. As you know the Crown Service will pay half his fee and you will have to find the rest. Do you have any source of income?"

"No, sorry and I have no savings apart from what they took from me. About 100 pounds."

"Well that is something we will need to sort out. Michaels fee is 500 pounds per day and the trial could last 3 or 4 weeks depending on your plea. You are looking at finding about 5000 pounds."

Harold blanched at the news. "Where can I possible get that sort of money, even if I was working that is a year's wages".

"We will work that out later if Michael takes your case, so over to you Michael".

"Thanks".

Harold noticed he had a voice that was not loud but carried a great deal of importance, a good thing for a jury he thought.

"I have looked over your case notes and I believe we can win this as the witnesses are not very impressive. A jury likes to hear firm, convincing testimony in order to give a decision. What I would like you to do is to go over what happened that night and clarify a few details for me. Is that alright?

"Yes".

"Good, so tell me everything you remember from leaving the pub until you got on the train".

"Well, I left the pub after the argument and I admit I was angry and humiliated by what had happened. I didn't have any idea of where I was going or what I was going to do. After walking around for a while, about an hour, I think. I passed by the Centre café and realized I had not eaten since lunch time. I went in and sat in the corner, the waitress came along an she spoke in a friendly way and I felt better. I ordered a meal and when it came, I asked her to talk to me. All went well but I think I upset her by asking for a date. I became angry again and put some money on the table and walked out.

I then walked up past the needles and down the road to Old Market where my flat was. When I got in, I lay down and I think I slept for a bit, when I woke up I decided that there was nothing for me here so I packed my bag and walked down to the station. I bought a ticket to London and went onto the platform, when the train arrived, I got on".

"Thanks. Just a few questions. When you left the café what time was it?"

"I am not sure".

"You left the pub at 8.45 according to several witnesses, you arrived at the café at about 9.30 according to the waitress you left at just after 10. how long is to walk back to your flat?"

"I think about 15 minutes"

"And the attack occurred between 10.15 and 10.30, according to the only witness. How far is it from the café to Queens Square?"

"Not far I would say about 5 minutes"

"Well that seems to indicate that if you left at 10 pm you would be in Queens Square at about 10.05 or so, which would be about 10 minutes before the attacker was seen. But of course, the tramp didn't have a watch so the times he gave are probably not accurate. Also, he woke up while the attack was happening, so he didn't see it start. We could say that the attack started at about 10.12 to 10.15.

The prosecution could therefore infer that you had the time to walk from the café to Queens Square and then attack the woman, before going home and getting your luggage and going to the station."

"Are you saying I am guilty?" Harold exploded; he didn't like what he had heard.

"No, of course not. As your attorney I need to think how the prosecution will probably think so I can prepare a defence to their arguments. One lesson I learnt many years ago was "Know your enemy"."

"Oh! I understand now. Well as I didn't go that way but up by the needles I wouldn't have been anywhere near the Square".

"That's true, what we need to show is that you did. On your way home did you see anyone at all?"

"No. at that time of night there wouldn't be many people because it is the business area so nobody would need to be there".

"That's a pity it would have been great if you had seen any-one. How about a policeman on patrol? Someone going to the hotel around the corner. A courting couple?".

"I am sorry, but I didn't see anyone, especially as I wasn't really thinking because I was upset about the waitress. I wish I had, but there you are".

"Right, well I will go and prepare the case and come back nearer the date. Do we have a date yet?" he turned to the solicitor.

"No, but the session starts on September 3rd and I would hope for an early date".

"Right, well let me know as soon as you can. Well Harold with what we have now I really believe we can prove your innocence, let's hope the prosecution doesn't turn up any other evidence".

"I will keep in touch, once I know the trial date, I will come and see you to explain how it all will work. See you then", he shook Harold s hand and left.

They then said goodbye, and Harold returned to the garden to consider all he had heard, he was in a confident mood as there didn't seem to be any strong evidence against him.

As the days passed Harold tried to keep himself confident about the outcome of the trial but it began to weigh heavily on his mind and made him short-tempered, this resulted in a problem.

At dinner one day Harold knocked someone's lunch from their hands, he was a long term, prisoner in for manslaughter and he turned on Harold.

"What the F.. k do you think you're doing?" And he aimed a punch at Harold, but he was no match for Harold, who deflected his arm and hit him with a solid right. Down he went like a sack of potatoes, he lay on the floor as two guards rushed over to see what was going on.

They took Harold by the arms and pulled him away and had him put in a holding cell while they decided what to do.

The Chief Guard came in and asked him what had happened. "Well I accidentally knocked his arm and he tried to punch me, but I was quicker than him. I didn't mean to cause trouble I need to keep clean for my trial".

"Well I understand the stress you are under, but we can't have violence it will spread and could cause more trouble. You will have to go to the governor and see what he says."

They took him back to his cell and he waited feeling sorry for what had happened and prayed that it would not affect his trial.

The next morning after breakfast he was escorted to the governor's office. The governor was a middle-aged man who always tried to keep a fair jail, so he listened to what the two men had to say.

"Well, as I see it the start was an accident which happens, your reaction was over the top, but Harold was quicker on the response, so it was over quickly. You should not have reacted as you did so I will give you 10 days in solitary.

Harold you have been the model prisoner so I will not be punishing you, but I warn you that his friends will be out looking for trouble so be careful".

Harold was escorted back to the garden to carry on his work and told Richard all about it.

"The governor is right some of his friends will be looking to pay you back so make sure you keep in company and not alone".

Harold was a little worried about further trouble and it didn't take long before it appeared. He was sat in his cell when three men entered and shut the door.

"We don't appreciate our mate being in solitary, so we need to teach you a lesson".

They approached him and started throwing punches, but they were no match for Harold and he deposited them on the floor in no time, they looked up at him in fear and then crawled to the door and let themselves out. Harold hoped that would be it and it was, the news flew around the jail and he got a lot more respect and a call from Mr Big.

"Well, you have got yourself a reputation now and I approve, I would like to help you but as a remand you can't officially associate with long termers. But what you can do is go along with my boys as a witness to those who need punishment, you won't do it but the mere sight of you will probably teach them a lesson and I will get you some reward. Do you smoke?"

"No, sir"

"Well, I will have to think of some other reward, by the way my name is Jack Hudson".

Mr. Hudson nodded, and Harold left the cell and returned to his own, wondering if he was doing the right thing.

A week later his solicitor turned up with the news of the trial. "You are due to go to trial on September 23rd at the Gloucester Assize Court. Michael will be along to see you next week and to explain what will happen and our strategy to get you free".

"Thanks, I hope that the time would pass quicker but I can't control that"

"Yes. By the way I hear you had some trouble last week".

"Yes, some prisoner got uppity because I accidentally hit his arm and he dropped his dinner, but the governor decided it was all his fault".

"Did anything happen after?"

"Well, three of his friends turned up but I persuaded them to move on and not cause any trouble".

"Good, we don't want any trouble to bring to the trial. O.k. I will see you next week".

Harold returned to his cell feeling quite hopeful about the outcome, now he had a date he could start planning towards it.

As promised Michael Springsteen turned up on the Thursday. As Harold entered the cell, they both stood up and shook his hand.

"Well Harold, we now have a date and my planning is almost complete.

I need a list of people we can call as witnesses in your defence. Give me the names of people who like you and will give a good character reference. We need to show the jury that you are a good, honest person who would not do such a crime".

"Well there are quite a few people who knew me but only two or three I was friendly with"

"We'll let us start at the beginning. When you left home, who did you have as a friend?"

"The first person was John, he and I met down by the canal and we became mates".

"What was his full name?"

"Hmm. Not sure it might have been England, but that could be untrue".

"Right, next?"

"There was a waitress who liked us and gave us big meals for the normal price, she was kind and I wasn't used to being kind. I her name was Lucy, not sure about her surname. If the café is still there, then they would know it."

"Right we will investigate. Next?"

"Well, John and I had a good mate in the market his name was Mark, don't know his surname, never asked, I had no need to".

"When was that? What year?"

"That was between '52 and '60, when I left for London". "Well I am sure someone will remember him. Next?"

"There were the four of us in the pub, we always sat together. That was Charlie, William and Jim. Unfortunately, Jim died, I was very upset. We were great pals".

"What were their surnames?"

"I have no idea, never had any need to know". "Well I am sure the landlord will know them". "I think that's about it".

"How about people in London?"

"Never thought about them. Well I am sure my boss at the garden would be a good witness, I worked hard for him and made him a lot of money, you could ask him".

"Good, sounds a good witness. What was his surname?"

"Not good with surnames. I think it was Owen, yes that's right it was on the board above his pitch".

"Well done. Anyone else?"

"No, I don't think so. I am not a person who makes lots of friends".

"There is one other person who we thought might be useful". "Who was that I can't think of anyone else".

"How about Diane?"

Harold gasped and almost leapt out of his chair.

"What after I assaulted her, and she didn't press charges. Then she told me never to see her again. I loved that woman and I am so sorry about what happened".

"Would you mind if we approached her? She may have changed her mind since then and it would be a great witness".

"But what about the assault charge? Wouldn't that count against me?"

"Possibly but we might be able to handle that. Do you agree?" "Well I would love to see her again, so give it a go".

Harold was excited as he went back to his cell, to see Diane again would be wonderful, but then he thought what she had said the last time they met.

Two weeks later they returned, and Harold was happy to here, what they said.

"Well, we have been pretty successful. We found your waitress, Lucy, and your friends from the Pub, Mark still works at the market that was good. But we couldn't find John".

"Well that's great, someone to speak for me". "But we have some bad news."

Harold stopped and looked intently at them, what could be bad?

"Diane, cannot testify for you", Harold's face fell, "Because she is being called as a prosecution witness".

"What!! I don't believe it. I am sure she would never say anything bad about me".

"Well, they will use the charge of assaulting her, even though she dropped the charge. It may not all be bad we just need to wait and see what she says".

Now Harold was in despair, if they got Diane to say nasty things about him, he could be in trouble, but there was nothing he could do now.

A week later they returned and told him what was to happen next and gave him some advice.

"Today, I just want to go over what will happen in three weeks' time. First always maintain your composure, the judge will not stand for any outburst. Whatever you hear just ignore because the prosecution will be trying to get you riled up and say something that can be taken as guilt. Just stick to your story and I think we have a great chance of finding you not guilty. Is there anything you need to tell me before we go forward?"

"No, I can't think there is anything new you need to know".

They rose, shook his hand and left. Harold was full of confidence and felt that in another month he could be free.

Meanwhile life continued in its monotonous way, he kept out of trouble and tried to be friendly with everyone but kept a look out for the men who had assaulted him especially after their mate came out of solitary.

They met in the dining hall and the man said "Sorry about what happened, I was having a bad day and just reacted, but I found out you were quicker than me. I offer my hand". Taking his hand Harold said "I don't want to be unfriendly with anyone so thanks".

After that Harold got on well with almost everyone and was treated with respect as someone who could take care of themselves, a great asset in prison where everyone was trying to be top dog.

Then he had a call from Jack Hudson, as usual he was escorted to his cell and he was resting there as was his custom.

"Hi. Harold. Glad to see you again, I hear you have a date for your trial".

Harold wondered how he knew; he hadn't told anyone just another example about who knew what in jail.

"Yes, another 3 weeks then I hope all will be over".

"Good. Now you said you would do me a favour, remember?" 'Yes", Harold wondered what was coming next.

"Well, I need to send a letter to someone in the court and I want you to deliver it".

Harold froze, how could he deliver a letter while he was under close guard?

Jack continued "All you have to do is to pass it to a guard called Bill James. That's it".

Harold was worried what if he got caught? That would not go down well with the judge he was sure.

Jack continued "Bill will be the guard who stays with you in the cell so you can pass him the letter then, no one else will be there, O.K.?"

Harold was still unsure but said "Well, as long as it does not get me into any trouble that will be bad for me

"No worries, all will be fine. I will send you the letter before you leave, put it in your trousers and it will not be seen. Doing this will go down very well with my friends. If by chance you finish up in prison again just give the leader my name and he will make sure you are looked after".

Harold hoped that would not happen and left to go back to the farm. The day before the trial Charles arrived to give him some last-minute advice.

"So, Harold tomorrow is the first day, but don't expect much to happen. There will be jury selection and it could take all day so you may not appear at all, if you do it will be to enter a plea, of course, Not Guilty.

Do not say anything else unless you are asked a direct question by the Judge, nobody else can speak to you. Then on day two the prosecution will begin its case; it could take two or even three days. Then it will be our turn and I will speak to you before then to tell you how we will proceed. O.K.?"

"Yes thanks, I can't wait to get started".

"Unfortunately, our court system is not the fastest so just be patient and say nothing to anybody, absolute silence. Well I see you tomorrow before court sits".

"Thanks for all your help". "Just doing my job, all success".

CHAPTER 14

The Trial

Harold hardly slept that night although he felt confident that he would be found not guilty he still was a bit worried about what would happen, it was a relief when he went down to breakfast although he didn't feel like eating. He was surprised by the number of people who wished him well, it felt good to be liked he got little enough of that in his life.

After breakfast he waited impatiently for the guards to come for him, then one of the prisoners arrived slipped him a white envelope and disappeared. Harold felt worried, he thought about leaving it somewhere, but he knew that jack would not be very forgiving, so he shoved it down his trousers and hoped nothing could be seen.

Eventually the guards arrived and handcuffed him before taking him to the yard where the van was waiting. It's about 30-minute drive from Horfield to Gloucester Assizes but it seemed to take for ever to him. When they arrived, he was taken down to the holding cells as he expected, but in the cell were another two prisoners and two guards. Which one was bill? He wondered.

Then one of the guards took a prisoner up to the court and Harold casually as he could asked "Do you know Bill?" The guard glanced around nervously and walked over to him, standing over him he said,

"Who wants to know?"

"Jack sends his regards".

"'Oh, did he, well tell him thanks and I will see him soon". Then he held out his hand so the other prisoner could not see, and Harold slipped him the letter. Without glancing at it he shoved it in his pocket and walked back to his place by the door.

Thank God that is over, thought Harold, at least he had done his job for Jack and hoped it would be a help in getting him help.

Lunch time came and went, no sign of anyone them about 3 pm his solicitor arrived and informed him that the court was finished for the day so he would have to come back tomorrow, one good thing most of the jury had been selected they needed two more in the morning then they could start.

All the way back to prison Harold was quietly fuming, a whole day wasted and nothing to show for it. All night he was turning over in his mind the waste of time and just couldn't seem to get to sleep.

Next day after breakfast they started back to court, the two from the previous day must have been dealt with as there were three new faces. Nothing was said each was in their own worlds.

Back in the cell he had hardly had time to sit down when the guard "Bill" approached him and standing close to him he pushed a letter into his hand. Harold tried not to take it, but he had little choice so glancing around he stuffed it down his trousers.

His solicitor came in and told him that the trial would start at 11 am, and not to forget his comments especially about not talking. Harold nodded and waited for the call, now he was beginning to feel a little shaken not knowing what was going to happen. He was called and the guard took him upstairs to the box, Harold looked around and was surprised to see so many people even the public gallery was full.

The court was called to order and the judge came in and sat down. He was quite old, thought Harold, maybe in his sixties and somewhat overweight. When he spoke, he had a soft lilt to his voice, maybe Scottish.

He called for the charge to be read.

"Harold Wilson, you are charged that on or about the third day of August 1960 you did rape and kill Suzanne Johnson. How do you plead?"

"Not guilty".

"Do you have a representative?" asked the Judge.

"I represent Mr. Wilson, Your Honour", said Michael Springsteen.

"Thank you, sir I recognize you. O.K Mr. Sweeting please commence".

"Thank you, Your Honour. This is a simple case. The accused was unhappy because of a previous fight that night and had come from a café near to where the event took place. He was in a bad mood and wanted to have sex, he saw this young woman, and raped her and killed her. He then made his escape to London, he was arrested some years later after being accused of assaulting another lady, but she refused to press charges. It was discovered he had been living under a false name and was wanted in connection with this event, so he was arrested and brought back to Bristol.

We will prove that he committed this crime, we will prove his motive, his opportunity and his association with the place. It is a plain case of an opportunistic man looking for sex and attacking a young lady of 21, Suzanne Johnson, and raping her and then killing her.

We will prove all these facts and ask the court that he receive the maximum sentence".

"Mr Springsteen, your opening argument please".

"Thank you, Your Honour. As my friend Mr Sweeting said this is a simple case but the case is about mistaken identity. The only person who saw what was happening was a homeless man who was sleeping in the park. He awoke and thought that the couple were having sex and went back to sleep. At the pre-trial he was not able to identify my client as the man he saw as he was groggy from sleep. My client only went to London as a result of the altercation at the Pub and didn't want any more trouble.

He has worked in London for three years and had a regular girlfriend, they had a bit of an argument which came to nothing. So it was that the police identified him as a suspect in this crime. We will show that Mr. Wilson was nowhere near the scene and is not guilty of this charge.

Your Honour, I wish to apply for dismissal of this charge as the only witness is not reliable, there is no other evidence against my client and I do not wish to use more of the courts time to come to the same verdict".

"Thank you, Mr Springsteen. I have looked over the papers and it would seem there is a case against your client, be it not very strong but I wish to hear some more evidence. Motion dismissed. Mr. Sweeting, as it is near to lunch, we will adjourn until 2 pm.

Harold for a moment had hope that it was all over but his heart sank with the judges' comments.

Harold went back down to the cell and had his lunch, then he was led to the interview room. His solicitor and Q.C. Were there. "Well we tried; it might have come of but not this time. Anyway, don't worry we still believe that you will be found not guilty". said Mr Springsteen.

"Now the prosecutor will try and make his case, but we can't see that it will be very strong, but let's just wait and see", said Mr Supworthy.

Harold went back to his cell and thought about what they had said, he still believed that there was no evidence to convict him.

After lunch he was escorted back to the court. After the judge had entered and sat down, he said,

"Mr. Sweeting please bring your first witness"

"Call Mary McKenzie"

Mary entered confidently; she had been in court many times before for soliciting so knew the procedure.

Once she was sworn in Mr Sweeting approached.

"Do you know anybody in the court today?"

"Yes, Harold Wilson in the box" "How do you know him?"

He was a regular at the pub I go to and we had sex once". "Miss Epstein, please answer the question you are asked and don't give any additional information" said the judge. "Sorry your honour"

"How well did you know the accused?"

"Not that well, he came in most evenings but only sat with three other men".

"What sort of man was he in your opinion?"

"Well as I said I didn't know him very well, but he never caused any trouble, just had a beer and sat with his friends".

"You have already said that you had sex once, how did that occur?"

"Well, he was only young, I think about 17 and had never had sex so his mates goaded him to sleep with me. He obviously did not know anything about sex, so I had to teach him".

"During sex was he in anyway violent or abusive?" "No, as I said he didn't know anything".

"Can you tell us of the incident on the evening of the third of August 1960?'.

"It started off as normal and I was talking to my friend Harry when he came storming in and grabbed my arm and said I was his girlfriend and to come with him. He had obviously taken our previous meeting the wrong way. Anyway, I refused and tried to get away from him, Harry told him to go away as he was only a kid. This made him angrier than ever and hit my friend who respond and knocked him to the floor. He got up shouted at me and Harry then stormed out".

"About what time was this?"

"Not sure but I would say about 9.30". "Have you seen him since then?". "No, not until this minute".

"Thank You. Your witness".

Mr. Springsteen got up and walked towards her.

"Now Miss Epstein, can I say that you are experienced in dealing with young men who have little or no experience of sex?".

"Well, some"'

"In your experience do men who have had sex for the first time get the wrong impression about the relationship".

"Not often, but there are some who think that it is more than a business".

"In those times do they react like Mr. Wilson did?"

"Yes, they try to make more of the meeting than it is".

"Good, so Mr Wilson's behaviour was not unexpected?"

"No".

"Thank you".

"You may step down" the judge said.

Well that didn't seem to bad thought Harold, well done by me Q.C.

"Call Harold Smith"

"Mr. Smith can you tell me what happened on the evening of August 3rd, 1960?"

"Well I had a few drinks and was talking to Mary when this young man came charging in and told me to leave her alone, she was his girlfriend. Mary tried to pull away, but he wouldn't let her, then he hit me, and I hit him back harder and he fell. He got up and swore at us and then ran out of the pub".

"Had you ever seen him before?"

"Well I had noticed him a couple of times with his mates, but not particularly".

"Thank you, Your witness".

"Did you ever observe Mr. Wilson to be violent before this event?"

"No, but as I said I didn't take much notice of him". "No more questions."

"You may step down now" said the judge. "Call Michael Walsh"

After being sworn Mr Walsh confirmed what the others had said and agreed that he had never seen Harold violent or lose his temper before.

At this point it seemed to Harold that the prosecutor was stating the case for the defence which seemed odd to him but perhaps he had some trick he was going to play.

Next was Emily Woodhead the waitress from the café where Harold had bought a meal. She related the events and said that he had stormed out when she refused a date with him. She didn't understand why because they had only just met.

"I call Jim Smith"

"What is your name and occupation?"

"My name is Jim Smith and I work as a Booking Clerk at Temple Meads station".

"Do you recognize anyone here today?".

Pointing at Harold he said "Him".

"How do you know him?"

"He bought a ticket to London"

"Can you confirm the date and time?"

"It was about 3 and a bit years ago, and he bought a ticket to London at about 11.30 at night"

"How do you remember that?"

"After the last trial I checked my records so I would not forget next time".

"Very admirable". "Your witness"

"In your witness statement you said you remembered Mr. Wilson because he was "Shifty", is that correct?"

"Well, as I said before he looked a bit upset and anxious"

"I see, so because someone looks "a bit anxious and upset" they are unusual in your opinion?"

"Yes, I see many people and you notice those who are different, and he certainly seemed different to me".

"Let me tell you that I have difficulty remembering people I met more than 3 years. Please tell the court again why he was distinctive?"

"Well, I am not sure now. But he definitely was different" he finished lamely, seemingly now not sure of his ground".

"That is all for now". "Call Albert Stevenson"

"Place your right hand on the bible and read the words on the card".

"I swear to tell the truth the whole truth and nothing but the truth so help me God"

"Is your name Albert Stevenson?" "Yes"

The prosecutor stands and comes towards the witness box.

"Please state your occupation and where you work"

"I work for British Rail as a ticket collector at Temple Meads Station".

"Thank you. Would you please look around the court and tell me if there is anyone here you recognize"?

He looks around the court and when he comes to the dock he points at Harold and says "Him".

"Are you sure? And where have you seen him before?"

"He came to the station late at night to catch the London train about 3 years ago".

"How can you be sure it is the same man, after all this time?

"As I said before I remember him because he was young and had blood on his cheek".

"Yes, in your statement you did say that. You also stated that you were in the war and saw enough then, so you were not mistaken"

"Yes".

"Now you also said that you did not do anything about it at the time because you didn't think it was important. How and when did it become important?"

"When he was arrested and charged with murder, I knew that my evidence might be important".

"That could be the case, so I want to make very sure that you recall exactly what you saw. I don't want the court to take the wrong decision because your memory is not as good as you think it is".

"I ask you again, how you knew it was blood and how much was there?"

"I have already said I have seen enough blood to last a lifetime".

He said angrily.

"Mr. Stephenson, please control your temper, or you will be in trouble", said the judge.

"Sorry, your Honour".

"And how much blood was there? Please indicate on your face where it was".

Reaching up he traced a line from behind his ear down to the hairline.

"Thank you, no more questions".

"Call Martin Rush".

He appeared and had certainly tidied himself up since the last trial, dressed in an old suit with a not too clean shirt and a pair of runners.

"Mr Rush please tell the court what happened on the night of third of august 1960".

"I was homeless then and I was sleeping in the bushes on the square, I was woken by a commotion and looking around I saw this couple. I thought they were having sex, so I took no notice and went back to sleep".

"This was Queens Square?" "Yes".

"What did you do next?"

"When I woke up it was dawn and when I got up, I saw this young woman lying there, not moving. At first, I thought she was asleep but coming closer I could see that she was dead. I went down to the Centre and told the first policeman what I had found. They took me to the station and questioned me, I think they half-believed I had done it, but why would I report a murder I had done? Anyway, eventually they decided it was not me".

"Thank you, your witness".

"Now Mr Rush, you identified the accused as the person you saw that night, is that correct?"

"Yes, it was definitely him".

"Let us get practical, Mr Rush, if I was woken in the middle of the night, I am sure I would not be able to focus on something in the dark. How far away were you from the incident?"

"About ten feet, I would say".

"And there are no lights near you?". "No, the nearest are on the road". "And how far away is the road?".

"I would say about twenty yards".

"So, let's recap. You were asleep in the bushes, which are about twenty yards from the nearest light on the road. You awoke and in your half-sleep you thought you saw a couple making love. But remember it was dark and you weren't really awake can you be sure who you saw?".

"Well, not for certain, but I am pretty sure it was him".

"Pretty sure but not certain! I would say that means you can't really remember who you saw".

"No, sir".

"Thank you, no more questions".

"Do you have any more witnesses?" asked the judge.

"One more your honour, but as it could take some time perhaps, we should adjourn".

"Yes, time is getting on, court adjourned until 10 am tomorrow".

Back in his cell Harold was feeling good. Doubt had been cast upon Mr. Rush testimony so that should go well with the jury.

The next day his team talked to him about how things were going. I think we had a good day yesterday; the prosecution did a good job for us and Mr. Rush was confused so I hope the jury took that as a good sign for us.

Today we have one more witness, I believe, and it is Diane. So please remember to keep quiet and make no comment on what she says. I believe it is as difficult for her as it is for you so let's hope that things go well".

Harold waited impatiently to go up to the court, but it seemed a long time before he was called. As he entered, he looked around and saw that the press gallery and the public gallery was full, there must be a lot of interest in the trial.

Nervously he waited for the usher to all Diane, then he did, and he looked down below as the door opened and she walked slowly in. His heart leaped as he saw her, how beautiful she was, how he loved her and wished the event at the café had never happened. No one had loved him like she did, and he destroyed it in one fell swoop.

She entered the witness box and took the oath in a very quiet voice not daring to look at him.

"Miss Epstein, I am aware that this may be an ordeal for you, the court only wants to hear the truth as you have just sworn. The jury will consider what you say in making their decision".

"How do you know the accused?".

"We met at my café in London when he came in regularly for his evening meal. He was always pleasant but a bit shy, we got on well and eventually he asked me out on a date. Now I hadn't been on a date since before my father died a year before, so I was hesitant at first. But we did go out on several times and I can say I fell in love with him. But there was one thing that stood between us ..."

"It's alright taken your time".

"It was sex" she said this so quietly that the judge had to ask her to speak up.

"It was sex. I was a virgin and Harold wanted it so badly, but he kept himself under control for months, until that one day when it happened

"So, can you describe what happened?"

"After we finished our meal, we were having some wine and he came to give me a kiss, but it became rough as he started to take of my clothes, and we fell to the floor. I banged my head and he then continued and had sex"

"Did you try and stop him?"

"Well, I was dizzy from banging my head and no I didn't because I did want to have sex but as I said I was afraid".

"How did you feel afterwards?"

"May I say that I don't blame him for what happened. I know he wanted to and really so did I, but I was scared never having had it before. But on that time, he had drunk more than he should have and lost his self-control".

"What happened next?"

"I called the police but decided later that I should not have". "So, did he go to trial?"

"Yes, and at the trial I refused to give evidence". "Why?"

"Because as I said I didn't really blame him and felt I was partly to blame as well"

"So how do you feel now that he has been charged with Rape and Murder?"

"I was shocked and at first I did not believe it" "At first! Did you change your mind?"

"Not exactly but I felt that after my experience perhaps the same thing had happened again".

"So, do you now think he is guilty?"

"I don't know, I don't want him to go to prison I am sure it would not be good for him. He needs love, he never had any growing up."

"Thank you, Diane. The court does not want to hear your recommendation".

"Your witness".

Harold stared at her, he loved her so much and he could see that she loved him but now all was destroyed. He wanted to cry, but he just buried his head in his hands and squeezed his eyes shut.

"Miss Epstein. Thank you for that honest and emotional testimony the court sympathises with you. You said that now you are not sure as to Mr. Wilsons guilt or innocence. I have just one question, do you love him?"

Diane hesitated, then for the first time looked to the dock. Her eyes were focussed on Harold and after a long time, with tears in her eyes she said "Yes".

The court and the jury made a slight gasping noise. "Thank you, Miss Epstein, no more questions".

Diane quickly left the stand and almost ran out of the court. "I think we need a short recess, 15 minutes", said the judge.

On returning the judge asked if the prosecution rested, they affirmed that they had.

Now it was the turn of the defence to submit their counter arguments to show that he was not guilty of any crime.

"Call Emily Jones".

She was sworn in and Mr Springsteen walked across to her.

"I just have a few questions to ask you. First of all, do you know anyone here in the court?"

"Well he has grown up a bit, but I recognize the man in the dock".

"And how do you know him?"

"Well about 10 years ago he and his friend came into my uncle's café. They were very nervous and not well dressed, they wanted to buy some breakfast, but they only had enough for one, so I gave them two plates and an extra portion of chips".

"And have you seen him since?".

"Oh yes! He used to come into my café about once a week as he was working in Old Market. We got on well and I was glad he had found a good job".

"Did he ever seem to be a violent person?".

"Well no, he was a perfect gentleman and so kind". "When did you last see him?"

"Hmm, must have been about three years ago, somebody told me he had gone to London".

Mr Sweeting approached, "Did you have any romantic association with the accused?"

"No sir, we were just friends"

"Did you want to have such a relationship?"

"Maybe but I am several years older than him, so it would not have worked out"

"Because of your feelings for the accused are you concealing the truth?"

"No sir!" Emily was angry at such a suggestion.

Turning away he walked back to his seat.

"Have you finished with the witness?" asked the judge.

"Yes, your honour"

"Then please say so in future" "Sorry your Honour, I forgot"

"Thank you, Miss Jones,".

They had managed to track down his first friend as a boy, John England.

"Call John England"

"Please read what is on the card"

He did so and glanced up at Harold with a half-smile.

"When did you first meet the accused?"

"Me and Harold met about 8 years ago when he had run away from home. We looked after each other and were great friends until I left the market and went to travel the world".

"In your time together did you ever see him be violent?"

"Never. He was the gentlest man you could know, and I didn't think he would hurt a fly".

"While you were together did, he have any girlfriends?" said Mr Sweeting.

"No, we weren't into girls, only to have a laugh with down the pub".

"So, he had no experience of a girl friend?" "Didn't I just say that!"

"Answer the question Mr England" said the judge.

"But I just did your honour, how many times do I have to say it?"

"As many times as Mr Sweeting wants you to say it. But I think you have asked that question too many times Mr Sweeting so move on".

"No more questions".

The next witness was Charlie Watson his drinking companion. He confirmed that Harold had never shown any sign of violence and blamed the attack on Mary who had led him on. He also told them about what had happened when their friend Jim had died. How he had raised money for the funeral and gave him a good send off. Many people in the pub liked what he had done.

His other drinking companion was Bill Watson who basically confirmed all that Charlie had said.

To Harold s surprise the next witness was his employer from Convent Garden, Sid.

"Thank you, Mr. Owen for coming all this way, Harold is most grateful. Now could you give us an impression of Mr Wilson when he worked for you?"

"Well his name wasn't Wilson when he came to work for me, but I needed someone, and he was a really good worker. Helped me make a lot more money and even when he was threatened by other traders he just smiled and got on with the job".

"You said he was threatened, how did that come about?"

"Well it was nothing really, he as you see is a big man and he just stood by my stall. This seemed to get customers to buy from me instead of pushing past him to others. They got angry and threatened to do him over if he didn't get out of the way, well the market manager and I didn't want any trouble so I told him to stand at the end of the stall not in the gangway. He did that and it all blew over.".

"I see, so you would say from your view that he was not a violent person?"

"No, until this case blew up, I thought he was a great bloke".

The prosecution couldn't get anything to blacken Harold's character so only asked a few questions.

Sid glanced up to the box as he was leaving and gave Harold a wave and a smile, Harold waved back and smiled as well. He really had enjoyed working with Sid and hoped he might get back again once this was all over.

Mr. Epstein called Lucy Hemingway a waitress at his local café, Charlie Mark and Jim Worthington friends from the pub. They all affirmed that Harold was a quiet, non-violent person usually. His Q.C.

"The defence rests, your honour".

Now the defence had finished it was time for summing up.

"At this late hour we will rise and resume on Monday at 10 am".

All rose and Harold went back to his cell. He met his legal team, and everyone was in a confident mood. Harold asked why they asked the question about romance, well it seemed that they were trying to say she was biased because you and her were involved. Harold said it had never entered his head, she was a good friend who looked after him when he was down and out.

CHAPTER 15

Summing up and Decision

Harold spent the weekend in an agony of depression, he wanted the trial to be over and now it was in its second week. On Saturday his legal team came into see him to discuss what had happened and what should happen on Monday.

"Well" began Mr Supworthy "Everything seems to be going well. The Prosecution case was not very strong as we believed, and I can't see any problems with the jury".

"Tomorrow I will sum up and so will the prosecutor, it shouldn't take more than half a day and then the judge will instruct the jury about what they must consider and those things to ignore. They must bring in a unanimous decision or if they can't then they will be sent back to bring in a majority decision. I can't see that they will have any great difficulty in bringing in a not guilty verdict" said Mr Springsteen.

"Please be patient and do not react to whatever the prosecutor says".

"Why didn't you put me on the stand?" Asked Harold.

"Well we didn't think it was necessary as the evidence against you is so weak".

"Oh! You know best".

"I suggest you try and have a rest this weekend, try not to worry we believe all is going well" said Mr Supworthy.

Harold returned to his cell and couldn't stop wondering about Monday. Come Monday and Harold could hardly eat anything before they went off to court, arriving there and waiting in the cell was a drag.

Then he was called, and they went up to the dock. The judge entered and sat down.

"Are you ready to sum up Mr Sweeting?"

"Your honour, I have some news, may we approach the bench?" "Yes, please do". Puzzled the judge beckoned them forward. "Well Mr Sweeting?"

"Your Honour I know that the prosecution had rested but on Saturday I received a phone call that will have a great bearing on this case, and I request that the prosecution be re-opened".

"This is a most unusual occurrence. I think we need to discuss this in my chambers". The judge announced an adjournment and rose and left the court.

Harold looked at his team and they just shrugged, before he was taken down to the cell.

In the Judge's Chambers the three men and a secretary sat down. "Well, explain what has happened"

"Your honour as I said someone phoned my office on Saturday and they phoned me at home. I spoke to this person and they said that they had been out of town until Friday when they heard about the trial. This person said that on the night in question they were driving past Queen Square and they saw someone running out of the square and up the road towards the station. They are sure they can identify the man who they saw and want to have a chance to set the record straight".

"Well that certainly is a bombshell. Are they in court?" "Yes, Your honour"

"Well Mr. Springsteen, what do you have to say?"

"Your Honour, this is most unusual. The prosecution and defence have rested so I believe that legally you cannot re-open the case".

"Yes, you may be right but I need to consider my options so we will adjourn for the day and I will give my decision tomorrow morning".

Back in the cells Harold wondered what was going on, and then he was called to the interview room. His legal team did not look happy.

"What has happened?" asked Harold.

"The prosecution has found a new witness who said they saw someone running from Queens Square on the night in question and believe they can identify him. Now normally at this point in a case it carries on and any new evidence would be on an appeal or a re-trial. Because the summing up had not been done the judge is of the opinion that he can re-open the case. He will tell us in the morning what he decides to do".

"So, if the trial is re-opened you will have to go on the stand and testify. Before that the police must hold an identity parade to see if they can identify the man they saw".

A policeman entered and said that Harold was needed for the identity parade. He reluctantly got up and went with the officer. The van took him to the central police station where he was held in an interview room while they found six other men who looked similar to him. This took a while, so he was in a very nervous state at the turn of events.

Eventually they called him in, and he entered a long room with a big mirror on one side, he guessed this was a two-way mirror. There were six other men there and the officer told him to find a place in the line. He chose the third place from the left and waited.

The room was soundproofed so they had no idea what was happening the other side of the glass, then an officer entered and told them they could all go. Harold was led back to the interview room to find his solicitor was there looking glum.

"Well, they identified you very quickly and were certain they were correct. Now we need to decide what action to take. We will come and see you at the prison later today".

Harold was numb as he was escorted back to the van and back to prison. In a daze he went to his cell and lay on the bed. It seemed all his hopes of freedom were shattered and now he faced many years in prison.

Later his team arrived, and he met them in the interview room. "Now you have been identified by two witnesses the whole case has changed. First of all, tell me truthfully did you commit this crime, your answer is private and privileged which means we cannot tell anyone what you say?"

Harold looked at them for a long time, his options going over and over in his head. "Yes, I did do it. But it was an accident I didn't mean to hurt her, I just wanted sex. Perhaps I was too rough, I don't know but when I saw she had died I panicked and ran back to my flat".

"Good, so that means we can go for a guilty manslaughter verdict if the prosecution agrees. You will probably get ten to fifteen years and be out in about eight".

After some discussion Harold and his team decided not to change his plea but to try and show that the witnesses were not reliable and he was not the person they thought they saw, hoping to convince the jury to not convict him.

"Mr Sweeting, please call your new witnesses".

"Call Clara Jones"

The lady entered, she was middle aged with short blonde hair, wearing a white blouse and black skirt down to her knees. She took the oath nervously and glanced up at Harold before turning to face Mr Sweeting".

"Please give the court your name". "Mrs Clara Jones".

"Can you please tell the court your account of what you saw on the evening of 3rd August 1960"

"We had been to the Empire Theatre and were on our way back home in the car, as we passed through Queens Square, I noticed someone running along the pavement towards Temple Meads station. At first, I did not think much of it as I thought it might be someone rushing to get to the station to catch a train. I did say to my husband that it looked like someone was going to miss their train. I didn't think any-more about it until we came back from holiday last week and saw the report in the newspaper, so I contacted the police who told me to phone yourself which I did".

"Thank you. Now you identified a man at a police line-up. Do you see that man here?"

"Yes, the one in the dock".

"Are you absolutely sure that is the same man you saw nearly 4 years ago?"

"Yes, I am certain".

"No more questions".

Harold's Q.C. approached the witness with a stern face.

"Mrs Jones, how can you be so sure this is the man you saw? After all it was dark, and it was years ago, I can't remember some people I have seen a year ago let alone 4 years. I ask you again, how can you know?"

"All I can say is that the man who I saw was big, young and dressed in working clothes. I was particularly clear about his age as my son was about the same age at the time".

"But it was dark, and I don't think the streetlights are very good about there".

"Yes, it was the lights are good just along that road, so my view was very good".

"Thank you. No more questions". "Call Philip Jones"

He was older than his wife and appeared more nervous than her. "Mr Jones, please tell the court what you saw on that night in August".

"Well I was driving and concentrating on the road when Clara mentioned that someone looked like they were running to catch a train. I glanced over and saw this young man running fast".

"Do you recognize the man here today?"

Looking around he stared at Harold for some time and then pointed his finger at him "I think it was him"

"No more questions".

"Now Mr Jones this is very important. You said you **think** that it was the accused you saw that night. Out of ten where ten is certain and 0 is not at all sure, what score would you give yourself?" said Harold's' Counsel.

"Well, I think that I would say six".

"Only six! That is not very high are you sure that is the man?".
"Yes, I am sure".

"No more questions". "Prosecution rests".

"Are you both ready to sum up?"

They both replied that they were.

"We will start summing up after lunch, court adjourned".
Harold didn't feel much like eating as he sat in the holding cell,

thinking that he was destined to spend several years in another cell. There was no-way he could see of the jury coming to any other verdict following the mornings evidence. After lunch court re-started.

Mr Sweeting approached the jury box, "Members of the jury, you have heard the evidence against the accused. The events happened nearly 4 years ago so memories can be vague, but we have heard from three witnesses that the accused was the man in Queens Square was Mr Wilson and he was seen by Mr and Mrs Jones fleeing from the scene.

As you see he is a big man and we have heard from many witnesses about the events at the pub. He had an encounter, his first sexual encounter, with a prostitute. But he mistook it for a love affair, being young and naive he had no experience to rely on, so he took the wrong idea and when he saw her with some- one else he lost his temper. Unfortunately for him his adversary was bigger, older and stronger than him, so he finished up on the floor. He then ran out scared, angry and beaten. In his state of mind, he wandered around until he needed to eat. The episode in the café was pleasant until he was again rejected. Now he was really angry and searched for a victim. He wanted sex, he wanted to assuage his anger, he had enough of being put down abused and made to feel alone.

Unfortunately for Suzanne Johnson who had been to the theatre and was making her way home she was seen by the accused who followed her into the square. He grabbed her and dragged her into the bushes where he savagely assaulted her, raped her violently and then fled from the scene. His tale of going home and then deciding to go to London was a complete lie. He fled to London because he had killed this poor young girl in rage and anger intending to escape justice.

Which he did for over three years but following another viscous attack on a young lady he was arrested, and the police identified him as the wanted person. We have here a viscous young man who got what he wanted by violence. Raping two young women, there may be more, but we don't know about them. I submit to you that the evidence is clear that Mr Harold Wilson raped and murdered Suzanne Johnson in a pre-meditated attack to salve his anger.

This is murder. A pre-meditated attack is murder not manslaughter, so I ask you to convict him and send him to prison for a long time to protect other young women from his attacks".

"Mr Springsteen".

"Ladies and gentlemen, here we have a young man who has suffered more than us in his short life. Beaten and starved by his parents, neglected, unloved rags for clothes, no shoes. Hardly ever went to school because he was bullied there as well so he ran away from home at the age of 11 looking for a better life.

Luckily, he fell in with Michael England who helped him to survive on the streets and together they became friends. The first time anyone had shown him any affection or care, Lucy Hemingway also showed him some affection and he repaid her with a great friendship. With his background he knew nothing, virtually nothing of the world and how to behave so he had to learn as he went along. As a young man he obviously began to think of women, like we all did at his age, but he did not know how to approach or talk to women romantically.

At the urging of his older friends in the pub he went with Mary Mackenzie. A complete revelation to him, having sex for the first time, being held romantically was a complete knew experience and he didn't know how to handle it. Thinking Mary loved him for himself he was upset when he saw with this other man. I am sure you can imagine how he felt. Thinking that his girlfriend was with another man inflamed him and he wanted to show she was his girlfriend. Unfortunately, she rejected him and when he tried to physically pull her away her client attacked him and knocked him down. Demoralized, upset, not sure what had happened he left the pub.

Walking around town helped him to calm down and as we see from the events in the café he was back to his normal pleasant self. Again, due to his lack of social graces he tried to date the waitress but was knocked back. Well we all get knocked back, but he was in a very fragile mental state, so this was doubly bad to him.

When he left the café, he was intending to go home as he had to go to work the next morning but seeing the young lady, he foolishly decided to have one more try and being loved. But when she resisted his mental state was such that he forced himself on her. When he realized what had happened, he panicked and ran away. Just remember that he was in a fragile state of mind and I believe he did not know what had happened and was now regretting what had happened.

Again, he took the wrong decision and ran away to London. Members of the jury I respectfully ask you to consider his poor upbringing, his parents virtually threw him out, unloved and not wanted he did overcome these challenges to become a good young man. A hard working, pleasant manner and good company who was not ready to face the problems he came upon. I ask you to find him not guilty of murder".

"Thank you. We will have a 30- minute break before I sum up" said the judge.

"All stand!"

The court re-started, and the judge turned to the jury.

"Members of the jury you have listened to all the evidence and later you will discuss it and make a decision. But first of all, I have to give you some instructions as to your conduct and what I will require.

First, you must not discuss this case with anyone outside of the jury room, you will be escorted by the bailiff if you need to leave for any reason.

Secondly your brief is to examine the evidence and come to a decision. Your decision must be unanimous, anything else will not be accepted. If you need any help or advice you may ask the bailiff and he will decide what action to take. If you cannot come to a unanimous agreement today, then you will be sent to a hotel and start again tomorrow.

I hope that you can make a decision in good time but please do not feel rushed.

Now as to the charge, the defendant is charged with Murder. This is a very important decision you need to make. You must examine all the evidence and decide if, in your opinion, that the evidence is sufficient to show that his actions were pre-meditated. You must be sure that he was pre-meditated in order to declare him guilty. But if you are not certain that the evidence is not fully sufficient then you must find him not guilty.

Under the law you may decide he is not guilty of murder but of a lesser charge of manslaughter. This means that he did kill the lady, but he did not do so with malice afore thought, in English this means that he did not intend to kill her, so it was not pre-meditated but an accident. Only consider this verdict if you cannot agree on the murder charge.

Finally, you may decide that the evidence is not strong enough to convict him of any charge, in which case you will declare him not guilty.

Under the justice system you must be absolutely sure that the accused did the act, either deliberately or by accident or the evidence is not sufficient to convict.

You will now go with the bailiff to the juror room and will not leave until you have decided on a verdict".

Harold watched as the twelve people who held his fate in their hands rose and followed the bailiff out of the court. Then he was taken down to the cells to meet his legal team.

"Well, I am not sure how they will see the evidence" said Charles Supworthy.

"Yes, we may have made the evidence of Mrs Jones unsafe and the evidence of the tramp is definitely unsafe. It all depends on how the jury saw their performances; all we can do now is to wait until they decide" said Mr Springsteen. They shook Harold by the hand and left him to his own thoughts.

Come five the jury was still out so Harold was taken back to his prison cell for the night. The next day he returned and sat in his cell again, just waiting and wondering. Mr Supworthy came by and said not to worry taking this long could mean good news as they are not sure of their verdict.

Lunch came and Harold could hardly eat anything, he wished the jury would make a decision soon. Then at three the warden took him back upstairs as the jury was coming back. He watched them as they entered trying to see what they looked like, a few glanced up at him and one half smiled.

"Members of the jury have you made your decision?" Said the judge.

"Yes, your honour we have". The foreman handed the bailiff a piece of paper which he handed to the judge. The judge glanced at it and gave it back to the bailiff, he returned it to the foreman.

What do you find against the defendant on the charge of murder?" asked the bailiff.

"Not Guilty" Harold breathed a sigh of relief.

"What do you find on the charge of manslaughter?"

"Guilty"

"Thank you, members of the jury, for your service, you are now discharged and may leave" said the judge.

"Defendant please rise" said the bailiff.

Harold rose and held on to the bar in front of him in despair.

"Mr Wilson you have been found guilty of taking another person's life. Even if it was accidental or not you have caused not only another person's death but distress to her family and friends. Losing a young member of your family is very distressing and society says that you must be punished.

Taking into account your attack on Miss Diane Forrest which she decided not to charge you because she told us she still loved you, still casts doubt on your temper. You had the fight in the pub before and then in a temper you were refused by Miss Woodhead so your temper was not in control so when you saw this defenceless girl you raped her for your sexual satisfaction.

Then as you were so angry you caused her death and then ran away to London. You have not been put on the stand so I cannot judge your character by seeing you, so I have to take the evidence I have heard in deciding what my sentence is.

Taking all these things into account I sentence you to 12 years in jail and no parole for 8 years. Take him down. Case Closed".

Harold was taken down put in the van and taken back to jail to begin his sentence. On his return to prison this time he was not greeted so happily, now the guards were more official, they treated him strictly and changed his green uniform for an orange one to show he was now a convicted prisoner.

He was led back to the cells but now in the long-term wing, so he had a new cell and a new companion.

The verdict was still buzzing in his head and the thought of years in prison was horrifying and he wasn't sure how he was going to manage.

Going down to dinner he noticed that the prisoners regarded him differently, they knew of his strength and therefore were polite too him especially as they knew he could be with them for some time.

The next day his solicitor visited him. "That was unexpected, but I think that we got the best deal we could. You have already been in jail for ten months so that will be considered in your eight years. If you keep yourself clean there should be no trouble in getting parole, then. There is the matter of your expenses. Being in here you won't get much money so when you come out you will have to pay the bills then. Any income you may receive will be deducted from your bills so pass any money on to me whenever you can. We won't be making an appeal; therefore, I won't be seeing you again. I like you and wish I could have got a better deal but there you are that is the law. Goodbye". He held out his hand and Harold grasped it and nodded; he was too emotional to say anything.

Then he was escorted back to the leisure room to start his long sentence, he could not see the end at this moment, so he believed his life was over.

Two days later he was called into the Senior Wardens office and told he was being transferred to Nottingham Jail as Horfield didn't have facilities for long-term prisoners.

Before he left, he was taken to see Jack. "Sorry about the verdict, you can never know what the prosecution is going to spin on you. I hear you are going to Nottingham, when you get there ask to see Bill James, he will make sure you get a good job. Tell him I send my regards and he will see you right".

"Thanks, Jack you have been good to me and I will try and live up to your faith in me".

He went back to his cell and then he was taken to the van to make the long drive to Nottingham.

So ended that chapter of his young life.

CHAPTER 16

Penny and John

As I sat there thinking someone came and sat next to me, at first, I was too absorbed in myself to notice who it was then he spoke. "My name is John; I have wanted to speak to you ever since you came and enrolled at the Union table". He spoke in a soft sympathetic voice and I looked at him and knew he was sincere; this could be my friend to help me through the rest of college.

I looked at him and saw a plain looking young man with a mop of blonde hair, a bit overweight, but who isn't? I liked the look of him and said,

"Hello, I remember you from when I enrolled in the union. How are you doing?"

"Well, pretty well. I am not finding the course too hard and studying is good, but I don't have many friends, in fact I don't have any".

"Well that makes two of us, I am friendless as well, so perhaps we can join up and be friends".

"Yes, I would like that. So where do you come from?" "I come from Ipswich, and you?".

"I come from Swindon. I don't have any brothers or sisters, do you?"

"No, I am an only child as well".

"We seem to have a lot in common, that is a good start. Shall we go and get a coffee in the Rec?"

"Yes, that is a good idea".

We walked over to the Rec and I felt safe with him and believed that I had found a true friend. We talked quite a lot over our drinks and over the following days got to know each other pretty well.

As we were studying the same courses, we also spent many hours in the library reading up and making notes. It was so good to have someone to talk to and to help in my studies, and I never felt threatened by him. The affair with Robert gradually faded into the background, it had been good, very good, but I couldn't get over the way he just threw me over.

Summer recess was coming up and I wondered what I was going to do. I ought to go home as I hadn't been home for a year and my parents had written several times asking why I didn't go home. I had made excuses and told them I had been to Worcester for Christmas.

With three weeks to go before the end of the semester, John asked me what I was doing for the vacation. I explained to him that I must go home for a little while as I hadn't been home for a year.

"I understand that, so should I. My family have been asking when I was coming home as well. May I make a suggestion?"

"Yes, of course".

"I could come home with you for a couple of weeks and then go to my parents for some other weeks".

"That sounds a good plan. I will tell my parents and you can tell yours".

So that was agreed, I phoned Dad and he was pleased I was coming home and seemed even more pleased I had a boyfriend. John said that his parents were delighted as well.

We travelled back home to Ipswich on the train and told John about my parents and he told me his father was a solicitor and his mother worked in an office as a secretary.

When we arrived at the station Dad was waiting for us, he gave me a quick hug, that is unusual for him, then we got in the car to drive home.

"How was the trip?" he said.

"O.K. I don't like train travel much, but it was alright as I had John to talk to ".

"How are things with you, John?"

"Fine thanks sir. And you?"

"Yes, not so bad. Well here we are at our house".

As we drew up mother came out, it looked like she had made some effort to be presentable, unfortunately mother's sense of dress is not very good. I was happy that she had made the effort this time.

"Welcome to our home, glad to meet you".

She shook John's hand but just sort of waved at me. She didn't like personal contact and she had never shown me any physical affection growing up, so I am sure she wasn't going to start now. We went into the house and into the living room. I observed that absolutely nothing had changed since I left home almost two years ago.

The same flowered wallpaper, the same old red three-piece suite, even the same brown carpet.

"We hope you will enjoy your stay with us, and we can get to know you better", she said.

"Yes, I am sure we will get on famously. I like your house it is so homely just like my house in Swindon".

"Well there you are, we have already started to get to know each other. I believe you are doing English as well as Penny?".

"Yes, I am doing English with History, but Penny is doing English with Literature. But we study together, and it is nice having someone to talk to".

"Good. Well it's time for dinner would you want to go and wash up first?"

"Yes, please"

Mother took John upstairs and showed him his room which was next to mine, she never thought that we might be sleeping together, which we weren't.

John came down freshly washed and dressed in his slacks and blue shirt, I thought he looked quite handsome. I had not thought much about it before just as a friend but now I thought well he would make a decent husband with no great demands, in any way I thought.

After dinner we sat in the living room and dad said, "Have you two decided when you are getting married?"

I recoiled in horror, what a thing to say after he had barely met John, I waited in anticipation to see what he would say.

After pause John looked at me and said,

"I have thought about it, but we haven't discussed it yet. We probably will later, but I think it would be a good idea". He smiled wanly at me and made a questioning look.

"We hardly know each other, dad, we need time to know what we want in life. I am sure we will tell you if we have any such plans". Having got over that challenge the rest of the evening was spent talking generalities. I was basically side lined, and they only spoke to John, eventually I got up and got a book to read.

Eventually we all went to bed, I said goodnight to John and went to enter my room when he grabbed me and gave me a hard kiss, then jumped back as if he had been shot. Getting very red in the face he quickly went into his room and shut the door. I stood there for a while, dazed at what had happened. Then I went into my room and undressed, as I lay on the bed my mind was in a turmoil. I quite liked John and he would make a sensible husband, but did I want a sensible husband?

After my affair with Robert anything else would be boring, I thought. But I only had boyfriends who wanted me for my body, they couldn't wait to get my blouse of.

The next day John was more quiet than usual and after breakfast I suggested to go and see the town. John agreed with a smile, so we walked out of the house and down the road towards the harbour. We sat down by the quay and nothing was said for a moment then he said

"I hope you weren't upset by last night. It was just an impulse".

"No, just surprised. I never thought of you that way".

"Oh!" he appeared disconsolate.

"But I think we might make a good couple, just give us a few more months".

Brightening John smiled and said,
"Great, yes that's a good idea. Perhaps we can decide by Easter".
Not liking deadlines, I said,
"Yes, that seems a good idea".
We went and had a cup of tea and cake in the little café and then walked around the town Centre before going back home in time for lunch.

We spent the rest of the week enjoying each other's company and I showed John the countryside and the local villages. He did not attempt to kiss me again or even hold my hand, I was feeling a little unhappy at this but accepted it for the time being and waited to see what happened.

At the end of the week we said goodbye to my parents although it seemed that they were more John's parents than mine by the way they hugged him but not me. I was glad to be leaving and looking forward to meeting John's parents.

We arrived in Swindon at 3.30 and on leaving the station we were met by his parents. Instantly I liked them. They were both about the same age as my parents but much more sociable.

"Welcome, to Swindon we have been looking forward to seeing you both" said his father giving John a hug and then me as well. He was smiling and excited to see us both, his wife was similarly happy she hugged John and gave him a peck on the cheek, and she hugged me for what seemed an age and then kissed me on the cheek. Not being used to this affection I was taken a little aback, but I loved it.

They had a new ford car and it smelt of new leather and was so comfortable that the journey didn't last long enough for me. All the way home they both kept up a chatter asking us questions about my parents and how we had met.

Their house was a large in grounds of its own, much different from our little terrace house in Ipswich. Entering the large hall there was a winding staircase on the left going up to the next floor.
"Just follow me Penny and I will show you your room".
The room was nicely decorated with Pink walls and a double bed with a red bed cover and white pillows. I hung my clothes in the wardrobe and sat down at the small dressing table. I looked at myself

in the mirror and thought how well I looked, it was probably because I had a no stress, John was a nice gentle soul and I felt safe with him unlike with Robert when it was exciting but would be stressful in the long run.

I checked my make-up and changed into trousers and shirt, something my mother would have frowned at with disapproval. Going downstairs I found them out in the back garden sitting on some cane chairs and sipping drinks.

"Well, I hope your room is O.K."

"Yes, fine thanks".

"Well come and sit down and have a lemonade and tell us about yourself, John hasn't really told us a lot" said his mum.

"Not a lot to say really, my parents both work for the local council in Ipswich, I am an only child. I had some problems growing up because I am a big girl but now, I have got over it and I accept me as I am".

"Too right too, be right in yourself and ignore the comments of the world. That way you will have a happy life. But I must say that you are a very pretty woman and I can see that John likes you a lot" said his dad.

Blushing a little I nodded and said "Thank you. We seem to get on well together even though we have not known each other very long".

"We haven't really introduced ourselves yet, I am Arthur, and this is my wife Mary. We are both solicitors but don't work in the same office, so sometimes we don't see each other a lot but when we do, we can enjoy each other's company".

"What are your plans when you graduate next year?" said Mary.

"Well my intention was always to go into teaching and I still think I will try that. I had hoped to be in Ipswich, but it depends where there are vacancies for English Teachers".

"Yes, I think that is John's plan as well, but I don't think he is bothered about where".

"Where is John?" I asked.

"Oh, he has gone to get his hair cut, he said it was too long. Shouldn't be long now".

John returned all spruce with his short hair and I thought that he looked great, my feelings for him were growing all the time and I don't think that I could wait until Easter to give him an answer.

Getting him alone I said, "Can we go out to a restaurant to night and have a dinner, just us?"

He paused and I thought he was going to say no but instead he said.

"Great idea, I know of an Italian Restaurant that I am sure you will love. I will just tell my parents not to make us dinner". For a reason I can't explain this dinner was exciting to me and I couldn't wait to get dressed up.

Coming downstairs into the living room I met Arthur and Mary,

"Wow! You look great" said Arthur and Mary smiled with approval.

"Is this going to be a big night?" Mary asked.

"No, we have never been out together before, so this is our first time".

"A first date! Huh!"

Blushing a little I just bowed my head and couldn't look him in the face.

"My you look great!" broke into my thoughts, it was John who stood in the doorway smiling all over his face. "Perhaps I should have dressed up a bit, I didn't think this was anything special but now I see it could be". Laughing he took my hand and led me to the door, I tingled as this was the first time, he had actually touched me apart from that brief kiss.

We got into the car and drove away under the smiling gazes of his parents. They lived about 20 miles out of Swindon, so we had a pleasant drive, we didn't talk much but I felt as if we didn't need to. Arriving at the restaurant we were greeted by the Maître D' enthusiastically,

"Why Mr John haven't seen you in ages. How are you? And who is this beautiful woman on your arm?"

"Hello Armand, I am at university, so this is my first-time home in nearly two years, and this is Penny my G – Friend from University". He had nearly said girlfriend but stopped himself in time.

"Right I have a booth for you both and the meal is on me so order whatever you want".

"Thanks Armand"

"It's a pleasure, see you later".

"As you see I am well known here, we come here often, and Dad and Mum have business meetings here. I hope you like it?"

"Yes, its delightful and so romantic". John looked at me with a new interest then resumed his smile.

The wine waiter came, and John ordered a Burgundy and an Alsace.

"I wasn't sure what wine you like so I have ordered a red and a white".

"To be honest I have never had any wine so this will be a first".

"Really! Well I promise I won't get you drunk, well not tonight anyway" he said with a smile. I thought what a charming smile he had and so attentive, I was going to enjoy this evening.

We had an enjoyable meal the food was great most dishes I had never had before, and the wine just suited the food. Obviously, John was well educated in Italian food and wine. As we had our coffee and mints I said,

"John, you know we said we would wait until Easter to decide our relationship!"

I had John's full attention now as he looked at me earnestly not sure what was coming next.

"Well, I have decided now what my answer is"

"And what is the question?"

"Well I was hoping you would know and could ask it?"

He looked at me for what seemed ages and I thought I had done something wrong then he reached across the table and held both my hands in his. Looking embarrassed and not sure what to say he eventually said,

"I don't know what question you wanted ask but I will ask my question. Penny I have loved you since the day you walked into my office and I didn't know how to get to know you. Now that I have, I have found how wonderful you are, and I want to be with you forever. Will you marry me? But I don't have a ring yet".

"We can get a ring tomorrow, Yes I will".

My heart was leaping, and I wanted to shout out loud as John got up and came around the table and held my head in his two hands and kissed me. I was in heaven; this time I knew I was in love with John not money or power and prayed that it would last for ever. Armand rushed over and said,

"What has happened?"

"We are engaged!" shouted John.

"Champagne here, let's toast the new couple!"

The champagne arrived and everyone in the restaurant toasted us, I thrilled to John having his arm around me and loved every minute. Armand gave us another bottle of champagne to take home to toast with his parents. The drive home was like a dream, when we arrived his parents had gone to bed.

"Better not wake them" I said.

"Nonsense they would be very upset if we didn't".

I went into the drawing room and sat on the big settee; John came rushing down.

"I only told them we had some exciting news; I didn't tell them what".

After a few minutes Arthur and Mary came in dressed in their dressing gowns, curiously showed on their faces.

"Father and Mother please meet the new Mrs Stephen"

"What you have got married?"

"No mother just engaged; you will have plenty of time to arrange the wedding".

They both hugged us, and the smiles were fantastic, we all sat down and talked about what had happened, drinking Armand s champagne.

We went to bed late, but I still woke up at 7 am thinking the previous evening had been a dream, but I knew it wasn't. Today we were going to get an engagement ring, something I had sometimes thought I would never get but it was happening today.

When I went down to breakfast Arthur and Mary were there and they both rose and came and gave me a hug, "Welcome to the family, we are so glad to have you", I was quite taken aback by their manner I would never have got this from my parents.

"Well thank you, I hope we will all get on well".

"Sure, we will you are just the right woman for John, ha! Here he is. Morning John how are you today?" said Mary.

John looked a little embarrassed as he sat down and glanced at me and then his smiling parents,

"I am fine, thanks".

"Well doesn't your new fiancée get a kiss?" said Arthur. Awkwardly John got up and quickly brushed his lips against mine,

"Not much of a kiss" said Arthur. John sat down quickly and started his breakfast. I felt a little embarrassed for him and could see he didn't like public displays of affection, well I thought I will have to get used to that.

After breakfast we borrowed the car and drove to town, parked it near the town Centre and went looking for jewellery stores. I tried to hold John's hand, but he didn't want to, so I thought another example of his antipathy at public displays. We looked in several stores, but I didn't see anything I liked.

"How much can we spend?" I whispered to him, he looked at me and said

"Well, I am not sure how about 500 pounds!" From what we had already seen I realized that nothing too big was in order. We went to several stores and I only looked at prices first, eventually I found a dinky ring for 550 pounds. Trying it on and showing him, I said,

"Is this O.K.?"

He looked at the price and said,

"Yes, that's fine, looks lovely".

As my hand is quite big the ring needed to be enlarged so we were told to come back in 3 days. When we got home, I explained why we had no ring and so they waited until we got it back.

I decided I ought to tell my parents and phoned them but as it was a workday there was no answer, I thought about leaving a message but decided that would not be nice.

All afternoon the subject was weddings, we decided that we would not get married until we graduated, John seemed pleased about that. Where? That is a difficult question, usually the bride gets married in her own church or town. As I never went to church neither did my parents, we did not have one in mind.

Arthur said "Look, I know that usually the bride gets married in her own town but as you don't have a church would you consider marrying here? We go to church regularly, it's C of E, and we know the vicar very well. I am sure he would be honoured to marry you both".

That seemed a great idea to me and I am sure my parents wouldn't mind; they could travel down to Swindon and spend a few days here with the family. Now all I had to do was to tell my parents and hope they were agreeable.

As it was after dinner, I thought they should be home, so I gave them a ring. On the fourth ring I was about to give up when mother answered.

"Hello, it's me".

"Well hello dear what is up, are you in trouble?".

Typical of my mother if you called you must be in difficulty.

"No, I just called to say that John and I are engaged".

There was silence on the other end then I heard her call,

"Father Your daughter has got engaged".

"Who too?"

Who too indeed how many boyfriends did I have, I thought?

"Congratulations dear, is it John you are marrying?"

"Yes, Father".

"Oh! Good. You had better talk to your mother. Your mother here. What arrangements do we have to make?"

"We have been discussing what to do and we have decided not to get married until we graduate".

"That is a sensible idea". "Arthur, Johns' father has suggested we get married here as they are regular church goers and know the vicar well".

"I will have to discuss that with your father, we have plenty of time so when you next come home, we can have a family discussion".

"Alright, we will see you then and get the details sorted out".
"Goodbye".

Typical abrupt ending from my mother and I was not happy with the reception of the news, no smiles or laughter just the sort of reception I would have expected. That put me in a bit of a bad mood, but Arthur soon got me out of that, such a funny and understanding man.

We went back and got my ring and it fitted well, I liked it very much and was pleased when Arthur and Mary approved but I noticed that Arthur glanced at John with a wry smile. Later I overheard him telling John that he had been a bit ungenerous with my ring, John protested that he didn't have that much money. His father said to him,

"You are our only son and everything we have will be yours one day so don't be so parsimonious. I don't know how well-off Penny's parents are so I intend to make sure that she gets the best wedding I can give her and you".

I was delighted but of course couldn't say anything then, I knew that my parents never spent any money if they could avoid it and they must have saved a considerable sum. But I knew they would try and cut down all the frills from the wedding and keep the guest list as short as possible.

I was glad that I had a wonderful future Father-in-law who would see I got the best.

It was time to go back to college and Arthur and Mary took us to the station, just before we boarded Arthur grasped my hand and I felt him put something in mine. Not looking I realised it was an envelope, I quickly put it in my pocket and kissed him on the cheek and Mary hugged me and kissed me as well. John being his usual self-abased person just waved and got on to the train first.

We sat down in the carriage and prepared for our journey. John didn't say a lot, but I had already realized he didn't speak much unlike his father. The journey was not too long, and we got back just before dinner, so we went into the refectory and ate. Then after dinner John said he was tired and wanted an early night, so we left, and he gave me a quick kiss on the cheek and was gone. I was feeling really down, what sort of relationship had I got myself into? I really hoped that once we got more intimate, he would show more affection, I could only hope.

Once we got back to college, we had to get down to studying and we got back into our routine quickly. We spent most of the day together apart from when we had separate lectures or sessions with our professors.

Most evenings we spent in the common room, watching T.V. Drinking lemonade and talking with a few friends we had managed to get to know. They all were surprised at our engagement and all pretended to love my ring, but I felt as if it was not really wonderful. As Christmas approached, we discussed where we would go, as there was 3 weeks, we decided to go to my parents first for a week and then to his for Christmas itself and new year. When I told my parents, they didn't seem very impressed, but I let it pass. Johns parents were much more excited and told us they had great plans for the holiday season.

We took the train to Ipswich and there was no-one there to greet us, not surprised I called for a taxi.

"I wonder why your parents didn't come to meet us", John said.

"They may have been busy or just forgot", I said.

Arriving home, we found no-one there, luckily, I still had my key, so we let ourselves in. I was surprised or shocked to see that there were no decorations, no tree and no sign of festivity. My parents arrived home at 6 pm, explaining that had to work that day so couldn't come and get us.

The atmosphere was chilly, over dinner not much was said, and John didn't say much either. Once it was over, they cleared the dishes and washed up before coming back to the living room. They sat in their usual chairs and we sat on the sofa, close but not close enough for my liking.

"Would you like to see my ring?"

"Yes. Looks very expensive" said my father.

"I am sure John can afford it his parents are solicitors" said mother with sarcasm. John and I looked at each other, this were not going well.

"What is the problem then?" I asked.

"No problem. Just that our daughter got engaged miles away to a man we hardly know and now wants us to travel miles to her wedding because we are not religious people. That' s all!"

Dumbfounded I looked at them both, I saw a middle-aged couple who never had an exciting experience in their lives and now begrudged their daughter getting married to the man she loved. I bet they were thinking of the expense!

"And we have to pay the fare all the way to Swindon, hotel costs, food and take time off from work as well".

At last John spoke up.

"You don't have to worry about expenses, you can stay at my parent's house and we can help to pay your fare if you want".

"You don't need to take time off from work you can take some holiday, you never seem to take any holiday so now you can" I said.

"Don't you tell us how to run our lives, young lady. We are too important to take time off the office couldn't run without us". Retorted my father.

"What! I don't believe you. You think you are indispensable? No way, I am sure the people at your office would be glad to see the back of you both for a while".

"How dare you! You know nothing about our work or the people we work with, they rely on us entirely".

I just shrugged my shoulders, looked at John and said,

"Well I wish we had not come here; I am off to bed, and we will leave in the morning!"

I got up and expected John to do so but he didn't, for a long time I looked at him and then stormed off to my bedroom. The situation had got to me and I started to cry, I needed John to come and hold me to tell me he loved me, but he never came. Eventually I dropped off to sleep.

In the morning I went down to breakfast and discovered they had already gone to work; John was not up yet so I went up to the spare bedroom and knocked on the door. "John are you awake?". There was a movement and then the door opened a little and John peeked out.

"What is it?"

"It's time to get up and have breakfast and for me to have a morning kiss".

John looked perplexed and then said,

"I am not dressed yet I will be down in a little while".

I stared at him, I was ready to cry again but held it then turned and ran downstairs to have something to eat.

John came down about half an hour later and sat down. I got up and walked behind him and put my arms around his shoulders and bent down to kiss him. He pulled away and said,

"I am not really romantic in the morning".

"In the morning!" I exclaimed "When are you romantic? Not in the morning, not during the day, not in the evening, not at night, never! We are supposed to be getting married, yet you cannot even give me a hug or a kiss, how romantic is that. Do you want to marry me?

He turned and looked at me, "Yes, I do but I need time to get used to the idea. I never had a girlfriend before, so I don't know what to do".

"Well let me teach you. First you kiss her every morning, you hold her hand when we are out walking, you hug me often during the day, you compliment me on my appearance, you say I LOVE YOU often. Anything else you need to know?"

"Don't get angry I don't like people being emotional. I will try and do what you say but it will be difficult".

"Right so start off with a kiss". I grabbed his head and held it firmly then gave him a passionate kiss. He stared at me as if I was a witch or something.

"Please don't do that again, I didn't like it".

"So, we don't have passionate kisses? What do we have instead?"
"Well I can give you a kiss on the cheek".

"What!" I stormed "I will be your wife not your mother or friend. You will kiss me on the lips whenever I want you too, do you understand?"

He looked at me scared and said,

"O.K. Whatever you want, but please don't get angry with me".

I was perplexed, who was this person? He was still a child, so I must treat him like a child until he grows up. We left the house and took the train to Swindon, when we arrived the parents were shocked and surprised. I told them of our experience with my parent, but nothing about John and me.

We discussed the situation and it was decided that Arthur would phone my parents and try to reason with them, I didn't hold out much hope, but it was worth a try to heal the rift.

Being close to Christmas Mary said, "It's time to get the decorations up, would you like to help me?" Never having had any decorations in my life I was pleased and excited.

"Yes, where do we start?" "Come up to the attic and help me get the boxes, John you can help as well".

We climbed up the stairs and up the ladder into the attic, John knew where the boxes were and picked them up and carried them to the hatch. I then lowered them down to Mary. There were 6 boxes and I wondered what was in all of them, downstairs I found out.

There were strings of lights, paper bells, streamers, balloons and a big box of tree decorations.

"John you go with your father and get a tree, about 6 feet would be good". So off they went as directed and left us to our work.

Mary got a step ladder and started to hang the lights, I assembled the bells and such like. Then we put them up as Mary directed. Within an hour we had decorated the living room, dining room and hallway. I loved the new look it was so jolly and exciting.

Then Arthur and John returned with a tree.

"This was all we could find but we got a good price on it" said Arthur.

"Well that's a bit more than 6 ft, I would say more like 7" Mary said.

Arthur found a big tub and he and John managed to get it installed securely. Then came the job of decorating it, Arthur got his 10-foot stepladder from the garden and started at the top, we started at the bottom. When it was finished, I admired it and then Arthur turned on the lights, they twinkled like stars and I loved it.

This was going to be a great Christmas, I was sure, and I gave John a big hug and a kiss, he did respond, and I was so glad he was warming up our relationship.

The rest of the day was spent getting the house ready for the party tomorrow, Christmas Eve, so Mary and I did lots of cooking and Arthur and John set up the dining room for 14 people.

The next day John and I went to the town to get some last minute gifts, I had bought John a leather notepad that he could use to keep all his notes in, it came with a calculator and 4 pens. But we needed to get his parents a present and as I had not known them long, I wasn't sure what to get. John suggested that we buy them a crystal horse, he knew that they loved crystal and didn't have this one, so we did.

After dinner we went to the living room and we talked on many subjects all evening, I loved it to have an intelligent conversation. Then we went off to bed, John came with me and at my door he touched my shoulder and turned me around and then gave me a real kiss, I was so happy as I went to bed.

After breakfast we finished off the preparations for the party, we were expecting about 10 guests about 6 pm. I looked into the dining room and was pleased with the layout, obviously the best china and glass was on display, with real Sheffield steel cutlery, napkins and down the middle were flowers and a real candelabra in the middle.

I had bought myself a new gown just for tonight and hoped it was not too out of the ordinary for the occasion. I went up to dress at 5 pm and so had plenty of time to get prepared. When I came down Arthur and Mary were there and they expressed how lovely I looked, I was so happy. John came down and when he entered the living room he stopped and gasped a little and said,

"Wow! You look wonderful",

I was so pleased he noticed and went over to him and gave him a kiss on the cheek, I didn't want to spoil my make-up.

The guests began to arrive and as I expected they were all in their line of business and mostly middle-aged or older. The men were in suits and shirts, some wore bow ties some ordinary ties, the ladies were in gowns of varying styles and colours, but I was glad that mine fitted in with what they were wearing.

I didn't get all their names, but one was a judge and there was a couple of Q.C. And the rest were in the legal profession in some capacity of other. Most of the wives it seemed didn't actually have a job but were engaged in what you might call "Good Works".

Before we started eating Arthur stood up and said,

"Friends today I want to announce a great event in this family, our only son John has become engaged to the beautiful Penny. John and Penny stand up please. A toast to John and Penny may they be as happy as his parents are. John and Penny".

"John and Penny".

We sat down a little embarrassed but happy at the congratulations. The dinner was a cheerful talkative time and although I didn't have much to say it was wonderful.

After dinner all the ladies gathered in one room and the men stayed in the dining room.

"Tell us all about you, we didn't know John even had a girlfriend".

"Yes, we thought he would never have one, he is so shy, but I can see you have already started bringing him out, good for you".

"Not much to tell. My parents are civil servants in the Ipswich Town Council, I grew up there went to Grammar School and then on to College as I want to be a teacher".

"What is your subject?" "English and History".

"Where did you meet John?"

"We met at college, but we have only recently become close and got engaged this week".

"Can we see the ring?" "That is beautiful"

"Yes, really pretty"

Obviously, some of them recognized that it was not a very expensive ring but were too polite to say so.

"When is the wedding?"

"We decided that we would graduate first and then get married, probably in August next year".

"Are you getting married here?"

"Probably, we haven't yet decided".

"Well I wish you well and look forward to the wedding". Wedding talk then started and most of it was about their wed-

ding or their children's weddings. I thought we ought to discuss this as well, but we could probably wait until Easter break.

Then the men came in and general talk ensued, plenty of laughter, drinks and cigars then we had a light snack before they all departed. It had been a great evening and John came and sat with me, he took my hand and smiled warmly, I was so happy and now that John was becoming unfrozen I could see we would be doing well in our relationship.

We said goodnight and then went to my room, John held me close and now I knew he was in love with me and would show it. We kissed several times and reluctantly had to say good night, no thought of sex before marriage for us.

I wondered if John had actually had sex, probably not I thought as he hadn't had a girlfriend before. Something I would have great pleasure in teaching him about, but carefully I wasn't sure what he would think of my previous relationship.

We still had new year to come so we just relaxed and began to enjoy our company, John now was getting into the romance mood and I was happy I had made the right choice.

The question of marriage came up and we sat around discussing what we should do.

"Are we going to get the ceremony done here?" said Arthur

"Well, it seems very sensible to me", said John

"Although I am not happy leaving your parents out of the planning".

"Yes" I said, "I hope that they will come around, I am sure they don't want to miss my wedding"

"When I spoke to them, they did seem reconciled to coming here for the wedding and I assured them that we would look after them and make them welcome. They do not need to worry about expenses, we will cover them all. Your father did say that as the father of the bride he was supposed to pay for her wedding but I told him that he could pay what he could afford and we would make up the difference, that seemed to go down well with him".

"So, if that is settled then we need to start making some arrangements, we can talk to the vicar tomorrow as it's Sunday and make an appointment". Today was Christmas day we had an early breakfast but didn't open any presents until after church.

The church was a Church of England one and it was what is termed a "High Church" as its service and theology was near to the Roman Catholic church for example using incense and respondent prayers. As I had never been to church, I did not know the difference so just joined in. After the service we shook hands with the vicar and agreed to see him on Tuesday he seemed to be a nice middle-aged man and I looked forward to the meeting.

Mary and I were very busy preparing dinner, we only had some sandwiches and pastries for lunch as dinner would be early today. Mary had put the turkey in the oven before we went to church, so it was well on its way to be done by 4 pm. We did the potatoes, Brussels Sprouts, carrots, garden peas, Yorkshire puddings, and plenty of gravy.

We had an hour to relax before serving up and we had a pleasant chat while we sat with a glass of merlot in the living room. It was so different from my home routine when mother did everything, dad watched the TV and I spent time in my room reading.

Dinner was served and the four of us sat down to a happy, laughter filled meal, Arthur complimented the chefs on the food and John said he loved it as well.

After dinner we all helped to clear away and wash and wipe the dishes and made the place tidy again, then we all sat down in the living room. The presents were handed out by John and everyone said they loved their presents, and I think they did.

Then we watched the perennial film on BBC – The Sound of Music. Afterwards we said goodnight and went off to bed, John and I stayed downstairs for a while and had a kiss and a cuddle. We were now behaving like engaged couple and I was really happy to be with John. Eventually we went to bed and I slept well having had the best Christmas of my life, even the time in Worcester were not as good.

On Tuesday we went to see the vicar, his name was Weston and greeted us warmly, and ushered us into his study.

We discussed my situation and why we wanted to get married here instead of Ipswich, I was told that the church needed a written letter explaining why and stating that I did not have a church. I needed to attend the church for 4 consecutive weeks before I could be married and it would be good if I became a member, this entailed 4 weeks of lessons before taking my confirmation.

We needed to set the date for the end of August, that would be no problem. He also counselled us on what it meant to get married in the eyes of the church and the responsibilities of having a union.

When we got home, we discussed what he had said and agreed on the date of 22 August, Arthur phoned the vicar and he agreed the date.

"Now we need to get down to planning the wedding as we only have 8 months left" said Mary.

Mary was in her element, she didn't have a daughter and she now took over me and did something she never thought she would do, planning a wedding. She said she would keep in touch with my parents to make sure they were involved as much as they wanted to be.

We returned to college and worked hard until Easter then we returned back to John's place. The major event was finding out what Mary had been up to and I was surprised at the number of things that needed to be done and was grateful that Mary had taken on the task. She told me that my mother had initially not been too interested but as time went on, she became more involved.

The one question was what was I going to wear? My mother obviously felt I should go home and buy a dress in Ipswich, I was not so sure but Mary persuaded me and said she would come with me as moral support, so we agreed we would go home after graduation. Graduation was a fun time and both John and I enjoyed it very much and to my joy my parents turned up and we all had a meal together for the first time. I was a bit worried at first but they both joined in and by the end of the meal we were friends, John and I were so happy.

We arranged for Mary and me to come down to Ipswich the following week and sort out a dress etc... Mother raised the question of bridesmaids; I had not even thought about it. Well I didn't have any close friends so thinking of someone to assist at the wedding was difficult. I said I would have to think about it, perhaps one of mothers relations might do it.

We drove down to Ipswich and it certainly was better than using the train and was just as quick. My parents welcomed us warmly and I was so happy that they had come around. Mother said that when she had told her friends at work several people had volunteered to help out. Her best friend had said she would love to be my maid of honour.

We visited three dress shops and I found a dress we all liked and so that problem was sorted. Margaret, mothers friend joined us, and we found her a dress. She was a jolly person about my size, and we got on really well, she was not married but engaged. It was agreed that she and her fiancé would travel down 3 days before and we would find them a hotel to stay in.

The rest of the time became a blur as I started my confirmation classes, helped Mary where I could in the arrangements and being with John. It was decided that the wedding reception would be held in their back garden, with a large tent in case of inclement weather. Afterwards we would spend our first night at an hotel in Swindon before leaving for our honeymoon, I was not told where so I would have to wait for the surprise.

I found the classes quite interesting and was so pleased when I passed, the ceremony was great, and John and his parents were there. Then we had another talk with the Father, and he explained the wedding ceremony and what it meant, we arranged for a walk through in a weeks' time when my parents were due to arrive.

The wedding preparations I think we're going well but Mary controlled most of it, she was so happy to be doing it and I loved her for it. We did the walk through and it was strange to my parents as they had not been to any church and had got married in a Registry Office.

The men went off to town to hire their dress suits and hats, I am sure my dad was going to be embarrassed but he would get over it. I had my last fitting for my dress and the two bridesmaids.

Only one day to go now and I was getting nervous, so was John but we both were looking forward to the great day. All the preparations seemed to be done and we just had to wait one more night.

Wedding Day!

Mary and the hairdresser arrived about 7 am, the makeup lady at 8 am and the flowers arrived at 9 am. By 11 am I was ready and waiting to go, John had stayed in a hotel with his best man, so I didn't see him, which of course is unlucky. Arthur said I looked beautiful, well he would anyway, dad and I drove to the church and arrived 5 minutes early, not done! I had to wait around the corner for the correct time.

It was a lovely day, the sun was shining, the birds were singing (well I thought for me) then we drove to the church and Arthur helped me out and my bridesmaids helped with my long train. We waited at the door and then the wedding march started, I glanced at my father and I saw he was looking so proud and had a smile on his face I had never seen before. He squeezed my arm and we started down the aisle. It was magical, I can't describe everything because most of it was a blur, I remember exchanging the rings and seeing the smile on John's face, then we kissed and walked down the aisle as husband and wife.

The reception was a blur, too many people who I had never met, lots of food and drink, some silly speeches and my father made a very up-beat speech, not what I expected. Then we danced and finally went to our rooms to change and then met at the top of the stairs, kissed and held hands as we walked downstairs.

Our car took us to the hotel and when we arrived in our room, we looked at each other and said, "Alone at last", then laughed and fell on the bed in each other's arms.

Our first night was educational for John, I had to pretend it was my first time but also to guide him as to what I needed him to do. At breakfast we both smiled and laughed a lot and didn't really eat much. I kept asking him where we were going but he just smiled and tapped his nose (meaning I would find out).

At 12 pm the taxi arrived, and we drove off to the airport, I was excited wondering where we were going. The flight was to Jersey, I had never been there, well I had never left England before. The hotel was overlooking the long beach and we had a great week, site seeing, eating, making love, laughing and having a great time. Then it was time to go home, when we got home, we both had letters from the Department of Education.

Too our surprise and delight we both had jobs at the same school, but we were shocked when we saw where it was, Ipswich!!

We only had two weeks before school started so we left Swindon and went to Ipswich, we didn't want to be with my parents so we found a 1 bedroom flat not far from the school so we could walk to school. My parents didn't seem to mind us not being with them which was a relief, and we were busy setting up the flat and getting ready for school.

CHAPTER 17

Harold In Nottingham Jail

Arriving at Nottingham he found the regime was much tougher and soon learnt to keep his opinions to himself and not to get into trouble, but trouble found him soon enough.

On his second day he was in the toilet when three big blokes walked in and shut the door. Standing menacingly around him, he watched them for the next move he expected.

"We are the welcoming committee to Nottingham and want to ensure that you a good time here by knowing the rules" The middle one said quietly but with menace.

"That's fine, I don't want to have any trouble. I just want to serve my sentence and get out of here as soon as I can" Harold said soberly.

"Great. But we need to tell you the rules first, so you don't get into trouble. That O.K?"

"Yes, but first I need to talk to Bill James"

Taken aback the three of them stood stunned for a moment then the leader said, "How do you know Bill James?"

"Jack in Horfield told me to find him when I got here, and he would see me right"

Looking at each other they were not sure what to do this wasn't in their script. Finally, they motioned to Harold and shooed him out the door and down the hall and up to the second landing and to the cell right at the end.

They stopped outside and the leader knocked on the door, someone looked through the hole, closed it and then opened the door. The leader went in and had a muffled talk with someone inside. Then the door opened again, and he was ushered in to see a middle-aged man sat in an armchair smiling at him.

"So, you are Harold! Jack told me you were coming and to make you welcome. Sorry about the welcome committee they didn't know who you were. Jack has told me all about you and I am delighted to have you join us. Friends this is Harold who took care of three of jack's best men in one sitting and did him several other helpful things so I know we can trust him".

Rising from his seat he came to Harold with extended hand and a smile, his grip was strong, and Harold felt at home here. He wondered how so much information about him had travelled all this way but was glad it did.

"Let's get down to business. I run this place like Jack does so you have some idea of what happens. I want you to go with Sam, Jim and Charlie (the three greeters) and watch how they do things. Later I will give you some jobs of your own once we get to know each other better".

With that Harold was dismissed and went back to the canteen as it was time for lunch. After lunch he was summoned to the chief warden's room and told that as he was a good gardener he would be allocated to the farm. Harold was pleased about that he didn't want to be kept inside all day and did enjoy his time in the garden at Horfield.

He was told that he would be taken to the farm after breakfast tomorrow so be ready at 8 am to go.

The farm was about three miles outside of Nottingham near the famous forest, he saw the sign from the bus. There were about 25 men and guards on the bus, so this was obviously much bigger than Horfield. He found out it was 25 acres and grew mainly vegetables for the prison but also some flowers that were sold in the market that helped the income of the prison. He was allocated a job of weeding the salad crop, a back breaking job but it was better than being back in the prison. They worked until 12 and then went to a hut where lunch had been prepared, compared to Horfield food this was good, cooked on the premises from their own crops plus some meat that had been brought in. After lunch he was told to go and learn how to drive a tractor, having never driven anything before this was a novel and exciting experience for him. He found he had a knack for driving and in one day he passed his test so he could drive around the farm.

Working on the farm was great, work was hard, but he enjoyed it, driving the tractor sometimes was a great change and it also helped him physically. He had never felt so healthy in all his life, then one evening it all changed.

"The Boss wants to see you" came the curt command.

Harold followed wondering what was up, coming to his cell he was ushered in and saw Jack smiling in his seat.

"Well, I gather you have been out of circulation out at the farm, pity I needed you to learn about our methods, so I had a word and you have been re-allocated to prison services. In case you're wondering it basically means that I tell you what you need to do and where. The governor is very happy I am taking some work away from the guards, they have so much to do".

Harold didn't know what to say he was enjoying the freedom of the open air and didn't really want to come back here.

"Why are you looking so glum?" demanded Jack.

"Well I am an outdoor person having worked in the markets all my life and I like working on the farm".

"I understand but sometimes you have to make sacrifices for the good of all and not just for yourself. I am sure that you will get used to it and enjoy it. Take into account that there are more perks working for services than vegetables out at the farm".

Realizing that he had no choice, Harold raised a smile and said "Of course, I was just thinking of myself. What is my first job?"

"Great. I knew you would be just what I needed. Well we are having a problem with Johnson in B 122; he thinks that he can do whatever he wants and is causing some dissension in his block. He needs a visit to explain that he is not in charge over there and to remind him of his future if he doesn't toe the line. O.K.?"

"Fine, I will go and see him now".

"Great, take Jack and Charlie for support".

Harold didn't take kindly to this new role, although he was a big man and very strong, he wasn't a person who liked throwing his weight around. He had resisted many times being violent and had sometimes had to take action before people realized he needed to be left alone. The thought of intimidating someone was not something he wanted to do but he had no choice in the matter.

They arrived at the cell of Johnson who was relaxing on his bunk, entering and closing the door behind them, he jumped of the bunk and retreated to the wall.

"What to do you want?" he asked even though he knew very well what they wanted.

"We hear that you have been throwing your weight around without any permission", said Harold.

"Not really, just having a laugh. I didn't mean any harm. Tell Jack I won't do it anymore". He pleaded.

Harold looked at him with pity, just a little man who played it big, not really anyone to care about. Before he could do anything, Charlie pushed past him and punched Johnson in the stomach. He fell to the floor with a whimper and lay there in a heap not moving, just uttering little cries and holding his stomach.

"O.K." said Harold "Just a small lesson, the next one will be much bigger. Just keep yourself quiet and all will be well".

Johnson just nodded his head and they left him to his own devices.

When they got back Harold told what had happened, "Only a little wimp who got above himself, I don't think there will be any more problems there".

"Good" said Jack "I will call you when I need you again".

Harold left not knowing what he was supposed to do, he decided he would go to the library and sit down in the quiet.

The prisoner librarian greeted him

"I don't get many visitors here. How can I help you?".

"I only came in for some quiet, I am not much of a reader".

"Well, perhaps you could start now. We have some good books here. What are you interested in?"

"Well I have worked in the fruit and vegetable markets and I was on the prison farm, so I like that sort of thing".

"Splendid. I have some books on farm management that you might like to read".

Harold did not like to admit he couldn't read very well, or hardly at all, but the man was so pleasant that he said,

"I can't read". The man looked at him then said,

"My name is Robert and if you like I will teach you to read".

Harold looked at him and thought there are some nice people even in prison.

"Thanks that would be wonderful, I have 7 years so hopefully in that time I can learn to read".

"You will be reading in a month or so. Right let's begin" Robert got him a 1st year reading book and they started. At first Harold was slow but being an intelligent man, he soon got to grips and was amazed that as Robert had predicted he could read within 5 weeks.

Then he started reading more and more and found he loved it, the stories fascinated and amazed him and he regretted that he had not learnt to read before, but he didn't need to in his work so that didn't matter.

He had to use a dictionary a lot but as he progressed his knowledge of words got bigger and larger. The course on farm management actually had an exam at the end so he could get a qualification, Wow! He thought me with a qualification.

Every morning after breakfast there was an hour of exercise before starting on your occupational therapy. Harold never went to these he went to see Jack and find out if he needed him, one day Jack asked him what he did all day and Harold told him he was studying for when he left prison. He explained that he wanted to stay out of trouble and make a living doing something he liked.

Jack asked him what he wanted to do later, and Harold told him he needed to be outdoors and had liked working at the farm, so he was learning about farming. Jack said that was a great idea and if he needed him, he would know where he was, he also said if he needed anything from outside just let him know. Harold thanked him and so his daily routine began. Breakfast, Exercise, report to Jack and then to the library. Sometimes he wondered why the guards never asked him what he was doing, he guessed it was down to Jack.

Life in prison is monotonous and can be mined bending if you have nothing to do to occupy your mind. There was some work that they could do, like making mail sacks, building small furniture, and working on the farm, kitchen garden or library. Most inmates were uneducated in that if they could read, they didn't find it interesting, they had no ambition apart from getting out and going back to their illegal ways to earn some money. Many ex-con found it almost impossible to get back into the regular job market so they had to work for cash for example like Harold they could work in markets, building sites and any place that would pay them cash, if not they went back to robbery, burglary, violence etc..

Fortunately, Harold had a more ambitious mind and didn't want to get into trouble with the law again. Hence his studying to be a farmer. He studied diligently and then came the time for his examination. He needed to take a written examination and also a practical one, so he spoke to Jack.

"Well I don't see any problem with taking the written exam, you can do that in the library, as regards the practical you will need to go outside. I will find out if our farm has the necessary facilities and let you know.

A few days later Jack told him that it was OK for the written exam, but our farm did not have all the necessary activities. Jack suggested that they have a meeting with the governor to see if he would allow him a day pass to go to a farm that was suitable.

The Governor was surprised at the request and initially said he couldn't see how it could be arranged so sorry he couldn't go.

Harold felt his anger rising but controlled it, he had worked hard for this exam and now was being prevented from taking it. He went to the gym and beat a punch bag to death for an hour, relieved he then went to see Jack. Jack was unhappy and he could see how unhappy Harold was. "Look, leave it with me and I will see what I can do, in the meantime don't do anything silly that might prevent you going out, O.K?"

"Thanks, I will not get into trouble I need to take this examination so I will do whatever you say".

For two days Harold fretted and fumed but managed to keep himself out of trouble with the help of Robert in the library, then he was called to the Governor's office again. When he entered, he was surprised to see Jack and Robert there.

"Wilson, I have been thinking things over and discussed the situation with Sampson and Warner". For a moment Harold wondered who they were then realized they were Jack and Robert, he had never known their surnames.

"As a result" continued the Governor "I have decided that as you have worked so hard in your studying and Warner tells me he is confident you have a good chance at passing the exam I have authorised you to have a day pass to go to Montgomery Farm to do the practical test"

Harold couldn't help but smile broadly and felt like jumping up and down but didn't.

Outside he thanked Jack and Robert for their help.

Came the day of the written exam, an outside invigilator arrived and came to the library. He gave Harold the instructions for taking the exam and then the paper. Harold looked at the words and suddenly he realized that he knew most of the answers. He completed the paper with 5 minutes to spare and as he had been told he checked his answers. He did find one error which he quickly corrected. The invigilator took the paper and he and Harold signed a form to show it was the correct paper and answer sheet. The invigilator told him he would be receiving a letter telling him when the practical was, it would be in about a week or two.

Waiting for the next test was more stress on Harold but he had learnt over the years that getting uptight did no good, so he was alright. The letter arrived 2 weeks later, and he was to do his test next week. He was taken to the farm the next day to talk to the farmer and to do the activities in the exam. Harold was a quick learner and the farmer was very impressed and told him "if you want a job come to see me", Harold mentioned "I still have three years to go before I can get parole", "fine" the farmer said "I will still be here".

On the day he was escorted to the farm by two warders and met the farmer who had agreed he could do his test there. The invigilator arrived and checked the farm was suitable, finding everything alright he instructed Harold as to what he had to do. There were various activities including ploughing, planting, milking the cows, mucking out the cowsheds and various other things.

He had to wait three months before he got his results. He was called to the Governor's office again; this time Harold was in an excited mood hoping everything was great. "Well Wilson, I have here the results of your examination". Passing a piece of paper across the table to Harold who scanned it quickly then re-read it slowly.

Mr Harold Wilson has passed the examination in Farm Management.

Written Examination 92%

Practical Examination 89% Congratulations

Board of Agriculture

"Congratulations, you have done well". Said the Governor.

Harold was elated and went to tell Jack who was as excited as him. That evening when he was going to the mess room to his surprise Jack came by his cell. Now Jack never ate in the mess hall, so Harold was surprised.

Jack took his arm and said "I need to blindfold you, so you don't see what is going on" Harold looked at him but trusted him, so he was blindfolded and led downstairs. When they got there, they stopped inside the door and Jack removed the blindfold.

There was a big cheer and clapping and shouting "Congratulations". The entire prison including many warders were there and Harold could hardly stop the tears coming. There was a special meal that night, a big cake and lots of laughter. Everyone seemed genuine happy for him and Harold was beginning to become more human every day.

The next day he was called to the chief warden's office, Harold wondered what it was this time. On entering he saw that the Chief

Warden was not alone, but he had the farm manager with him. Harold greeted them both and he was motioned to sit down.

"Well, Wilson, once again congratulations on your success. Mr Morris, the farm manager, and I have been discussing what is the best for you with your remaining time here. We agreed that you should put your qualification to use so you are being re-assigned to the farm to act as assistant to Mr Morris. The Governor wants all his inmates to be as happy as is possible. So, he thinks this is a good idea as well. What do you say?"

Harold knew this was a rhetorical question he was going whether he wanted to or not, but he wanted to desperately.

"Thank you, Sir. I would love to go back to the farm and be useful to all the inmates and myself. Thanks again".

"Good. You will start tomorrow, be ready at 7.30 am to catch the transport".

Harold was overjoyed as he left the office and hurried to Jack's cell. When he told him at first, he was not too pleased but then he said. "Sorry to see you go but I can see it's best for you and you can still be useful to me by keeping an eye on anyone who is not toeing the line and keeping me informed of what is going on out there".

Harold was not too pleased about that but saw it as a small inconvenience to be doing what he was happy doing.

Harold could hardly sleep that night and was first for breakfast and waiting for the transport, he could hardly contain his excitement and some of the men looked at him a bit strangely but wouldn't dare to say anything.

Once they were at the farm Mr Morris took him aside and showed him the administration details and his duties as an assistant. With his knowledge Harold was able to help a great deal and introduced improvements to the farm so that more food could be produced. Mr Morris was very pleased with him and gave him more authority as time passed.

The years passed and prisoners came and went and one day he was called to the chief warder's office.

"Come, sit down I need to have a word with you. You will be due for a parole board meeting next week and I am recommending you be released on licence".

Harold was so pleased, and he had forgotten his time was nearly up as he had enjoyed the last three years. In a way he felt some trepidation leaving his "Home". He was used to the routine and wasn't sure he could cope with looking after himself after all these years, but he wasn't going to object just now.

"Thank you, Sir. I hope all goes well"

"Well with your record you have no need to worry, just make sure you tell them that you are sorry for what you did and have no intention of getting into the same trouble again and you will do well".

"I am most grateful for your advice and I will follow it so that I get a good result".

The next Thursday he was called to the interview room for his appearance. When he entered there were three people there, a lady of about 50, a thin man who looked about 45 and had a sour face, and the third person was another lady of about 40 who was plump and had a kind looking face.

The older lady was the chair and she started by saying "Mr Wilson, we are empowered to make sure that any person released will be a valuable member of society and has learnt their lesson for what they did. We will take into account your conduct in here and you will be able to tell us how you feel about your crime and what you will do outside".

Harold just nodded; he wasn't sure what to say.

The sour faced man spoke in a harsh voice "So it looks like you have been an exemplary prisoner, but you are still the man who killed a young lady and assaulted another. How do we know you won't do it again?"

"Sir, when I committed the act, I was not myself, I had a terrible day and being rejected twice by a woman made me angry. Now I have learnt my lesson and learnt how to control my temper and I am sorry for what happened, and I would ask for her family to forgive me for taking their daughter away from them".

"Well you haven't seen a woman in eight years so how will you behave when you see one again?"

"I honestly don't know but I do know that I won't behave the way I did before".

The plump lady asked, "What do you intend to do when you get out?"

"Well I have a farming qualification and have been working on the farm for three years so I will hope to find a job in farming".

"Yes, I see that you did get a qualification, congratulations on that. There are plenty of farming jobs around here so you should have no difficulty in getting employment".

The chair said, "Thank you Mr Wilson, we need to have a short discussion so would you just wait outside".

Harold left with the warder and sat outside; it didn't take them long before he was called back in again.

"Normally we give the Governor our recommendation but, in your case, we think that you should be told now. We have considered all sides and decided that you are a good case for release on licence". Harold smiled. "But remember you are on licence for the remainder of your sentence, seven years, so you will need to report to the nearest police station once a month. If you fail to report for three months you will be found and re-arrested to serve the rest of your sentence. Do you understand?"

"Yes, I understand. Thank you".

He was handed a piece of paper, his parole letter, and left the room happy and delighted things had gone his way.

The warder told him that he would be released tomorrow after breakfast so report to the office after breakfast to get his personal belongings back.

Jack was pleased all had gone well and told him he had come to like him and hoped he would stay out of trouble once he was released. He warned him that in eight years a lot had changed I the world so be ready to accept the changes and keep his mouth shut. Harold thanked him and said he had made his time here much more pleasant than it could have been.

The next morning after breakfast he presented himself at the office. He was given a plastic bag that contained the clothes he had when he came in, they looked strange to him after all this time, his purse with three pounds six shillings and his comb. He was taken to the cashier's office and given thirty pounds and a travel warrant for ten pounds that he could exchange at the railway or bus station for a ticket to wherever he wanted.

Dressed in his clothes he felt awkward as he was taken to the prison entrance and the door was unlocked and locked behind him for the last time, he hoped.

He stepped out into the world of 1973.

CHAPTER 18

Penny and John Married Life

Once we had established ourselves at school and got our little house in a liveable condition, I had hoped we could get our marriage to be more romantic.

Unfortunately, John didn't seem to want much romance. I know that we were busy during the day teaching and we had to prepare lesson plans and mark homework etc. but I had hoped there would be some time for us to be together.

Instead John just went to bed and was asleep in no time at all while I was hoping for some physical touch, a cuddle or a kiss or even a word of romance or love. Nothing!

I was beginning to think that it had been a mistake marrying him, I couldn't help but think of the times with Robert, although he turned out to be a rat. At least we had a great romance and he taught me a lot about sex, now I couldn't get my husband to even kiss me let alone do anything else.

On several occasions I tried to bring up the topic, but he usually said, "Not now, I am busy" and that was that.

I needed to have a new strategy to get what I needed, but how?

Now Saturday was our quietest day so I decided that this would be the day to start. On Friday night I said to him "John, we haven't had a break since we arrived how about tomorrow, we go for a drive and have a meal in a nice restaurant?".

He looked at me for a while then said,

"Well it sounds a good idea, but I have some work to do before Monday".

"Well you have Sunday to do that, we need a break so tomorrow we go for a drive".

I said with finality. He stared at me and was going to say something but then he didn't. He turned and went off to the bedroom, by time I got there he was asleep, or was he just pretending?

The next morning, I woke him up and told him we were going out. He grumbled that he needed to rest so I said don't worry I will drive so you can relax. He didn't like the sound of that but acquiesced and had his shower.

After breakfast I prepared a picnic lunch and packed some night clothes including a negligee that Robert had bought me. I smuggled the suitcase into the boot of the car so John would not be aware of my plans.

John made a great fuss about going but I was determined he was going to do what I wanted, he tried all his tricks but eventually he had to give in. We managed to get away by 11 and I drove in the direction of Southwold. I tried to get some conversation going but John was sulking like a spoilt child and refused to talk.

Just before we got to the town I pulled of the road into a lay-by and got out of the car.

"Why are we stopping here?" John asked.

"We are going to have some lunch over there by the tables".

"But I don't like eating out of doors".

"Then you will have to get used to it, we are having a picnic. I am fed up with you constantly complaining and never doing anything so today you are going to do what I want for a change. Get out the car and come over to the table".

John looked at me with amazement and I detected a little fear, he didn't like me to be boss, but he had no choice I had put up with his behaviour for long enough.

We sat down and I put out the food, some cold chicken, salad, apples and lemonade to drink. After a while John decided he was hungry, so he started eating and soon was enjoying himself I thought.

After we finished, I said "Now we are going to talk, TO each other. We need to sort out your behaviour it is really upsetting me, and I need to understand what you want".

"I have behaved perfectly well, I never shout at you, or complain or leave you alone at home while I go drinking".

"That's because you never do anything except work. We are now married, and, in a marriage, we need to talk to each other. We need to touch each other; we need to kiss and have a cuddle and have sex".

John was obviously embarrassed at the word Sex. "I don't think we need to talk about that it is private"

"What! Private! Who do you think we are? Strangers in the night? A husband and wife need sex, it's part of being married. Otherwise I might as well be a nun and join a convent. I need you to love me to touch me to kiss me to say you love me to make love to me. I am a woman and I need all these things and as my husband I expect you to do these things".

John sat there for some time looking puzzled as he thought about what I had said, then he got up and walked to the car got in and shut the door. I wasn't sure what to do so decided I would stay here for a while until he decided what he was going to do.

I was beginning to think that I was wrong as he never moved for half an hour, then as I was about to move, he opened the door and came back to the table.

"I think you are being completely unreasonable; I am not a romantic person and just want a quiet life with no distractions. I think I understand your problems, but I don't think it's my duty to fulfil what you want".

"So, you don't think a husband should show some affection to his wife? Shouldn't make her happy by doing some small things for her? Not having sex. Why did you get married then if you didn't want to be a proper husband?"

John was silent for a long time then he said "Well, I wanted a wife. But I didn't want to be a husband".

I stared at him and said "So you just want a trophy wife? No affection or love? Is that right?".

"Well, yes I think that's it".

"O.K then we might as well get divorced, I am not going to live as a nun. I will find a proper man".

"No! We can't do that my parents would kill me. They have been married a long time and expect me to do so. They would never countenance divorce I would be cut off for ever".

"So, what are you going to do?"

"I will try to do what you want; I do love you in my own way but obviously that is not sufficient for you. I can't promise everything, but I will try to make you happy".

Getting up I move around behind him and placed my arms around his neck

"John, we can have a good marriage if you just become a bit more romantic. I just need you to be more attentive and touching".

He touched my hands and I felt happier, just a start but I hoped that it would grow to be a better relationship.

We drove on to Southwold and when we arrived, I drove to the Beach Hotel and John was surprised but said nothing. We entered and booked in, we had a room overlooking the sea and promenade. It was a pleasant room with a queen size bed, drink making facilities, mini-bar and a 24-inch TV.

We unpacked and I suggested we should go for a walk before dinner, so we went downstairs, and the receptionist said go along the promenade to the right.

It was a pleasant day and we walked along the prom then I slipped my arm into his and he did not protest so we had a pleasant walk, then we sat down and looked at the sea. Water I find has a very calming effect, and as we sat there, I placed my head on his shoulder. I felt he wanted to move but didn't. We sat there for about 30 minutes and then as we were about to get up, I moved his head to mine and kissed him. To my surprise he responded, and we had the best kiss since we had met. I held him close and prayed that this was going to be the start of our physical marriage.

We slowly walked back, and I felt that John was feeling more emotional than I had ever known him to be.

We went to our room and had a shower, not together that would have been too much I think, then got dressed for dinner. The restaurant was a pleasant room in the old Victorian tradition with 10 tables. The waiter showed us to one by the wall and brought us the menu. I liked the menu it was a good English menu and I decided to have the steak and kidney pie with boiled potatoes, cabbage and carrots. John ordered a 6oz steak rare with chips and peas.

"This is a surprise, I never suspected you to be such a schemer" John said.

"I wanted us to get away from home and the work and to just enjoy ourselves for one night, have a good meal and relax".

"Well, I want to thank you for your effort. I am afraid I was never very romantic, but I do love you and will try and be more what you want".

I was so happy that I wanted to kiss him, but I just reached across the table and held his hand.

The food was excellent, and we talked more than we had ever done before, we had some wine and a coffee before returning to our room.

I undressed in the bathroom and when I came out John was already in bed I slipped in beside him, I was a little nervous but John responded to my touch and I helped him to enjoy the best sex we had ever had. We fell asleep in each other's arms and I was so happy. In the morning he kissed me, the first time ever in the morning.

We had a good English breakfast and then paid and left.

The drive home was delightful, and I discovered that John had a wicked sense of humour that I had never seen before, I was so glad my ruse had worked.

From then on, we had more physical contact, but sex was still rationed, at the best was once a week and sometimes not for 2 or 3 weeks. But when it happened it was pretty good and John did try hard to be more romantic, one Saturday he went out and came back with a bunch of flowers. I was so overcome I grabbed him and kissed him and held on to show how much I appreciated his thought. He was a little embarrassed but also happy he had done something to please me.

Then in November I had to tell him I was pregnant; I wasn't sure how he would react because we hadn't really talked about children.

He was so excited that he was going to be a father he hugged me and kissed me several times and couldn't wait to phone his parents and tell them the news. I was more circumspect with my parents, although we only lived 2 miles from them, we hadn't seen them since the wedding. I was not surprised when my mother hardly reacted when I told her she was going to be a grandmother. Well, I thought that is up to them, perhaps when it comes, they will be happier, we shall see.

William Arthur arrived at 4.55 am on April 2, 1972, the birth was not difficult, and I was only in labour for 5 hours, so it was good. When I held him for the first time my maternal instinct kicked in and I loved him so much. John arrived at 8 am and once he had held him even, he began to be much more loving and cradled the baby in his arms.

William was a good baby and all my fears about raising a baby were put aside as he grew up. In August after school was closed, we drove down to see Arthur and Mary, they were overjoyed at their first grandchild. It was difficult for me to get any time with him as they wanted him all the time, luckily, he needed breast feeding so I had that time with him. John was a loving father and husband; he certainly had changed since the birth. I was really happy for us and our marriage, Mary had noticed his change as well and congratulated me on making him into a good husband and father.

On our return from Swindon my mother phoned and complained she had not seen her grandson; I was a bit short with her and told her she only lived around the corner so come and see him whenever you want. She did not take kindly to my remark, so she and dad did not come around until his first birthday party. They did not stay long, neither of them was very maternal as I knew to my cost. We did not see them again until 1975 when our daughter, Mary Penelope, was born. Sometimes I felt that I should have been more welcoming to them but my experience growing up had not been good, so I did not do anything to help.

Our married life was contented, I stayed at home looking after the children, William went to pre-school when he was three, but we had to take him away because he constantly upset the other children.

I had him at home until he was five when he went to school, when Mary was three, she went to a pre-school and loved it, so I had no qualms about going back to work. I arranged for Mary to be looked after in the afternoons and as she was the only child got along well with the adults.

John enjoyed being a teacher and had been promoted to head of English. Our physical marriage was the same, sex about once or twice a month, John was more physically affectionately and I had grown used to the attention and did not demand more from him, I knew he was doing his best.

Our children were complete opposites in character my son was a charmer from birth, he seemed to be able to get anyone to do anything he wanted and if we tried to discipline him somehow he always got us to be blamed not him. When he was five, he started in school and he was very intelligent, some might say too intelligent. He learned quickly and then got bored, so he started playing around, upsetting the other children and getting into trouble with the teacher.

We had to go to the school several times a term to sort out his troubles, but of course he never saw that he was to blame it was always someone else. No matter who spoke to him he basically ignored them and carried on in his own way. Then the final straw was when he damaged the classroom, this was too much for the Head and he was expelled.

What to do? We discussed it far into the night and we came up with several options, one tries and find another school who would accept him, two find a private school and three teach him at home.

Number one seemed very difficult because of his record, two would work but would cost us money and three we didn't think we could cope with him as he was so ill-disciplined. We decided that the only way was a private school, then the question was home or boarded. I was loath to send him away and being here he would probably be in the same situation as before. We consulted an educational psychologist who having taken all the facts talked to him he recommended we send him to a school that specialized in unruly children.

The school was in Derbyshire, so a fair way from home but he would board there and only come home for holidays.

"William, we want you to try and understand what we are going to say, please pay attention because it is very important for you and us. Alright?" John said.

William looked at us and he could see that this was not the usual telling off session, so he nodded his head.

"You get bored at school and then cause trouble; you won't listen to the teachers and so you got expelled. We cannot find another school who will take you because of your disruptive behaviour. That means we have to send you somewhere else. You remember Mr Baker who talked to you about your behaviour?"

"Yes, he was a nice man. Didn't shout or yell and listened to what I had to say".

"Good. Well he thinks you should go to a school that has a more disciplined approach and mix with boys like yourself. The school he recommended is in Derbyshire, a long way from here. This is a boarding school so you would live there and come home in the holidays, do you understand?"

William looked a little bewildered and then started to cry, I took him in my arms and held him close.

"I don't want to go away from you, I promise I will be good from now on and not upset the teachers".

"That is good" I said, "but we can't find a school who will accept you, at least not here in Ipswich". I said.

"We have one other idea and that is that you are home-schooled. You would stay here, and a teacher would come in and teach you by yourself. This would mean that you must behave yourself, do as the teacher says and get good marks. Are you willing to try this?"

"Yes, I promise I will be good and cause no trouble".

We looked at each other and agreed it seemed the best answer, for the time being.

"Good, we will give it a try until Christmas, if it works out well then we can continue but if it does not you will have to go away, understand?"

"Yes, I promise to be good".

He clung on to me like any seven-year-old would who was afraid and scared. We found an agency who would supply three teachers to give William all that he needed, we registered with the Education Department and they came and saw us and gave us loads of documents to read and sign.

In September the teachers arrived, and we agreed a schedule with them to teach him 3 days a week, the other two days we would teach him.

I can say it was almost a great success, William did as he promised and got good marks and comments from his teachers. We were so happy.

The problem was his sister who had just started school and wanted to know why she had to go, and he didn't. Trying to explain to a five-year-old the situation was very difficult, and she caused many an argument in the house and tormented William a lot. Eventually she gave in and went to school because she had found many friends and enjoyed the social atmosphere, unfortunately her learning was not very good and had consistently low marks and reports saying she did not pay attention and did not do her work.

We had to monitor what she was doing and punish her when she went astray. She only wanted to play and was forever asking to go out with her friends. She got grounded at least once a week, but she didn't seem to care.

As they grew up our family was rent by arguments and rows, William was the calmest of all and just went to his room and shut the door when Mary was in one of her tirades. The situation became very stressful and we had to get her professional help. This helped to an extent she didn't blow up so often and learnt to behave better, she now just sulked and stomped of to her room. At least we had some peace and quiet.

Most of the pressure was on me as John basically abdicated his father role and went out or sat in the garden until it was over, when he was there, he just sat in the chair and said nothing. I could not get him to support me in anyway, so the stress on me was terrible. At one point I had to take some anti-depressants, but I didn't like that so stopped as soon as I could.

Just after Mary's twelve birthday she informed me she was going out with her boyfriend.

"What boyfriend? You are only twelve and you won't have any boyfriend yet".

"Well I'm going to whether you like it or not". She retorted.

"Don't you argue with me, young lady. Girls your age don't have boyfriends and I am certainly not going to let you have one? She stormed off to her room making as much noise as possible and slammed her door. I was really feeling at the end of my tether. With no help from my husband, a daughter in a constant state of rebellion and no family to support me, I had not spoken to my parents since Mary was born, I really didn't know where to turn.

The only people I felt I could rely on were Arthur and Mary, but I didn't want to inflict my problems on them although I was sure they would come to my aid if I did ask.

Once peace had descended on the house, I got my shopping list together and drove to the supermarket to get the weeks groceries. All the way there I was not really watching where I was going, I was on automatic pilot trying sort out in my mind what I should do. But no solution came to me. When I arrived at the supermarket, I parked the car as usual and set out to do the shopping.

Little did I know that this trip would be like no other!

CHAPTER 19

Harold goes to London

Once he had left the prison he needed to find somewhere to live and a job, his small amount of money would not last long.

The prison visitor had given him the address of someone who would be willing to take in an ex-con. He found out where it was and knocked on the door. A small rounded lady answered, "Mr Simpson said that you would be willing to let me a room" She looked at him and said "Yes, but I need a month in advance and a deposit against damage".

"How much is that?"

"Rent is five pounds a month and a deposit of five pounds"

Harold was relieved that it was what he could afford so he gave her the money and she showed him to his room. It was a pretty room with flowered wallpaper, cream paint and a single bed, small cupboard and a lamp. Harold thanked her and she gave him a key,

"Door is locked at 10 so be home in time".

"Do you know where I can get some farm work?"

"Well, I think you have to go to the corner and wait for a hirer to come along, but you may be too late today".

Thanking her he walked to the place she had said and found one other man waiting, they nodded but said nothing. He was about to give up after waiting an hour when a small bus pulled up.

"Looking for work?"

"Yes"

"Hop on, wages are one pound a day as long as you fulfil the requirement".

Harold had no idea if that was good or bad after being away for so long, but he got on the bus with the other man. They drove out of town about 3 miles and pulled up alongside a field with several men working. Harold tried to tell the man he had a farming qualification, but he said this was the job. The job was digging up potatoes and he had to do 50 pounds in a day to get his wages. The job is hard back-breaking work and although he was fit from the farm work, he found it hard going. He managed to get his quota and sat down to rest. The foreman said he should carry on until 6 pm for some extra money. Harold didn't want to, but he needed money. At six a whistle blew, and all the men came in to be paid. Harold got one pound 2 shillings.

The next day he was there earlier, and another gang-master came along and wanted men to pick berries. Harold thought it might be easier than potatoes, but the pay was not as good only 18 shillings per quota. He went along and soon realized picking berries is just as bad as potatoes and he had to work hard all day to get his quota.

He kept at this for a month and each day he hated it more, he was a qualified farmer but all he could get was slave work. One day he didn't get his quota and the gang-master refused to pay him anything. Enraged Harold attacked him and took his money then jumped on the bus and drove away. Reaching town, he drove to the railway station and got on a train, he didn't care where it was going, it was going to London!

The train arrived at St. Pancras at 8.25 so Harold was hungry as he had not eaten since a sandwich at lunch time.

He found a small café just outside the station and went in, he found a table and was soon served by a young waitress. Harold was getting wary of young waitresses they had caused him no end of trouble. He ordered a meal and enjoyed it a lot, he hadn't realized how hungry he was. Now he had to find somewhere to stay, he asked the waitress and she said there was a B & B just around the corner. He discovered that there were many such establishments and found one with a vacancy sign. He found they did a room and breakfast for a good sum, so he booked in.

Next day he had to find a job. He didn't think that he could go back to the Garden so he asked the landlady if there were any vegetable markets near here. She said not only some shops, but she said I could try Portobello Road they had a market there.

Thanking her he went to the tube station and asked how to get to Portobello Road, the clerk said Westbourne Park was good. Arriving there he walked up the road to the market, it was more of an antiques and general market but there was one area where they sold fruit, vegetables and flowers. He asked one of the stall holders if they had any work, he was directed to the manager who offered him a day's work as a labourer. At the end of the day the manager was pleased with his efforts and said could he come back next Monday?

He found out that the market was only open from Monday to Wednesday. Having nothing else in mind Harold agreed, the man also gave him the name of a grocery store around the corner who might have a job. Going there he discovered that they could give him a job from Thursday to Saturday, gratefully Harold accepted the job. He had a week's work now and could afford to find somewhere to stay. He was lucky to find a top floor flat not more than half a mile away, it was well lit and clean. The rent was only four pounds a week, so Harold paid over the thirty-two pounds for one month's rent and security from the money he had stolen from the gang-master.

He remembered that he had left the flat in Nottingham without notice so he got some paper and wrote a brief note to the landlady, his security deposit would cover the next month's rent, so she was not out of pocket.

Harold found that he enjoyed his two jobs and as they were day jobs he could go out and explore the area in the evening. On his walks he came across a pub called the Moon at Night and it was a Victorian type pub with a small garden. He started going there most evenings and got to know a few of the regulars.

He had been in London now for three months and he thought of Diane, he wondered if he should go and see her if she was still there after all it was now ten years or more since he had seen her. One evening he decided to go and have a look, down to Leicester Square and he walked around the corner to Convent Garden and down the road to her café. When he got there, he saw it was much changed with a new front and was now an Italian Restaurant, as he hadn't eaten, he went in and found a table.

The waitress came over and said,

"Welcome, Sir, what can I get you to drink?".

"Do you have a beer?"

"Yes, sir. Would you like a Pilsen?" "Yes"

She brought him the drink and a menu, he quickly looked down and picked a 12 oz steak with chips and tomatoes.

"Nice restaurant you have here, how long has it been open?" "About five years"

"Do you know what happened to the previous owner?"

"Not really. I think she had some sort of personal problem and sold up. I don't know where she went, sorry".

He wasn't going to find her here and had no clue as to where she might be, going home he felt a bit depressed but then he reminded himself that she probably didn't want to see him anyway.

He celebrated his one year back in London at the pub with his few mates and they all had a good laugh. As he was at the bar fetching the next round a thin man stood next to him and asked how he was. Harold did not know him but was polite, the stranger asked him if he was looking for a good paying job. Harold said wasn't everyone. Well the stranger said if he was interested meet him here tomorrow at eight. Harold agreed, not knowing what the job was and forgot all about the conversation.

The next night he was in his usual place when the stranger approached him and said if he was still interested in the project come with him now. Harold was reluctant but curious, so he told his mates he had an appointment for a new job. They went outside and a car was waiting, not being that interested in cars Harold had no idea what make it was, but he knew it was expensive with the leather seats. The stranger sat next to him and he said that it was a strange request, but he needed to blindfold Harold, a little upset he thought about it and then agreed. When the car stopped, he was helped of the car and into a building, the door closed behind him and the blindfold was removed.

In the room were four men, one sat in a chair facing him and was obviously the boss.

"Tell me about yourself" he commanded.

"My name is Harold Wilson and I have just been released from Nottingham Jail after serving 10 years of a 15-year sentence. I came back to London because I couldn't find any work in Nottingham".

"What was your crime?"

"I killed a young woman by accident when we were having sex". "I see. What are you looking for now?"

"Well I have a qualification as a farm manager but can't get a job, as you will understand, so I am working in the market".

"Would you like to make some money, that won't involve too much work and will be more than you have seen for a long time?"

"Well I am always ready to earn more, who wouldn't?"

"We are in the business of re-distributing wealth to more people". One of the men guffawed but stopped when the boss glared at him. "To continue, we take money from the rich and after our commission we pass it on to others".

Harold listened and began to understand what he was saying, they were thieves.

"I am always looking for good people to join our firm and you look like you could be an asset to me. Are you interested in helping us?"

"Sounds interesting, what exactly do you want me to do to help?"

"Well I need someone big like you to explain to the people that they should co-operate with us without any fuss. I am sure you would be ideal for the job".

"No guns are involved. I don't like guns".

"No, we don't need to use guns, but we do sometimes show one to help our project move along smoothly, we have never had to use one though".

"Right, when do I start?"

"Not so fast. I think you should carry on doing what you are doing until I have planned our next collection. Jack, here" he indicates the man who spoke to him, "will be in touch as soon as we are ready. OK?"

"Yes, I will be waiting".

"Good, thanks for coming Harold, Jack will take you back to the pub. See you soon".

Jack took Harold back to the pub and dropped him outside. Harold was still in a state of shock and realized he had missed his dinner, so he went to the café to et and then went back to his flat.

Harold didn't hear anything for days and was beginning to think it was all a ruse, but then that evening Jack appeared and beckoned him to come outside. They got into the car and drove to the house, this time no blindfold was needed, he was in the gang.

Entering the house, they went to the room and met the rest of the gang. "Welcome back. Let me introduce the members. Jack you know, this is Bill (he was a thing wiry man with what appeared a constant sneer on his face, about 5 feet 5 inches tall), this is Sid our driver (he was about 30 years of age, five feet 8 inches, with a paunch but a cheery expression) and this is Charlie our agent (he was about 5 ft 6 inches tall, average build and thinning hair on top) and my name is James but you can call me Boss".

"Right let's get down to business".

He drew out a large sheet of paper and they all crowded round. "The target is Bondsman Jewellers in Shepherd Street, near to Green Park. This is a quiet road with exits at both ends. They are open until 6 pm so there is not much traffic around that time. We can go in as they are closing, Bill will go to the cashier and get any cash they have, find out where the safe is and I will go with a member of staff to open it.

Charlie will examine the goods and pick out the stuff we can easily re-sell and is expensive. Sid will park outside keeping an eye out for any trouble. Harold you will go with Jack and help the staff to co-operate, I don't want anyone hurt and just the threat should be enough. We will have ten minutes to get in and out. Make sure all the staff are tied up and can't raise the alarm, we need time to get away. Any questions? Right we will meet here at five on Wednesday".

After they all left and jack took Harold back to the pub, he was quite a jolly person and told Harold he had a wife and an adorable girl who was 5. He wanted to get enough money to take them to Spain where they could live in the sunshine.

On Wednesday Jack arrived to take Harold to the meet, they were the last to arrive. The Boss went over the plan again and they all got into a van marked, General Electricians. They drove to the shop and went down the street and back again to see if there were any problems. They didn't see any pedestrians and saw that the shop had three assistants, so they stopped just past the store and they all got out.

Quickly James led them into the store, Jack had a gun which he assured Harold was not loaded and they pointed it at the cashier. James found the manager and he and him went to find the safe. Jack put the money from the till into a black bag, the others selected the items that Charlie picked out. The staff were tied up and gagged, within eight minutes they were out and piled into the van and Sid drove away naturally. They arrived back at the house and Harold felt relieved that everything had gone well.

They were told to come back on Sunday when the money would be split. On Sunday there was a happy atmosphere and James told them that he had got a good price and their share was one thousand pounds. Harold couldn't believe his ears; he had never had that much money before. Then he had to decide what to do with it, he had lost money before because he had not put it anywhere safe. This time he decided to ask James and he said he would get his man to contact him and tell him how he could invest it.

Three days later he had a message to go to an office in St Johns Wood there he met a portly middle-aged man who went by the name of Sylvester Moon. He explained that trying to post a large sum of money would be suspicious so he should only pay in small amounts and open several accounts. He said he would do this for a ten percent commission, Harold thought it was worth it so agreed. He gave him eight hundred and Sylvester said he would see him again on Friday to give him the details of his accounts.

Going back on Friday Sylvester gave him six pass books for six different accounts so each had about 120 pounds in each. Harold was happy now he had secure accounts and he had the two hundred he had kept back, Sylvester warned him not to spend on anything expensive as this could arouse suspicion, Harold understood. He did buy himself some new clothes and a ring. He carried on his jobs and after a few months he stopped the shop job and just did the market, giving him more time to travel all over London.

The gang did about three or four jobs in a year, as James said doing too many would get them caught eventually. Harold didn't mind because each job gave him more than a thousand each time and he invested it in the accounts he had. Most of the time on the jobs Harold didn't have to do much, on two occasions he had to be a bit rough with an assistant who didn't want to do as he was told, but the threat of a six foot two man weighing 20 stone soon ensured they did as they were told. Mostly the robberies went of smoothly with no trouble, on one time the assistant had set of the alarm, so they had to rush the job and get away. But he still got six hundred pounds so was quite happy.

Love Life?

Now that he had money, he went to other entertainments like night clubs and cabaret clubs. Here there were lots of young single girls looking for adventure and sex, Harold decided to investigate. He was not really into any type of music or dancing he just wanted a girlfriend. Since his incarceration he had become much more circumspect when it came to women.

At one club he got to talk to one girl whose name was Jill, despite the noise of the music and people they did manage to talk a bit. Harold suggested they go somewhere quieter to talk. She was a bit reticent but eventually agreed so they went out and found a café nearby where they ordered coffee and talked. They seemed to get on well and Jill suddenly realized the time, she had to get home. Harold found her a taxi and gave the driver enough money to take her home, but not before getting her phone number.

Over the next few days, he wondered about calling her but decided it was worth the risk. When the phone rang it was answered by a lady.

"May I talk to Jill please?"

"Who shall I say is calling?"

"Harold, we met the other day",

"Just a moment", he waited in agony hoping she would answer then a breathless Jill spoke.

"Hi, I thought you would never call", well that seemed a good start.

"I was not sure if you wanted to see me again, but took the risk",

"Yes, I enjoyed our talk".

"Will you be free tomorrow night?"

"Yes"

"What would you like to do? A meal, go to the cinema?"

"It would be good to go to the cinema I haven't been for ages"

"Good, where is the best one for you?"

"Well I live in Romford, but I could come up to the West End or Leicester Square"

"I think there is a good cinema in Leicester Square shall we meet there?"

"Great, about six. Is that good?"

"Yes, fine. See you then",

"Good, see you then. Bye".

Harold came of the phone in ecstasy, then he had to see what was on at the cinema, he remembered his first date with Diane at that cinema, when he had never been to a cinema before. He found that the latest James Bond film "*Live and let Die*" was showing and he had heard many people talking about it.

The next day he wasn't working so he went and had his hair cut, bought a new shirt and coat and had a bath (not something he did often). He got to the cinema at quarter to six and waited impatiently outside. Six o'clock came and went and he was beginning to think it was a waste of time when he saw Jill running down the road from the station. Smiling he moved towards her and she hugged him and said she was sorry but there had been problems on the trains.

"Don't worry the film doesn't start until 7 so we have time, do you like James Bond?",

"Oh yes!"

They crossed over the road to a small café on the corner and had a coffee. Harold felt so at home with Jill and she seemed to like him to. They went to the cinema and Harold was now worried about what he should do, bearing in mind his previous encounters. After the first film, he had no idea what is was about he was concentrating on Jill. Once the film began, he enjoyed it and even more when Jill grabbed his arm in the scary bits.

He touched her hand and she looked at him and smiled. Feeling her soft hand in his was a wonderful feeling, but Harold went no further he had learnt his lesson and determined that Jill should make the move.

After the film they decided to go and have something to eat,

on the corner was a small restaurant so they went there and ordered a meal. The meal was one of Harold s most favourite and he would remember it for many years. They got on famously and eventually Jill said she had to go home so they walked to the underground station, Leicester Square. Shall I come with you to keep you company?" said Harold. "Well it's a long way, about an hour then you have to go home, where is that?"

"I have a flat in Portobello Road, but I can get there easily from Liverpool Street." "It would be nice if you are sure you want to?" at that moment Harold wanted nothing better. He bought them tickets to Romford. Took the train to Tottenham Court Road and then the central line to Liverpool Street. They had a 20-minute wait before the next train, so they found a seat and sat down. Jill cuddled up to him and he looked into her eyes and her sweet mouth was so close he wanted to kiss her, then she kissed him. At last he had found someone who liked him, and they were soon kissing each other. They caught the train to Romford and Jill said she would walk home from here, but Harold would not hear of it, especially as he found it was a twenty-minute walk, so they got a taxi.

Once they got to her house she got out and waved to him as she walked up the path to a 1930's style semi-detached house. He then drove back to the station and made his way home.

Once they got to know each other better they saw each other almost every evening, she worked in Ilford at a bookstore so she could catch the train into Tower Bridge from East Ham station. They usually walked down to the river and sat on the embankment or went and had a meal at a small café, going to the cinema, they even went to a concert (a new experience for Harold). Strangely his sexual feelings were being kept under control and they both seemed very happy.

One evening Jill said her parents would like to meet him, Harold was not so sure, once they found out about his background, they would probably ban him. For some time, he kept putting it off until Jill became not only exasperated but curious as to why he would not come and see them.

Cautiously he told her of some of his life, he didn't tell her the truth about his conviction he said he had a fight with someone, and they had died. Jill was sympathetic and understood now why he had not wanted to meet her parents. She said she would broach the subject with her parents and see how they reacted.

He did not hear from her for three days, then he phoned and was told in no uncertain terms that he was to have nothing to do with their daughter. Depressed Harold bought a bottle of whiskey and went home and drank the whole bottle. For three days he would not come out until one of his workmates came and saw him. This man was older than Harold and he understood what he was going through, eventually he persuaded him to come back to work.

Harold did but only for a while then his grief was too much, and he left, he moved to a new address as if it would help, but of course it didn't. Eventually his pain became a dull ache and he began to go out again but only to a local pub.

He and the gang had been working for about two years when trouble loomed for Harold. He was down in Brixton when a couple of West Indians accosted him and said to hand over his money. Well Harold was having none of that, so a fight ensued, he was getting the better of it when two policemen arrived and arrested all three of them.

At the police station they took his fingerprints and discovered he was an absconding prisoner. The visit to the magistrate was short and he was sent back to jail to finish his original sentence plus another five years for not reporting. So now he was in Brixton Jail and his life of leisure was over, he now faced another ten years in jail. But he was comforted by the knowledge he had a substantial sum for him to come out with then, he didn't know exactly, arithmetic was not his strong suit, but he knew he might not need to work ever again.

Now he faced up to the grim life in prison, the monotony, the terrible food, the uncaring warders, and his loss of freedom. And he had to bear the thoughts of losing Jill, just when he thought his love life was turning around and he had someone who cared. All his life he had wanted someone who cared, when he found Diane he thought he had but he ruined it by being in too much of a hurry, with Jill it was down to prejudice and he hoped she would find someone to love her like he thought he did. Well now he could forget women and sex he had to get thought the next years, but somehow being back in prison wasn't so bad as he had already had 10 years of it, so another 10 years was not so bad.

CHAPTER 20

Harold in Jail

Arriving at Brixton Prison Harold was confronted with a regime entirely different from Nottingham, the Governor here was hard because he had to control some of the most violent criminals in England. Some were serving life sentences and didn't care about what punishment he could give so they tended to do as they liked despite the constant threat of being in isolation for long periods.

The guards took their cue from the Governor and dealt harshly with anyone who stepped out of line, but they knew they were losing the battle so became even more cruel.

Harold found this out soon enough, he was lined up with the other new inmates and the guard walked down the line looking at them and at their charge sheets. When he came to one who had been sentenced for GBH or suchlike he hit them on the knee with his stick, causing them to fall to the floor, then shouted at them to get up or they would get some more.

When he got to Harold, he saw that he had been in a robbery but no violence, so he looked at him, he was at least 6 inches shorter so had to look up. Then he hit him in the stomach with his stick, he was amazed when it seemed to have no effect. Smiling he said "Tough guy, hey! Well in here we deal with tough guys all the time, just keep your nose clean and you may not be hurt. But take this advice, there are guys in here who don't like people who keep their noses clean. You have the option be good and the guys will deal with you or don't and we will deal with you" he sneered and then moved on to the next one.

Harold didn't like what he had heard but he had no choice so just decided to watch his step. They were marched off to the clothes store where they were issued with the orange suit and tennis shoes that was standard issue. His clothes and belongings were taken from him and put in a plastic bag with his name on, in case he got released. Not many did from here except to go to their funerals.

He was taken to his cell on the first landing and left there with an order to report for dinner at 5 pm. There wasn't anyone else there, so he sat down on the bottom bunk, then in walked a man as big as him.

"Get off my bunk, or I will get you off" he yelled.

Harold jumped up and apologised as he had not known it was his bunk.

"My name is Geoff and as the senior here you do as I tell you, GOT IT!".

Harold didn't care for his tone but was not in any position to start disagreeing so said "OK".

"What is your name? And what have you been sent down for?"

"Harold Wilson. I was convicted of armed robbery". He omitted his previous history although he expected it would become known fairly soon.

"Right, just follow my lead and everything should be fine. The boss will want to speak to you so just be ready when he calls, got it" Harold nodded. The bell went for dinner, so he and Geoff went down to the mess hall with the other 300 prisoners. He collected his dinner which looked particularly unappetizing, but Harold remembered the Nottingham food as good. Then followed Geoff to a table where there were four other men.

"This is Harold, jewel robber", they all nodded.

"Right, go and sit at that table over there, they are newcomers as well but don't listen to anything they say", dutifully Harold went to the table indicated. The three others looked at him and waited for him to say something.

"My name is Harold and I am in for robbing jewellery stores with violence, but we never used violence".

"I am Joe and in for GBH, Sam for robbery using confidence tricks, Jim for Fraud".

They continued eating there meal and Harold was advised about the nature of the place, he was told that if someone wanted to beat him up, which they would, he should allow it and all would be well but if he resisted he would get a worse beating later. Now Harold couldn't understand this but kept his own counsel. He was soon to find out for himself that what they said was true.

The next day he was in the showers where the guards waited outside for privacy, when three big men came in, one stood by the door and the one of the others grabbed Harold from behind and pinned his arms down. The third man aimed a punch at Harold s stomach, but he was not fast enough because he collapsed on the floor. Harold had brought his knee up and hit him in the balls. While the other man looked on in amazement, he pulled him over his shoulder and crashed him to the ground. The third man looked on not knowing what to do, this was not supposed to happen.

Eventually he went to help up his mates and Harold stood over them and said, "Thanks mates, tell your boss that Jack Hudson from Nottingham said hello".

They staggered out of the door and the guard was astonished, he expected to see Harold carried out but instead the gang did. He opened the door and saw Harold getting dressed, none the worse for wear. He passed the information back to say this man needed to be watched and he could cause trouble if they were not careful.

Nothing happened for the rest of the day except Harold was detailed to work in the Laundry, one of the worst jobs in the prison. Hot, sweaty and hard work all day washing the clothes and linen of the prisoners. Harold didn't mind the hard work it kept him fit and although not keen on the heat he didn't make any complaint.

The next day after dinner he was approached by the three men who had attempted to rough him up but now, they kept their distance and were more circumspect. The boss wants to see you, can you come with us? More a request than an order they obviously had respect for Harold after their lesson two days before. They took him to a cell on the first floor and knocked on the door, unusual because all cell doors had to remain open during the day so the guards could see in. But this door belonged to "The Boss" so he could do what he wanted.

Entering Harold saw a large man about 50 with thinning brownish hair and a decided paunch. The man looked him up and down and then spoke

"You didn't like my welcoming committee? Sorry about that but we have processes to follow here so we know who we can trust".

Harold said nothing just looked the man in the eye with a questioning expression.

"You told my guys that you had a message from Jack Nottingham, is that right?"

"Yes"

"How do you know Jack?"

"I worked with him for eight years".

"Right. Now I know that I can trust you because you come with Jacks' recommendation. In fact, he was very complimentary about you and the work you did for him".

Harold was surprised that word had got to Nottingham so quickly but said nothing.

"Don't say a lot, do you? That's good I don't like people who talk too much, I find they don't do much either. Well tell me a bit about yourself so I can see where I can fit you in to my organization".

Harold gave a brief overview of his life and how he came to be back in jail, he knew that the man probably knew already so made sure he told the truth, or as much as he thought he should.

"Good. How do you like the laundry?"

"It's a bit hot but I like the physical work, it keeps me in shape"

"That's true, let me know when you need a change and we can arrange it"

"I have a gardening certificate and I like the outdoors, does the prison have a garden or farm? I would like that a lot"

"Yes, as it happens, we do have a farm and I need someone there to keep an eye on what is going on and to keep them in order. I will get your transfer tomorrow. I will expect a report from you about the activities and who may not be doing the right thing. O.K.?"

Harold was so pleased he wanted to shake his hand but refrained.

"Thank you, Sir just what I wanted".

"No need to call me sir, my name is Henry to my friends, and you are my friend for now. Just don't cross me because friends who upset me get more severe punishment than others. Got that!"

"Yes sir, Henry. I understand exactly".

"Good, can I offer you a drink?"

"Would you have a beer?"

"Of course. Give the man a beer".

Harold gratefully accepted the drink and spent an hour with the new gang before returning to his cell on lights out. The next morning at breakfast a guard came over to him and told him he had been re-assigned and was to report to the waiting room at 8 am.

Arriving there Harold saw that there were about 20 others waiting, they eyed him, but his reputation had already travelled, and they kept their mouths shut. They got on the prison bus and drove off to the farm. The farm was some distance away in Croydon, so it took about 30 minutes to get there. Harold was excited and interested to see what sort of farm it was and was pleased to see that they had not only vegetables but cows and a few sheep and pigs. He found out that it was 20 acres so there was plenty to do and they worked hard all day except for half an hour break for lunch.

The head guard spoke to him and said as he had some knowledge of farming he could act as a foreman, to start with he would oversee the vegetable garden. Harold was glad to be outside again and quickly got into the routine, he noticed that the men just worked haphazardly going to wherever they wanted. The guards had no idea of what they were doing so ignored them, as long as they weren't causing any trouble, they were happy.

So Harold called all the men together, ten of them, and explained that they could work much more efficiently and with less effort if they did things methodically, he explained about working down a row, weeding as you go, removing any plants that were not any good and making sure all the plants were healthy. At first, they were a bit suspicious but as the explanation proceeded, they saw the wisdom of Harold s' words and were enthusiastic to get started. The guards were also impressed by what they heard and saw that if the prisoners were happy then they wouldn't have any trouble.

The men got to work to the plan and were surprised when they got to lunch time that they had done a lot more than they usually did. Harold spoke to the guards and suggested as the men had worked so fast that they should get a longer lunch break, discussing it between them they saw no harm as the work was proceeding so quickly. The men all cheered when they were told that they could have an hour for a break and several of them clapped Harold on the back for his work and advice.

At 5 they boarded the bus and went back to Brixton, because they had missed the usual dinner, they had a special dinner just for them, not that it was anything special just the usual kept warm so it was almost inedible.

The mood on the bus was much different now from the men who worked on the vegetables, but the others were not so happy seeing them get a privilege of a longer lunch break and complained amongst themselves about it. Later that day the Head Guard called Harold to his office and said he had done a good job with the men but now he had caused the others to be jealous and feared they would cause trouble, he didn't need trouble.

Harold noted what he had said and suggested that he have a look around the rest of the farm and see what he could suggest making things better. The head guard agreed as he wanted the men to work hard and be peaceful. Harold walked around the farm and talked to all the workers, examining their work practices he was able to suggest new ways to get the jobs done and give them the same privileges. Now all the men were happy because they had a longer break and still got the work done.

A few weeks later Harold was told not to get on the bus but go and see the Governor. The governor was not a pleasant man, he believed that all prisoners were useless and should be treated harshly so that their life was miserable, and they would not come back to prison again. This was a view of most prison governors at that time, but things were beginning to change with more thought being given to rehabilitation over punishment.

"Wilson, I hear you have been changing the procedures at the farm and giving the prisoners extra breaks, is that true?"

"Yes, a happy man gives you more work than an unhappy man. I have tried to make them happy in their work and you can see that the productivity is way up and the men are happy".

"Well I don't think you are right. You are a prisoner and don't have any authority to change my rules. This is a place of punishment not rest, all the prisoners need discipline and harsh treatment to make them stop being criminals. You are back in the laundry and my rules will be re-instated at the farm".

Harold was mortified, not only had he lost his outdoor work but now the prisoners were going to be punished. The next week he spent in the laundry, but he heard that the farm workers were on a go slow and their productivity was way down. They were being hit and punched by the new guards, but this only made matters worse as they were reporting sick so even less work was done. Many prisoners came to Harold and asked him what to do, as he explained the Governor didn't believe in rehabilitation but punishment. Well the solution came from an unlikely source, the prison visitors. They came ever couple of months and checked how the prison was running, the treatment of prisoners, food and conditions.

When they did their inspection, they heard about what had happened and saw the number of prisoners being treated every day for injuries received from the guards they were not pleased. At the end of each visit they spoke with the governor and his deputy, the doctor and the priest.

"Sir, we have conducted our inspection as per instructions and we have a report that does not bear good reading. We inspect many prisons and yours is the worst in terms of discipline, food, accommodation and health. You have more prisoners in hospital than any other prison, your officers are the most brutal we have come across, the prisoners are unhappy, and the food is virtually inedible. Talking of food, we found that one of the prisoners, Harold Wilson, has an agricultural certificate and was given some charge at the farm.

We heard that his changes not only increased food production but also the prisoners were happier, then you took him away and now the place is terrible. Your new guards beat the prisoners with sticks and fists, they have caused so many injuries to prisoners that the food production has almost stopped. What do you say to these findings?"

The governor was in a rage and could barely hold himself back from attacking the visitors. "This is my prison and I run it as I see fit. Prisoners need discipline they are criminals and should be treated as such so they don't come back. As far as the farm goes my rules were changed and nobody changes my rules. Wilson has caused no end of trouble and will be dealt with later".

"Sir, we warn you that if you take any action against Mr Wilson then you will be reported to the prison authorities. As it is once they see this report, I believe that you will not be a governor for much longer. Times are changing and physical punishment is being banned, if you cannot change your attitude then the prison service does not want you. I suggest you carefully consider your attitude before you go to the Home Office for a de-brief".

Following the meeting the governor thought long and hard and then decided that if he was going to be sacked and lose his pension then he would resign, which he did.

When the new governor arrived, Harold was summoned to his office. He was middle-aged with black hair; a paunch was beginning to appear, and he wore a serious expression. "Wilson, I have heard tales about your exploits and getting the previous Governor sacked so I am not pleased to have you here. Because of your record of trouble making I am having you transferred, you will be going to Nottingham tomorrow to finish your sentence".

He left in a daze, he was only helping the prisoners and the governor had been a bad person and deserved to go, anyway he was going back to his first prison where he had a good life. It had been over seven years since he was there so he did not know who might be still there from his last time, well tomorrow he would find out.

The journey to Nottingham is not long and he arrived at lunch time, his greeting was not good, and he hoped it was not a presage of what was to come. Most of the warders were new so did not know him and he was treated like any other prisoner. Searched, showered and given a clean set of clothes then taken to the canteen to have his dinner. Not many prisoners seemed to remember him as he sat down at a table, dinner was almost over so there were not many prisoners there. Once he had finished his meal, he was taken to see the Governor.

This was a new person, so Harold had no pull with him. He was an older man with thin wispy grey hair, he wore a worried expression, he was thin and spoke with a high-pitched voice. He examined Harold and his folder, glancing up as he came to certain parts. Finally, he spoke,

"Wilson, I see that you were here before, and the previous governor seems to have treated you lightly. Well get this straight there are no favours here and you will do as you are told when you are told. Any violence will be harshly dealt with, I won't have any in my prison. Right to you understand what I have said?"

"Yes sir"

"Good now off you go, and I don't want to see you here again in your next 4 years".

Harold was led to a cell on the first floor near his old cell and he discovered that the occupant was a thin weedy looking person who he soon discovered was a tell-all, so he didn't tell him anything of his history.

The next day at exercise time he talked to a couple of prisoners and discovered that Jack Hudson had left 2 years before and the prisoner who had assumed his role was not a nice person, Harold didn't remember him from his last time so he must have transferred in. His job was now to help build the new wing, it was a hard-labouring job and not one he liked or wanted but being a strong and healthy person, it was no great burden.

Most of the day he was mixing cement or mortar and carrying bricks up to the bricklayers. At the end of the day even he was exhausted so after dinner he was quite happy to go to his cell and sleep. His cellmate didn't say much but was always on the look out to see what he was doing, Harold ignored him most of the time and just slept or pretended to sleep.

After he had been there for three weeks he was visited by the minders, Harold had wondered why it took them so long so was glad to meet the new boss. He was large, even bigger than Harold, but out of condition and had a bad temper. He looked at Harold and motioned him to come closer,

"So, you are Wilson! Well I have heard some tales about your past and how Jack looked after you, well I don't want any trouble here. The governor can be pretty mean if things get out of hand so ensure it doesn't. Just keep your nose clean and don't interfere with what is going on. I can't stand people who can't keep their nose out of other people business. GOT IT!?

Harold just nodded he didn't see any sense in antagonizing this person, all he wanted was a quiet life and get out in time. Nothing much happened to Harold, he did his job, obeyed the warders and slept a lot. Three months later his cellmate was released and for two days he had it too himself then his new partner arrived. This man, Dave, was very friendly and allowed Harold to be in charge as you might say. Harold and he got on well and now they sometimes chatted for ages and life was a lot more pleasant.

It was now June 1983 and Harold had done eight of his ten years, he was now due for a parole hearing and hoped he might get out soon. The parole board was the usual three people, two men and a woman, they were not overly suspicious, and Harold thought he had done a good job.

Three days later he was called to the chief warder's office and given a piece of paper, Harold excitedly read it hoping for good news. His face dropped as he read his parole had been refused but they did say in six months' time they would re-consider.

Harold was depressed at the verdict but at least he only had to wait another six months to try again, the time passed quickly and Harold did all he could to ingratiate himself with the staff, this time the meeting was quickly over and the next day he was told he was to be released on licence.

Harold was over the moon and gathered together his few belongings and reported to the warder's office. He collected his few belongings that had been sent up from Brixton and was so pleased to hear the gates slam behind him.

CHAPTER 21

Nottingham

Here he was in Nottingham again, remembering the last time he was unsure of what to do, he had his rail pass and his thirty pounds plus his fifty pounds of his own money. After nine years things had changed a great deal and he gazed around him at all the new buildings, all the cars and people's clothes. He wandered around looking at all the new things that had happened over the last nine years.

The fashions were now more relaxed, and many people no longer wore suits, but the new Jeans and leather jacket were popular. Harold decided he needed to get some new clothes, so he went into a department store and looked around the men's section. He bought two pairs of jeans, a leather jacket and six shirts plus a suitcase to carry them in. He changed into his new jeans, shirt and jacket putting his old clothes in the suitcase.

He treated himself to a meal at a Pizza Restaurant, he had never had a pizza so wanted to try it. Then he thought about where to live so he got a newspaper and looked up the accommodation to let. He remembered the place he had stayed before so he went there but was disappointed to find she had died. The new owner was quite pleasant when he saw the suitcase and clothes, he assumed that Harold was a decent person so let him rent a room, the price was double what he had paid ten years before. He now went to get some money out of his savings accounts and faced a lot of questions about why it had been ten years since he had accessed the accounts. He didn't want to say he had been in prison so said he had been working overseas and had now returned to England. Eventually they accepted his story and was able to withdraw 250 pounds, the maximum they would allow although he now had over five thousand with interest.

He had somewhere to live he had money, but he should have a job to tell the probation officer that he was working otherwise they would be suspicious of where his money came from. He went to the probation office and after a wait of over an hour managed to see one, he was overloaded with work so didn't ask many questions. Harold gave him is address and said he was looking for a job, he was told to go to the labour exchange and register there. Out on the street Harold felt happy and confident that his new life was just beginning, and he would enjoy it as much as he could.

During the next week he went to various pubs and night clubs and found that he liked the new life. He found that the people were very friendly and struck up a couple of friendships that helped him to feel much more part of the town. Nottingham is a small town of course dominated by the castle and full of stories of Robin Hood, who may or may not have been a real person. Harold went to some of the exhibits and the castle, although not particularly interested in the past he found it good to know something about the history of England. He did feel that he needed more education but felt at his age it was probably too late.

At least thanks to Jim he could read and write and do simple sums, that was really a great help to him, and he didn't feel so alone. He went to the cinema and remembered going with Diane and pangs of sorrow overcame him, so he had to leave. For a while he was really depressed but after a few days he was back to his old self, but he would never forget her that was for sure.

But he had to find a job to satisfy the probation officer, initially he looked at the agriculture jobs, but he remembered the gang master before who he had punished so severely. The work was hard and poorly paid, and he had the education to do better, there were a few farm jobs but when he looked into them, they were poorly paid and not what he wanted. He looked around the vacancies board and had no trouble in getting a job at that time there were many vacancies, so employers did not delve too deeply into an applicant's past. Harold told his story of having been abroad for ten years and had now returned to the UK, if anyone asked he said he had been in South America as he expected very few people would know anything about there, well neither did he so he hoped that no-one asked any questions. He did not have a national insurance card, and he had never had one as he had only worked in the cash industry. He knew if he went to the Department of Employment he would be questioned and could be in trouble. He was talking to a man in a pub one day and told him of his problem, the man looked at him and said,

"Do you have fifty pounds?"

Harold looked at him for a moment and said,

"I can get it, what for?"

"Well I can solve your problem for you, I can get you an Insurance Card, all legit, so you can get a job". Harold thought for a moment then replied,

"OK, how do I do it?"

"Right you give me twenty quid now and I will have a card for you in 3 days then you can pay the rest".

Harold was a bit suspicious and looked at the man quizzically.

"How do I know you will come back?"

"Yes, you will have to trust me then".

"Well I don't want to be taken for an idiot, I will give you a tenner and the rest when you come back".

The man thought for a while and then said

"I agree, but it will cost you another fiver".

Harold agreed and handed over the money. Well he was not convinced he had done the right thing and said goodbye to his tenner but three days later the man turned up with his insurance card, plus a Drivers Licence. He told him he could have it for another tenner. Although he could not drive it was good to have another piece of ID, so he paid over the money.

Harold was happy now he felt more like a legitimate member of society which he had never before. Now he could apply for a job as a legitimate worker. The Labour Exchange sent him to Sampsons to be employed to load the wagons using a forklift truck. He didn't take long to get the hang of it and as most of the supplies were palleted it was an easy job but busy. The pallets contained all sorts of food and drink to be delivered nationwide, so he had to be sure that he loaded the correct pallet in the correct lorry. Each pallet was checked by the loader so there were very few mistakes. The work was not exciting but at least it was a job and Harold needed one in order to prove he was a useful citizen to the probation officer.

His life now was pretty good, with money and gaining a good reputation with the probation officer and getting on well with his workmates, he felt that life couldn't be better. The only problem was that he needed to have female companionship, not an area had had much success with so far and having been in prison for so long he had lost any social graces he might have had. Luckily one of his workmates called Richard was very friendly and they started going out together. Richard was single and had a few girlfriends but nothing serious, so he was an ideal teacher for Harold.

They mostly went to bars and the occasional club; they saw lots of single girls and most of them were pretty keen on being friends. They had a number of dates with girls and Harold found that soon he was able to get a date and even have sex. Women were much more liberated now and took the initiative as much as men, so Harold was able to get back into the swing quickly. Although he had several dates none of them lasted more than a few weeks, one lasted 2 months but they all finished.

Harold didn't mind as he hadn't any ideas about getting married and having children, his own childhood was something that hung over him like a dark cloud, so he pushed all thoughts of marriage aside, he just enjoyed himself. This could have lasted for a long time when an event happened that caused his life to be upset and change direction again.

He had been at Sampson's for about 12 months when he first saw her, when lone lunchtime just as he was about to finish, she walked through the warehouse taking a short cut to the shops behind.

She was a little over 5 feet with short blonde hair and round steel glasses she had a nicely rounded figure and Harold was impressed with the shape of her breasts pushing against her suit jacket. She wore a grey suit a white blouse that gave her a look of efficiency and an air of being unobtainable or mysterious. Harold had not seen her before and decided to ask Jim the foreman who she was. "Jim, who was that woman in the grey suit who came through lunchtime?" he asked, "that was probably Lyn; she is the PA to the directors. Nice lady and she likes her job, works long hours. I always found her to be quite nice but has got a bit of a sharp tongue, so don't annoy her" Jim said.

Harold wondered how he could get to know her, she didn't seem to go to the canteen very often as she had her lunch at her desk, and he had no reason to go to the office. Eventually he discovered that she went to a health club once a week; on a Thursday so he decided that was where he needed to go. When he found out the price he was not put off as he had more than enough to pay for a year whether he went or not. Then he had a bright idea, he would ask Lyn about the benefits.

One lunchtime he wandered into the office area trying to look as unobtrusive as possible, but of course he did the opposite so all he staff there looked at him curiously. He approached the desk where Lyn was sitting eating her sandwich and reading her emails. "Excuse me" he began, Lyn started and stopped in mid-chew, she looked at him suspiciously then said,

"What are you doing here? You shouldn't be in this office" Harold reeled back as if he had been hit with a hammer, which he might have been the way Lyn spoke. Then taking his courage in his grimy large hands he said,

"I am sorry to bother you, but I was thinking of joining the Hearts Health Club and I believe you go there, and I wondered if you would recommend it?"

"Yes, I do go there once a week" Lyn said her face smiling now. Harold thought she had a lovely smile but still felt the sting of her tongue.

"I find it's very good, but I don't do a lot just keep in shape. Why are you asking?"

"Well I thought I might join but it is a bit expensive, so I wanted to find out if it was worth it"

"Yes, it is a bit expensive, look I am allowed to bring a guest along, why don't you come one evening and you can see what it's all about"

Harold couldn't believe his luck; she was inviting him along his mind raced at all the possible scenarios that could arise but was brought back down to earth.

"Well would you like to come along?" Lyn said quizzically.

"Yes please, how about this week?"

"Yes, that's good. I usually go straight from work, so meet me in the foyer at 5.30"

"Thanks, see you Thursday".

Harold couldn't escape fast enough as he marvelled at his good luck. The next day he put on clean shirt and trousers, tried to keep himself as clean as possible during work and impatiently waited for the end of the day. He rushed down to the foyer and saw she wasn't there, so he withdrew behind a pillar and watched, she arrived promptly at 5.30 looked around her and was about to leave when Harold appeared.

"Sorry, I hope I am not late?"

"No, your right on time"

They walked down the road, her at 5 ft nothing and him at six feet two making an odd couple. Nothing was said as they walked along and Harold had completely lost his power of speech, he looked down on her and felt he might be in love again.

Arriving at the health club they entered in and the receptionist registered Harold and gave him a visitor badge. He was disappointed when she said she was going to do her work-out and would see him later. The "see you later" to him seemed a good omen. He was show around the club but didn't really take in much he kept thinking about her and seeing her again planning to take her to a restaurant and maybe later. At last he got back to the foyer and sat down to wait her return, she arrived, and he thought she looked wonderful with her red cheeks and healthy body.

"Well, did you like what you saw?" "Yes, looks good" lied Harold.

Going outside he stood with her on the steps and was about to ask her to a meal when she jumped up and waved.

"Sorry, I have to go now my boy-friend is taking me to dinner. See you at work. Bye"

She ran across the road and met a man, they embraced and kissed and walked of down the road. Harold was fit to bust, his anger grew in his chest and he felt cheated by a woman again, but of course it had all been in his mind there was nothing doing in fact. He turned and walked in the opposite direction until he found a bar, ordering drink he sat down at the table and mused on his misfortune. Several beers and two whiskeys later he decided that he needed to get some air and vent his anger and frustration.

Coming out of the bar he walked fast to get of his anger, not sure where he was or where he was going, in fact he didn't care. Once again, he felt alone and betrayed would he never find the love he craved? He just wanted someone, anyone to love him to let him know they cared, in all his life he never had anyone who really cared apart from Jim and he had been taken away from him. Morosely he wandered around town his mind full of confusion not knowing what to do, he had a good life here but no companionship. The thought came that perhaps he might try somewhere else, where he was not sure but perhaps a new town would offer him the thing he hoped for. He came upon a used car lot and walked in for no particular reason, he found an old VW Camper van and decided he needed transport, so he paid the deposit and drove off down the road.

The next day he decided that he was going to leave Nottingham and go somewhere else, when he told Richard he said he didn't know yet just somewhere else. Richard wished him all the best, Harold went to the bank and took out five hundred pounds. He filled up the van with petrol and bought some groceries and then drove out of town. He didn't look at the signs just drove with his mind still fuming.

The area around Nottingham is quite pretty and of course there is the forest where Robin Hood was supposed to live. He stopped by there and looked at the tree that Robin supposedly hit with his arrow from his death bed. He then drove off not sure where to go not knowing the area eventually he looked where he was and saw that he was on the road to Melton Mowbray. Never having been in this part of the country he was quite interested and looked at the fields as he passed and noted what crops they were growing. When he arrived, it was eight in the evening, so he stopped at the first pub he found. It was a Hungry Horse pub and restaurant, it looked busy and he went in, the menu was good, and he ordered a meal with beer. When he finished, he asked the receptionist for somewhere to stay and she suggested the Queens Head, he took directions thanked her and drove off. The Queens Head was an old pub but with a good atmosphere, they had one room left so he took it. He slept well that night and found they did a great breakfast after which he wandered around town.

Melton Mowbray is only a small village, but it is famous for its Pork Pies, so Harold bought one for his lunch, he found a small grocery store and bought some tomatoes, cheese and bread plus an apple pie and three bottles of beer. He went back to his van and drove off in the direction of Peterborough. Along the way he found a lay-by and stopped to eat his lunch, the pie was great, and he enjoyed his lunch. He continued on to Peterborough and found it to be a pretty town with a famous Cathedral. He decided to stop and have a look around, he went to the market and the river and thought it was a nice place to live.

Then he thought that he hadn't considered where he was going just driving along enjoying his ride and the country- side. He loved the outdoors and hoped to find somewhere where he could work outdoors. As he had spent most of the day sightseeing, he decided to stay the night. He found a B&B in a backstreet and booked a room; he then went out to find somewhere to eat. There are many pubs, cafes and restaurants so he had many choices. Eventually he went into an Italian Restaurant, looking at the menu he didn't know most of the dishes so when the waiter came, he said what would he recommend, he said try the Carbonara. When it arrived, it was a large plate of spaghetti with bacon bits and parmesan cheese on top, Harold tried it and liked it, he also ordered a beer. When he was finished, he decided some ice cream would go down well. He had never tasted such delicious ice cream and he was well pleased that he had come in. Paying his bill, he left a good tip and went out into the night. The streets were very busy, and he enjoyed walking around then he went into one of the many bars. It was fairly crowded, so he sat at the bar with his beer.

A woman came and sat next to him, he glanced at her and saw that she was about thirty, bleached blonde hair, nice breasts and well dressed in a neckline that just about stopped at her nipples.

"Are you new here?" she asked,

"Just passing through".

"Would you be looking for some female company?"

Harold guessed she was a prostitute, but he didn't mind having sex with her she looked good. She suggested they went to a nearby hotel and had a room for a few hours. Harold agreed so they went there and obviously she had been there before as the doorman didn't make any comment. Going to the room she said,

"Well I like to be paid before, so that will be a tenner".

"What a tenner! That's a lot are you worth it?"

"Tell you what if you aren't satisfied, I will give the money back to you. How about that?"

Harold agreed and he certainly thought she was worth the money in fact he gave her an extra fiver. She was delighted and hoped to see him again. He told her he was leaving in the morning, but thanks for a great time.

The next day he left and drove down to Cambridge, a college town full of students and bicycles, and visitors. He couldn't find anything in town so drove out and found a pub with a room for the night. Talking to the landlord he was told that he believed around Ipswich there was plenty of farm work and they were always looking for workers. He decided to go there.

The next day he set off for Ipswich, on the way he stopped at Bury St Edmunds for a meal and a walk around the town. It is only a small town with the ruins of its cathedral that Henry VIII had pulled down. After lunch he set off again it was only about 40-minutes, so he arrived there in mid-afternoon.

Ipswich was only a small town; it had a small port that was still operating and a pleasant atmosphere. He liked the look of it and after walking around he started to look for somewhere to stay.

CHAPTER 22

Ipswich

He walked around and looked in the local paper for somewhere to stay, he managed to find a small flat about half a mile from the town Centre up on top of the hill on the main road. The Landlady was quite old, about 65 Harold thought, and was a widow. She let out two of her bedrooms and did a good breakfast. Harold liked her and they seemed to get on well, he was no trouble and she liked the company.

Every evening after dinner they sat in the living room and talked and watched TV. Harold hadn't seen any TV before, so he was fascinated, they did have some TV in prison, but he had never watched it. There was another guest, James Cameron by name, who only appeared at mealtimes. He was middle-aged and with blonde hair, average build and about five feet six tall. He didn't say much and as soon as the meal was over, he disappeared to his room. Mrs Norman, his landlady, said that she thought he had some marital problems and had been with her about three months now.

Harold told her some of his story missing out the prison bits and sticking to his South American story avoiding any details. He had been living there about three months when a thought struck him that he should have registered with the local parole office, he was going to but then thought he might be sent back to prison again for not telling them of his move so he decided not to. He didn't have a job so during the day he wandered around town doing some odd work when he felt like it, he didn't need money as he had plenty of his own. He liked the town and decided to explore the area.

He told Mrs Norman that he was going on a holiday trip so would be away about a week, she said good idea and said he should drive up the coast towards Great Yarmouth. He filled up the van with petrol and food and set off.

He went to Felixstowe to see the port and then up the coast to Great Yarmouth, he stopped a couple of nights on the way to enjoy the scenery. Great Yarmouth is a tourist town with a harbour that used to be very busy with fishing boats, but not so many now. He stayed at a B&B near the seafront and visited some pubs along the front. At one he had a bit of an incident; it was late at night and three youths had had too much to drink and were swearing and shouting at the other customers.

Harold decided they ought to go home so he approached them and suggested they should leave. In their condition they were not in any mood to take advice and decided they could deal with this old man. Unfortunately for them they were no match for Harold, and he knocked two of them down and told them to leave, they drunkenly held on to each other and left. Unfortunately, the landlord had called the police so when they turned up, they questioned Harold. He told them where he lived and that he was on holiday and thought that the youths were causing a nuisance, the land lord and several customers agreed, the police decided that he had done a good job but warned him not to get into any more fights. Harold was relieved he didn't want any trouble.

The next day he drove on to Norwich and found an old city with a huge castle, a big covered market and lots of places to stay. He had enjoyed his trip, but one thing was missing, a companion. He had met a couple of girls in Great Yarmouth but before anything could happen, he had left after the fight. His confidence was still low when approaching women, so he began to feel depressed and decided to return home to Ipswich. Now the feeling of being alone again was gnawing away at his heart and he knew he needed to find some female company. One night he was drinking in a pub and a pretty woman came and sat at his table. She asked if he minded and he said no, she began talking to him and said that did he want to be friends. Harold didn't want a friend he wanted a woman, but she seemed eager to please, so they agreed to go to the local fast food joint and have a burger.

They had a pleasant meal and Harold thought they were getting along fine, then she said would he like to come back to her place for a night cap, Harold agreed. She lived in a small block of flats just off the main road and it seemed a decent enough place. Now Harold had become more excited as they walked to her place but knew he had to control himself or he could be in trouble again. They had hardly got in the door when she began pulling his clothes off and he responded, they careered into the bedroom and finished undressing each other.

They had riotous sex and it lasted several hours, having sex three times. Then they lay exhausted on the bed, both fulfilled and for Harold happy. When he woke up, she was not there and although he searched the small flat, she was not there. As he got dressed, he noticed that his wallet was missing, so she had been a prostitute, well he didn't worry there had only been a few pounds and he had plenty more.

A few nights later he went back to the same pub, he waited and saw her as she entered. She saw him and was about to leave when he called her over, reluctantly she came but smiled sweetly at him. He told her that she had been good, and he had enjoyed their night, so she didn't need to steal from him. She sat down and they talked and decided they would like another night together but this time no stealing he would pay her.

They had several more nights together and Harold was beginning to think more of her but when he broached the subject she was horrified; she didn't want a long-term relationship. Harold was upset and protested but she would have none of it and left him in the pub. Although he went back several times, he never saw her again and when he went to the flat, he discovered she only rented it.

Now Harold was depressed again, another woman had betrayed him, why did they all do this? Why couldn't he find a nice woman who would love him? He determined that in future no woman would do this to him, and they would do as he wanted. With this new determination he set out to find that woman.

Penny was fuming as she drove along, the nerve of that girl not listening to me over her choice of boyfriends, for the life of me I don't know what is going to happen to her. John is not much help he just hides away and won't get involved; I feel so lonely with no-one who cares for me. I feel like that I should run away and never go back and see how they cope without me. She was getting very depressed and wasn't really watching where she was going but as she did this trip ever week it was a routine that didn't need much attention.

Harold was making his way to the supermarket not necessarily to buy anything but just to pass the time he was getting very bored and was thinking he ought to get a job of some sort, the supermarket usually needed help so perhaps he could get a part-time job there. He still had his money from the jewellery robberies, and he guessed it was over 10000 pounds, so he didn't need to work but he did need something to do.

Penny drove into the car park and parked her car in her usual place, she mused that everything she did was a habit, she really must find something that was different and get her out of her routine.

Harold noticed the woman getting out of the car and something inside him stirred, she was a nice shape, a bit plump and he liked that, she had large breasts and he loved that, she was middle-aged so that was good too she would know how to look after him. As she caught his eye he turned and went into the store. Penny noticed this man at the store entrance and somehow, he attracted her, she quickly turned away and walked towards the store to get her cart and do her shopping forgetting all about him.

As she wandered around the store almost mechanically picking things and putting them in the cart her mind was far away not concentrating on what she was getting. She didn't notice Harold shadowing her as she wasn't aware of anything at the moment.

Getting to the till there was the usual wait, being Friday every-one seemed to be getting their weekly shop. She patiently waited, what was the rush? She didn't need to get home and have more fights she wanted someone to love her and say she was beautiful and to hold her in his arms, unfortunately John did none of those things. She had hoped over the years that he would become more romantic, but he did not, in fact the opposite. They hadn't had sex for months; she couldn't remember that last time he gave her a passionate kiss. Then she got to the till, the girl seemed to take ages to tally her shopping but eventually she got out of the store.

It was dark now as she made her way to her car, opened the boot and put her shopping in. She took the cart back to the park and then got into her car and started the engine.

"Don't make a sound and do as you are told, and you will not be hurt"

She felt something cold and steely at her neck, she looked in the mirror but it has been turned away so she could not see. Frightened but somehow not scared she listened to what he had to say.

"Drive out of the car park, make no bad moves, turn left and follow the road until I tell you otherwise, got that?"

Penny nodded.

She did as she was told and drove along the road for a while.

"O.K. Pull into that layby on the right"

"Pull up behind that van and turn off the engine".

Penny wasn't sure what to expect, rape did enter her mind, but she dismissed it, surely a woman of her age would not get raped? Getting out of the car Harold led her to the van and tied her hands and feet.

"If you promise not to make a sound, I won't gag you. Alright?"

She nodded not sure to trust her voice.

Harold unloaded her groceries and put them in the van, then he drove the car down the road to a bend, put a brick on the accelerator and sent it into the river, people would think she had had an accident and drowned, he hoped.

Walking back to the van he felt happy, he had a woman and she was just what he had hoped for and he wanted her to look after him. Checking her ropes, he got into the driver's seat and set off, he realized he had forgotten to get some fuel so had to stop at the next petrol station.

"Don't make a sound or you will be in trouble".

Penny looked at him, a tall man with big muscles could hurt her so she nodded. Harold filled up and went in to pay, he bought two coffees and some cakes and as he returned to the van, he heard her calling out. Dashing into the van he hit her around the head, she fell to the floor dazed.

"I told you to behave or you will get hurt. So be quiet".

He now gagged her as he didn't want any more scenes. He drove for a couple of hours and then pulled into the side of the road. Untying her gag, he offered her a coffee and cake. She was feeling hungry, so she eagerly ate them.

"We have a long way to go so I suggest that you try and get some sleep, I will stop at a Motorway services and get us some dinner and I can't trust you to behave so I will have to gag you again".

He came to the M1 and drove northwards in the direction of Leeds; he stopped at the next service area and went and bought some food and drink. Untying her hands, he pulled down the table and they ate the food.

"What are you going to do to me?" Penny asked.

"Well, I have been looking for someone to look after me and act as my wife. I saw you and you looked an ideal candidate".

"What! I need to get back to my family they will be getting worried".

"Well I am your family now and you will never see them again". Penny gaped at him. He wants a wife, I was only thinking that I wanted a new husband. She thought about the family she had left behind and although her life had not been perfect it was alright. She began to cry softly, Harold came around to her and to her surprise he put his arm around her and said,

"I will look after you, I have never had anyone to look after me and I hope you will do that. I am sure your family will cope without you, but I need you".

Penny stopped and looked at Harold, this was what she had been missing all these years someone to hug her and care for her. She was confused, how could she desert her family for a man she had just met, who had hit her, but it was only because she didn't do as he said, and he had given her a hug.

Having finished their meal Harold drove off up the M1, it took about 4 hours to get to Leeds, so it was about midnight when they got there, Harold found a car park and parked the van there. He untied Penny and made up the bed, she looked at him and said, "Are you going to rape me?"

"Well what is rape? I want to have sex with you and if you agree it is not rape, but if you don't then I will rape you".

Penny could see that whatever happened he was going to have sex with her, she was a little excited but fearful. John hadn't made love to her for months and when he did it was a little perfunctorily and soon over. So, she tried to undress with her back to him,

"Let me see you, don't be shy I want to see your body".

She slowly turned around and finished taking of her clothes but kept her bra and panties on,

"Everything".

Since Robert no man had seen her naked, so she was a little reluctant but did as he asked. She saw that he had a big smile and drew her into bed.

Because he had not had sex for a while, he was a little rushed and urgent and Penny did not like it as he hurt her. He did apologize and say he hadn't had sex for a while. Then he began to use all that he had been taught by other women and Penny loved the feeling of his hands and lips touching her body and found herself ready for more sex. They had two more that night and both fell asleep in each other's arms.

Penny woke up first and felt wonderful she hadn't had such sex since Robert years ago, she looked at Harold sleeping peacefully and she like what she saw. Then her mind turned to what to do, should she quietly slip away and try to get home or stay with him. Before she could make up her mind he woke up and reached for her and gave her a long loving kiss. Penny's' mind was made up she was staying with him.

"So, what is your name? Mine is Penelope or Penny".

"My name is Harold. We need to find somewhere to eat and get freshened up, alright?"

"Yes. I am starving".

They got dressed and had quick wipe with a flannel.

"I need to get some make-up and other things; can I go to the shop?"

Harold looked at her and decided she could be trusted.

"Yes, but I am coming with you".

They drove along and came to a supermarket, parked and went in. They bought what they needed and then went to the restaurant and had breakfast. Penny went to the ladies and had a quick wash and make-up. She looked into the mirror and wondered what had happened. How did she come to be here? With a man she had never met until yesterday. Had sex with him, she smiled at that, and now she was going with him wherever he went. Coming back, she found Harold waiting outside the door, he smiled at her and touched her arm,

"I thought you were never coming out. But I see you are beautiful; it was worth the wait".

Harold couldn't believe what he was saying, all those years alone, all the women he had flirted with and now he was saying these words.

Penny was delighted, Harold was doing exactly what she had been hoping for and she was so pleased.

"So where are we going?"

"Well I am a farmer so I thought I could get a job on a farm somewhere in the Yorkshire Dales".

"I have never been to Yorkshire; mind I haven't been to many places".

They drove up the road to and stopped at a village called Malham. Enquiring at the local post office he was told that a lady had been recently widowed and needed someone to run the farm.

Harold couldn't believe his luck and excitedly told Penny and she was excited too. They drove up to the farm and knocked on the door. An old lady answered with a puzzled look on her face.

"Can I be of help to you?"

"Well I am hoping we can be of help to you. I believe you are looking for a farm manager and I would like to apply".

She looked at the pair of them and then beckoned them inside. Harold explained that they had lived in London and had decided to move to the country, he had a certificate in farm management, which he showed her, and it seemed that it was just what they all wanted.

Annie, that was her name, asked lots of questions but Harold was able to answer them all. She showed them around the farm it was a mixed farm with sheep, two pigs, some hens and vegetable fields. Her late husband had let things slip over the last few years, so it needed a great deal of work.

Harold relished the chance and Annie said he could have a six-month trial, there was a cottage a mile down the road that they could use. She couldn't afford to pay them much, Harold told her they had some money and would wait until the harvest was done to get paid. All in all, everyone was happy. Penny loved the little two bed-roomed cottage with a small kitchen and living room with a big open fireplace. She quickly set to work to make it into a home.

Penny knew nothing about farming or the countryside, but Annie showed her how to look after the hens, feed them, clean out the shed, collect eggs and later how to kill them for food and sale. Harold employed two workers to help him get the farm to rights, one of them knew about pigs so he made sure they were looked after and later sold.

The vegetable field was not in a good state but there were some vegetables he could sell, Annie told him the farmers market was on a Wednesday, so the next Wednesday they all piled into his van with as much of the vegetables as were worth selling and drove into the village. Annie introduced them to all her friends, and they made a tidy sum selling all their vegetables and eggs. They then retired to the pub, there was only one, for lunch and a celebration drink.

CHAPTER 24

Life in the Dales

Harold discovered that there was more to do on the farm than he had thought, as Annie's husband in later years was not able to do much, but he had two good workers, so they set to work.

Jim was to look after the sheep, repair the stone walls, make shelters for the sheep during the winter, Harold had been told about the severe weather they got here, could be snowed in for more than a week and very cold.

Martin was to look after the pigs and get them ready for market, Harold knew nothing about pigs and didn't think they were worth keeping, Martin agreed and got them ready and sold them at the next auctions, the money came in handy to pay for the expenses on the farm.

Martin was able to repair the tractor and to help Harold in the fields. The crops in the field were not very good, but Harold managed to save some of them, he gave Annie what she needed, kept some for themselves and the workers, there were even some left over to be sold at the farmers market.

Martin ploughed the fields and Harold bought the seeds for the next year, they decided to concentrate on cash crops like salad stuff, one field of potatoes and another of cabbages which he hoped would do well at the local market. He also planned to take produce to Leeds next year as he expected to get better prices there. He discovered that the house was badly in need of repair, so he and Martin set to work making the building waterproof and re-decorated it. They also laid in a big store of logs in the kitchen so that Annie would not have to go out in the cold to get them, there was also a large supply in the lean-to outside.

Whilst doing all this he and Penny had work to do on the house. It had not been lived in for some years so was badly in need of some loving care. Penny started by cleaning up the place starting with the bedroom, they had to have somewhere to sleep. They bought a bed from the store in Leeds and many furnishings that she needed. Harold visited his five banks and withdrew five hundred from each to pay for the goods. When Penny asked how come he had so many banks he said it was because he didn't want all his money in one place. Penny wondered where the money came from but decided not to ask.

Every day after feeding the hens Penny came home and continued making it a home and a pretty comfortable place to live. Penny was very happy, Harold looked after her well, he showed consideration and proved to be a good husband. Their sex life was also good, Harold of course had had his problems with sex, but he had learnt his lesson and with the help of Penny who had learnt a lot about sexual techniques from Robert they had a great sex life.

Penny rarely thought about her previous life, when she did, she marvelled at how different her life was now. She realized that the life with John had been boring and unfulfilling, her children seemed to resent her, and John had never helped to bring them up. She wondered how they had coped without her, but not in any concerned way she felt that whatever had happened was their own fault and not hers.

As autumn approached the work to get ready for winter became more Important, neither of them had any experience of winter in the Dales, although the neighbours gave them plenty of advice so they took all they said and got on with it. Because the lived so remotely they were told that they could be cut off even from the village for weeks at a time. So, they made sure that they had enough supplies to last them. The log store was full to overflowing, the house had been made waterproof and as warm as they could. The larder was full of food in tins mostly, but they had been able to buy a small freeze/ fridge, so they were able to store some meat and vegetables in it.

They made sure that Annie had all she needed, and Penny promised she would come up every day and look after the hens. The hens now had a nice new house where they could roost in warmth and comfort. Penny could collect the eggs either from outside or inside depending on the weather, the grain store was full, and the mash ingredients were in airtight containers.

On the 1st of December they all had a party to celebrate the work they had done, and the men would not be needed again until the new year for any lambs that the sheep might have. Harold gave them both a month's wages so they would not go short at Christmas, they both thanked him heartily and said they never had such a good boss, Harold was a little abashed he was not used to being praised but he was grateful all the same.

Some snow had already fallen so Harold took the men home on the tractor and it gave him a chance to see how it performed in the snow. He soon realized that even with the big tyres it needed careful handling, as he slid across the road but stopped before the ditch. Driving back up the hill to his cottage he was a happy man. He could never have believed this situation 20 years ago, he expected to be in and out of prison, no one caring about him and in debt most of the time.

Well he had done his time, although he had not completed his visits to the probation's office, he didn't think there was any chance they would look here.

Within a week the snow arrived and there was five feet of it, Penny said how lovely it looked they never had that much snow in Ipswich and Harold agreed he had never seen so much in his life. Now he said no matter how lovely it looked he had to go and see how the animals were and to feed the hens and see Annie. He and Penny wrapped themselves up warmly with several layers of cloths and hats. To his relief the tractor started straight away, they cleared away most of the snow on the short drive so that would make it easier to get out and also about 10 yards on the road. They were tired out after doing that so were grateful to climb on the tractor and start away. Harold found that with the new snow it was not too difficult to drive but it still took them a half an hour to drive the mile to the farm.

On arrival Harold went to look at the sheep and Penny went to the hen house. The sheep seemed to be alright, using the shelters that had been built was a good idea. Harold gave them feed and drew some water from the well that Annie said never froze. Satisfied that they were fine he made his way back to the farmhouse, calling in at the hen house he found Penny busy feeding the hens and collecting the eggs. They had 10 hens and there were eight eggs so that was a good return, they cleaned out the house and then went to the farmhouse. They were about to knock when the door opened with a smiling Annie.

"I saw you coming so I made some breakfast and tea, come on in the warm".

"Thanks" they both said and gave her the eggs.

"Well you have four and I will keep the others. What I usually do is to hide them in the snow, the cold keeps them fresh for about two weeks, otherwise you can cook them and use them later. If you can try and get down to the market people will be glad of fresh eggs".

"Yes, you're right, we will take them down on Wednesday, the tractor seems to cope ok with the snow".

They had a good breakfast and stayed and chatted with Annie most of the morning then they donned their clothes and drove slowly back to the cottage. They began to look forward to Christmas, Harold had never had a happy Christmas so was not sure what happened, he had seen all the shops full of presents and people but never had any money to spare. In prison they used to have a Christmas tree and a supposedly Christmas dinner but as usual it was not very good.

In Nottingham they were given a small gift usually shaving cream or soap. They did sing some carols but Harold didn't know any of them, when he was a child Christmas was the same as every other day for him, his sister got a present and they had a chicken but as usual he only got the left overs. Penny had never really enjoyed her Christmas's as a child, her parents were not into happiness and never had a tree, she did get some presents usually new clothes. Her friends had much more and once she had been invited to one of their houses and saw what others did, she refused every other time because she was ashamed of her lack of presents to give. She, of course, had that wonderful Christmas at Worcester but it ended so badly when she returned to college, still she had the memory.

Penny was determined that they would have a good Christmas, she bought a tree and ornaments, some balloons and trimmings. She also bought a turkey the smallest she could find, and with their vegetables it would make a good dinner, as a surprise she bought a Christmas pudding.

As for presents she guessed that Harold would not know about what to buy so she gave him a short list of things she would like and told him to buy just one of them. Her and Harold decorated the house and Harold loved every minute, it was so exciting to decorate the tree for the first time, to blow up a balloon, and when one burst, they both fell about laughing and hugged each other.

On Christmas day they had to go and feed the animals and see Annie was alright, they invited her to come to their house for dinner. She was so happy to agree so they wrapped her up and drove back home with an extra passenger. She loved all the decorations; she hadn't bothered this year. They sat down to a wonderful meal, Harold had never seen so much food and they all tucked in and there was lots of laughter and talk. Penny brought in the pudding and set fire to it; Harold was startled but then laughed as it burned out.

After dinner Penny and Annie cleared away and washed up while Harold listened to their new radio, another thing that Harold had never had. Now was the time for presents, Harold was excited like a small child and eagerly gave Penny every gift on her list, she protested that she only wanted one but laughed and kissed him many times. She gave him two new shirts, socks and a swiss army knife. He loved it all especially the knife something he had seen in the shops but never thought he could afford.

They gave Annie a new shawl, slippers and some soap and a flannel. She was over the moon and cried all the way through saying they were such wonderful people; God must have sent them to her. She apologized that she hadn't bought them a present, but they said she was their present and hoped that they would have another good year.

They talked and laughed a lot, listened to the radio and had some beer to drink. Then it was time to take Annie home, Harold told Penny to stay home and he would be back soon. It had begun snowing again so the road was a bit slippery, driving carefully Harold got Annie back home, saw her indoors and the started back home. Perhaps he wasn't paying sufficient attention to the road, but the tractor ran off the road into a deep ditch. Harold hit his head and was knocked out.

Penny was waiting at home full of love and happiness, but as the time went on and Harold had not returned, she began to be worried, eventually she decided that she would go and look for him. It was snowing heavily now, and she had great trouble walking in the snow she soon found the tractor and slipping down the bank she found Harold unconscious.

She tried to lift him, but he was too heavy for her, she shouted at him, slapped his face, kissed him but couldn't wake him. Getting desperate she didn't know what to do, the nearest neighbour was a mile away and she didn't want to leave Harold. She covered him up with a canvas that was on the tractor and set out down the hill, it seemed to take for ever before she found the cottage. Knocking on the door a light came on and a voice asked who it was. "It's me Penny, Harold has had an accident". The door swung open and the man beckoned her in. Penny told him what she had found, and he quickly got dressed and started up his tractor, it was bigger than theirs and much newer, so it didn't take long to get back to the scene of the accident.

He managed to get Harold out of the ditch and onto his trac-tor and drove them back to their house, putting Harold to bed they hoped he wasn't badly hurt. Penny watched over him and he came around not sure what had happened, Penny told him and kissed and hugged him telling him not to scare her again like that. Harold hugged her and promised to take more care.

The next day their neighbour came by to see how he was, Harold felt fine but was worried about his tractor, the neighbour said they could go and have a look. When they got to the scene it was not as bad as Harold had suspected. The tractor was soon towed out and Harold was towed back to the house. They thanked their neighbour and offered to give him something, but he refused and said he had only done what any neighbour would do.

Later Harold checked out the tractor and everything seemed fine, it started immediately, and he was so happy, they needed the tractor to get to the farm every day. That reminded him that they hadn't been up today, so they went to the farmhouse and explained to Annie what had happened. They checked and fed the animals and returned home. Penny fussed around Harold and he protested that he was fine now, but he secretly loved it.

The rest of the winter was without any great incident, the snow this year was not so great as at other times so that was good. But they did decide that next spring they would see if they could buy a new tractor, Harold wasn't sure how much money he had left so had to wait until spring.

They had a wonderful time together; it was if they were meant to be together. All the troubles and strife they had been through had just been a testing ground for them finding true love. Now Harold began to tell Penny about his life, he now trusted her to hear the truth and not to judge him. She listened to his tale and hugged and kissed him at times, she held his hand as he described his love of Diane and how it had all gone wrong, being sent to prison for manslaughter, the terrible conditions, how he had made sure he had a qualification which had now been the way to their current condition.

Once he had finished she held him for a long time and then told him about her life, its downs and ups, she told about Robert and his betrayal, her unloving husband and children and how she had found him, or had he found her? But now they had found each other and were so happy.

Come the new year and the sheep needed to be looked after ready for any lambs in the spring, Jim said that he thought about six of them were pregnant and they usually delivered in March or April. The ones who he suspected were pregnant were put in one of the shelters and the others were kept out.

In late February Penny called on Annie as she usually did after feeding the chickens but there was no answer to her knock, she looked through the window and saw that the fire had gone out so she tried the door and it was unlocked. Calling her name, she went into the kitchen which was freezing and then into the small lounge and then looked into the bedroom. There on the bed lay Annie and she was obviously dead. Penny cried a little then ran out to find Harold. Harold did cry when he saw the body and held Penny tightly, he remembered Jim lying on his bed and now another of his friends had died. Life was so cruel!

They tidied up the room and lay Annie out as best they could. Martin said he would tell the village doctor when he went home to come and give a death certificate. Now they had to organize a funeral in the depths of winter, the undertaker took the body to the lying-in room and got everything sorted.

Harold was surprised how many villagers came to the funeral but then he remembered that Annie had lived here all her life. She was buried next to her husband and Harold thought that was good as they were now together again, and he hoped when the time came, he and Penny would be together.

After the funeral they were asked what was to become of the farm and them, it had not entered his mind, but the local solicitor said they should look for a will. So, they looked around the cottage and found a tin box on a table, when they opened it, they found a single sheet of paper on it was written

"Leave everything to Harold and Penny".

They weren't sure of this was legal or not so took it to the solicitor.

"As far as I know they did not have any children and no family hereabouts. I am sure that the court would accept this a will. I will give it to the court in Leeds and see what they say".

A week later he called them and said the court had agreed in the circumstances that the document was a valid will so the farm now belonged to them. He had had it registered in their names and they just needed to sign the documents to make it legal". They were overjoyed, now they could carry on Annie's work and keep the farm running as well as having a property of their own.

They set to work and began renovating the farmhouse as they had decided that they would live there. During the renovation they found many things of Annie and her husband and they carefully collected them together. They made a display on one wall of some old photos and documents that they had found of the couple and were pleased to be able to look at it daily to remind them of a loving old lady who had taken them in and given them such a good life.

Running a moorland farm is hard work, but Harold and Penny didn't mind working hard because they were together, and they loved each other so much that they needed to be together. They managed to get the farm to be profitable and did not need to use anymore of Harold's savings. They even could afford a new tractor but kept the old one so that two of them could work on the fields at the same time.

The sheep flock increased to fifty and Martin had a full-time job looking after them and Harold made sure he was well paid. Penny and her chickens also grew, she bought 3-day old chick and grew them to 3 months and then sold them in the market, she also sold a dozen hens at Christmas so the income from the hens was good.

They celebrated ten years on the farm in June of 1998 and invited all their neighbours to a party, over the years they had become much loved and respected by the village for their hard work and generosity to their workers and the village.

Lying in bed that night cuddled together Penny said

"Thank you for kidnapping me and saving me from a loveless and dull life and giving me such a happy time. I love you".

Harold kissed her and said "And I thank you for giving me all the love that I never had before, I am so glad we got together. My life was a ruin when I first saw you but somehow, I knew that you were meant for me. We have been such a great couple and I love you every day more and more".

They kissed and made love again. Little did they know what fate had in store for them later, but for now and the next two years they enjoyed themselves, were happy and felt safe from the world. Harold never thought about prison or ever going back, nobody would find him here after all these years. Penny never thought about her family, they had all been a disappointment and did not wish to be reminded about them.

CHAPTER 25

Harold Arrested

Penny was driving down to the village and thinking about how happy she and Harold were, she was looking forward to her fiftieth birthday. How life had changed over these last twelve years before she had been unhappy and felt unloved. John had never been very romantic, and her two children seemed to not like her either, she had struggled and done her best for them, but it never seemed enough.

Meeting Harold, although his intention had not been very romantic, had changed her life and fortune. That day in 1987 was a turning point in her life and she could hardly believe how happy she was now. Harold had been a good husband and a great lover; she had so missed the physical side of her marriage with John and try as she might she could not get him to be more romantic or caring. Even now they enjoyed sex very much and she could not have asked for a better man to be her husband and lover.

He wasn't legally her husband because she had not divorced John, that had been impossible because they would have had to reveal their location, and more than likely Harold would be sent to jail. She couldn't bear not to have him with her, so they didn't discuss marriage but enjoyed each other's company.

The farm was doing well, as well as any moorland farm could, they also had extra income from letting out the cottage where they had first lived. All in all, her life was very good, and she would not ask for more.

Arriving at the market she was greeted with friendly smiles and hellos, she had become a big part of the market scene and got on well with all the people, she and Harold had helped some of them over the years and their efforts were appreciated.

She set up her stall and unloaded the vegetables and eggs from the VW and displayed them on her stall, most Wednesdays' the market was busy and today was no exception. By lunch time most of her stock was sold and looked forward to a lunch. Unfortunately, she was alone because Harold had so much to do and only had the three men to help him with the continual work on the farm. He worked twelve hours a day and she did her bit with the chickens and looking after the men with food and drink.

As she walked along to the pub where they always ate, she suddenly stopped and stared. There was a man walking along there who looked familiar, she looked again and suddenly realised who it was, it was her son! She stood in the middle of the pavement struck by the appearance of her son who was now 28. What was he doing here? Probably on holiday, was he married? Did he have any children? He was alone at the moment, so she had no clue. Indecision, should she talk to him and in consequence reveal their location or just forget she had seen him?

Finally, she walked over the road and approached William from behind, she hesitated to call his name for a while, then he sat down on a bench and she did the same. He glanced at her then looked away, then looked at her again.

"Mother?"

"Yes, it is me".

Angrily he turned to her,

"So, you are here, you abandoned me and Mary and dad to our own devices. We had no idea whether you were alive or dead. You should have stayed dead; we managed without you and don't want you back ever".

"I have no intention of coming back, I am more than happy here. I have a wonderful man who loves me and looks after me, better than your father did".

Perhaps she shouldn't have said that but was angry with him now.

"So, your shacked up with another man! Well I hope that he knows the trouble he has caused. Leaving two children to cope alone."

"How dare you! You were seventeen and an adult, quite capable of looking after yourself and your sister constantly fought with me over her life, so don't give me that nonsense of being abandoned".

"Even so you could have told us what had happened, dad was very upset"

"John was probably upset because he didn't have a slave to look after him, prepare his meals, keep his house clean and treat so badly"

William got up and said,

"Well at least I can tell them you are alive, but we don't want to see you ever again"

Penny said nothing as he walked away, at least she had seen him. She had a lunch and closed up her stall then drove home.

"You are very quiet tonight my love" said Harold

Penny looked at him with pain and indecision then burst out,

"I ran into William my son today and we had a big row"

Harold got up and came around to her, hugged her and kissed her.

"Don't worry my love I am sure everything will work its way out. What happened?"

"Well he was very angry at being "abandoned" but as I said to him, he was a man so could look after himself. At least he now knows the truth so he can tell the rest of the family. I just hope he goes home, and nothing else happens".

"Well now you can get a divorce and we can be married".

Penny looked at him, this was the first time he had mentioned marriage, she had not been sure if that was what he wanted. She hugged him tightly and kissed him,

"I am so glad; I wasn't sure if you wanted to marry me".

"Of course, I do we have been together now for a long time and I would so love to call you Mrs Wilson".

"But the might is not good for you, because the authorities might send you back to prison"

"Yes, they will but it might be only for a couple of years for not reporting and breaking my parole. I am sure we can survive that short time to be together legally"

"Yes, but I don't want to lose you for one day".

That night they made great love and were exhausted. Two days later it happened, a police car drew up and asked for Harold.

"Harold Wilson I am arresting you for breaking your parole, not reporting to the probation office and kidnapping"

"kidnapping? How did you come up with that charge?"

"We have had evidence that you kidnapped Mrs Penelope Stephen on 21st June 1987 and brought her here under threat of physical injury"

"Well I can tell you whoever told you that is a liar, I was not kidnapped I came voluntarily otherwise why am I still here?" Penny exploded.

"You will have to argue that in court we can only carry out our orders".

"Where are you taking him?"

"There are no local facilities so we are taking him to Leeds Central police station, and he will appear before the magistrates probably tomorrow".

The next day Penny came down and visited him, she couldn't believe the kidnapping charge and told it was probably her son who had brought the charge to try and hurt her. She was sure that the court would understand and drop the charge, if they wouldn't and he was found guilty he could get another 10 to 15 years in jail.

The next day he appeared before the magistrates, there were three of them two woman and one man. They were all middle-aged and experienced prepared to enforce the law as they interpreted it regardless of consequences.

Harold took the oath.

"Please give your name and place of residence"

"My name is Harold Wilson and I live at top farm, Malham"

"You are charged with not reporting while on parole, how do you plead?"

"Guilty"

"You are charged with the kidnap of Mrs Penelope Stephens on 21st June 1987 how do you plead?"

"Not Guilty"

"On the charge of not reporting for parole we order that you are returned to prison to serve out the rest of your sentence and one year in addition for breaking your parole"

Harold and Penny glanced at each other and somewhat relieved on the sentence, now they faced the more serious charge.

"Mr Jones are you ready to present you case?"

"Yes, Madam"

"We have evidence that Mrs Penelope Stephens was kidnapped from the Supermarket car park by Mr Harold Wilson on 21st June 1987. He forced her to drive out of town and somewhere on the way he put her in a VW Campervan that he owned. He then drove up to here and found work at the Top Farm. He and Mrs Penelope Stephens lived in a cottage on the farm for two years. On the death of Mrs Annie Postlethwaite in February 1990 they inherited the farm. Mrs Penelope Stephens was held against her will at the cottage and later at the farm. We are confident that the accused is guilty as charged"

The arresting officer was called to give his evidence and then cross examined by Harold's lawyer.

"Do you have any witnesses to these events?"

"No actual witnesses only the deposition of members of Mrs Stephens family"

"Are they being called as witnesses?"

"Not at this time, at the full trial they will be called"

"You have no actual witnesses to any of these events?"

"No"

"Right, now you stated that Mrs Stephens was held against her will at the cottage and later the farm, yes?"

"Yes"

"Have you interviewed anyone in the local area regarding these charges?"

"No, not yet. We will do so once the hearing is over".

"You seemed to think that the accused will be sent for trial but you have not got any evidence of the actual kidnapping, you have not talked to any of the villagers and all in all you have absolutely no evidence that Mrs Stephens was held against her will".

The policeman said nothing only looking confused and a little ashamed of the weakness of his case.

"Madam chair I think we can complete this quickly by calling the "victim".

"Yes, I agree"

"Mrs Stephens"

"Please call me Mrs Wilson, although not married I prefer to use that name".

"Very well. Please give the court your version of this 'kidnapping".

"I was very unhappy in my marriage; my husband was uncaring, and I had constant arguments with my two children and I was thinking about leaving. That day I had thought about it a lot and when Harold spoke to me and asked me to be his wife I did not hesitate for a minute".

"He asked you to be his wife even though you both had never met before?"

"Yes, he told me that somehow he knew we should be together and now thirteen years later he was right we are very happily together"

"So, he never kept you a prisoner? Never physically harmed you?"

"He is the best husband in the world, and I could have left at any time, but I didn't want to. For the first time in my life I am very happy".

"No more questions".

"Mr Jones do you have any questions?"

"Madam Chairman, having heard the evidence I will withdraw the charge of Kidnapping as it should never have been brought in the first place"

"I agree with you entirely, Mr Wilson the charge of kidnapping is withdrawn".

Penny and Harold smiled broadly at each other. Later while waiting for his transport to prison they met and hugged. A tearful Penny said goodbye and promised to visit him as often as she was allowed, once a month. Harold said he might get some time off if he behaved himself and promised to love her for ever.

He was taken away to serve his sentence in Leeds jail.

Penny returned home alone, this was the first time in thirteen years she had not had Harold by her side, when she got home, she couldn't stop the tears. She faced at least three years without him and wondered how she could cope. Then she straightened herself up and thought Harold is relying on me to keep the farm going and to be strong for him, I can see him every month so that is something for me to hold onto.

She realized that she could not cope alone so she called in the men an explained the situation, they both said they didn't mind working longer hours but she said thanks but we need another hand to do the work that Harold did. Martin suggested someone he knew in the village as a good worker and knew what to do so Penny said ask him to come and see me. He came the next day and Penny saw that he was a dependable and honest person, so she hired him. With the extra wages the budget would be stressed but she was sure that there would be enough.

Then she remembered all of Harold's bank accounts there might be enough money there. She found the bank books and altogether there was over ten thousand pounds plus some interest so she could use some of that. When she next visited him, she would ask him if it was alright to use that money.

Meanwhile Harold was being re-introduced to prison life, after all this time things had changed, and the regime was not so rough as it had been in the past. There still was the routine of cleaning out his potty in the morning, the food was a bit better but not much. Now there was some work that could be done with a small payment, but at least it was something to relieve the boredom. He was given the job of making small ornaments that would be sold in the stores, others were making cards, and various other jobs that changed as the contracts were filled.

Prison life is not very exciting, although not the same physical discipline as before being locked away for 12 hours a day was bad. Being used to working outside Harold felt it more than most, but he knew he had to put up with it for at least three years. At least he could look forward to seeing Penny sometime, he filled in the appointment card for her next visit in two weeks' time, he was allowed one five minute phone call once a week so on his next call he told her about her visit time. It was good to hear her voice but afterwards he felt depressed, but he had to keep going for both their sakes.

Penny was able to use the money in the bank to keep the farm afloat and she had many offers of help from the neighbours, she appreciated all they did and gave them produce when she had some. She contacted a solicitor to get the divorce from John, it was a long and painful experience, at first he said he would not divorce her but later realizing that she could get a divorce on being separated for ten years or more he gave in. She sued him for her share of the house, and he offered less than half, but she accepted that it was enough to pay the fees and leave a little over. When the papers finally came through, she was so happy and couldn't wait to tell Harold. He was overjoyed as well and now the remaining 18 months would not be so bad to bear.

Coming to the end of his sentence he looked forward to being with Penny again and getting back to the farm, she had done a sterling job and he was so appreciative. The day before his release a parcel arrived for him, it contained his best suit, clean shirt and underwear, new socks and shoes. He wondered why she had sent all these things but guessed she wanted him to look good when he came out. He dressed in his new clothes and put his old stuff in the bag and walked out of the prison, he vowed he would never be back.

When he walked out he was surprised to see a crowd of people waiting all dressed up and there was Penny looking beautiful in a new white dress and she ran to him and hugged him for a long time, they kissed several times.

"What is going on than with all these people all dressed up?"

"Well we are going to a wedding of course, what else could we do?" said Penny. Harold was moved to tears, he loved her so much and now she was going to be his wife! They got into the car and drove to the registry office. There they gave their vows and committed themselves to each other for ever. The reception was held in the village hall and almost the entire village had turned out, there was lots of laughter and speeches, lots of food and drink. The local band played the music and they danced together; later Harold realized that they had never danced together before.

Afterwards Penny and Harold got into the car but to his surprise it didn't go to the farm it went to the station in Leeds.

"Where are we going?"

"We are going to Scarborough for a honeymoon"

He hugged and kissed her, she had thought of everything, he was so happy that day, it was the best of his life. Returning from their honeymoon they found that the villagers had been looking after the farm and prepared a meal for them, Harold thanked them all for their kindness.

Harold and Penny continued to be happy and lived their life together in Top Farm.